# Jeremy

By
## HUGH WALPOLE

**CASSELL AND COMPANY, LTD**
London, Toronto, Melbourne and Sydney

| First published | *July* | 1919. |
|---|---|---|
| Second Impression | *July* | 1919. |
| Third " | *August* | 1919. |
| Fourth " | *September* | 1919. |
| Fifth " | *November* | 1919. |
| Sixth " | *December* | 1919. |
| Seventh " | *January* | 1920. |
| Cheap Edition | *October* | 1920. |
| Popular Edition | *January* | 1924. |
| 3s. 6d. Edition | *November* | 1925. |
| Second Impression | *June* | 1928. |
| Pocket Edition | *May* | 1928 |

*Printed in Great Britain*

# Jeremy

To
BRUCE
FROM
HIS LOVING UNCLE

" *It is due to him to say that he was an obedient boy, and a boy whose word could be depended on.* . . ."

—JACKANAPES

# CONTENTS

# JEREMY

## CHAPTER I

### THE BIRTHDAY

I

ABOUT thirty years ago there was at the top of
the right-hand side of Orange Street, in Polchester, a large stone house. I say " was "; the
shell of it is still there, and the people who now live
in it are quite unaware, I suppose, that anything has
happened to the inside of it, except that they are
certainly assured that their furniture is vastly
superior to the furniture of their predecessors. They
have a gramophone, a pianola, and a lift to bring the
plates from the kitchen into the dining-room, and a
small motor-garage at the back where the old pump
used to be, and a very modern rock-garden where
once was the pond with the fountain that never
worked. Let them cherish their satisfaction. No
one grudges it to them. The Coles were, by modern
standards, old-fashioned people, and the Stone Huse
was an old-fashioned house.

Young Jeremy Cole was born there in the year
1884, very early in the morning of December 8th.

He was still there very early in the morning of December 8th, 1892.

He was sitting up in bed. The cuckoo clock had just struck five, and he was aware that he was, at this very moment, for the first time in his life, eight years old. He had gone to bed at eight o'clock on the preceding evening with the choking consciousness that he would awake in the morning a different creature. Although he had slept, there had permeated the texture of his dreams that same choking excitement, and now, wide awake, as though he had asked the cuckoo to call him in order that he might not be late for the great occasion, he stared into the black distance of his bedroom and reflected, with a beating heart, upon the great event. He was eight years old, and he had as much right now to the nursery armchair with a hole in it as Helen had.

That was his first definite realization of approaching triumph. Throughout the whole of his seventh year he had fought with Helen, who was most unjustly a year older than he and persistently proud of that injustice, as to his right to use the wicker armchair whensoever it pleased him. So destructive of the general peace of the house had these incessant battles been, so unavailing the suggestions of elderly relations that gentlemen always yielded to ladies, that a compromise had been arrived at. When Jeremy was eight years he should have equal rights with Helen. Well and good. Jeremy had yielded to that. It was the only decent chair in the nursery. Into the place where the wicker, yielding to rude and impulsive pressure, had fallen away, one's body might be most happily fitted. It was of exactly the right height ; it made the handsomest creaking noises when one rocked in it—and, in any case, Helen was only a girl.

But the sense of his triumph had not yet fully descended upon him. As he sat up in bed, yawning, with a tickle in the middle of his back and his throat very dry, he was disappointingly aware that he was still the same Jeremy of yesterday. He did not know what it was exactly that he had expected, but he did not feel at present that confident proud glory for which he had been prepared. Perhaps it was too early.

He turned round, curled his head into his arm, and with a half-muttered, half-dreamt statement about the wicker chair, he was once again asleep.

He awoke to the customary sound of the bath water running into the bath. His room was flooded with sunshine, and old Jampot, the nurse (her name was Mrs. Preston and her shape was Jampot), was saying as usual : " Now, Master Jeremy, eight o'clock ; no lying in bed—out—you get—bath—ready."

He stared at her, blinking.

" You should say ' Many Happy Returns of the Day, Master Jeremy,' " he remarked. Then suddenly, with a leap, he was out of bed, had crossed the floor, pushed back the nursery door, and was sitting in the wicker arm-chair, his naked feet kicking a triumphant dance.

" Helen ! Helen ! " he called. " I'm in the chair." No sound.

" I'm eight," he shouted, " and I'm in the chair."

Mrs. Preston, breathless and exclaiming, hurried across to him.

" Oh, you naughty boy . . . death of cold . . . in your nightshirt."

" I'm eight," he said, looking at her scornfully, " and I can sit here as long as I please."

Helen, her pigtails flapping on either shoulder, her nose red, as it always was early in the morning, appeared at the opposite end of the nursery.

" Nurse, he mustn't, must he ?  Tell him not to. I don't care how old you are. It's my chair. Mother said——"

" No, she didn't.  Mother said——"

" Yes, she did.  Mother said——"

" Mother said that when——"

" Oh, you story.  You know that Mother said——" Then suddenly a new, stiffening, trusting dignity filled him, as though he had with a turn of the head discovered himself in golden armour.

He was above this vulgar wrangling now.  That was for girls.  He was superior to them all.  He got down from the chair and stood, his head up, on the old Turkey rug (red with yellow cockatoos) in front of the roaring fire.

" You may have your old chair," he said to Helen. " I'm eight now, and I don't want it any more . . . although if I *do* want it I shall have it," he added.

He was a small, square boy with a pug-nosed face. His hair was light brown, thin and stiff, so that it was difficult to brush, and although you watered it, stood up in unexpected places and stared at you. His eyes were good, dark brown and large, but he was in no way handsome ; his neck, his nose ridiculous. His mouth was too large, and his chin stuck out like a hammer.

He was, plainly, obstinate and possibly sulky, although when he smiled his whole face was lighted with humour.  Helen was the only beautiful Cole

child, and she was abundantly aware of that fact.
The Coles had never been a good-looking family.

He stood in front of the fireplace now as he had
seen his father do, his short legs apart, his head up,
and his hands behind his back.

" Now, Master Jeremy," the Jampot continued,
" you may be eight years old, but it isn't a reason for
disobedience the very first minute, and, of course,
your bath is ready and you catching your death with
naked feet, which you've always been told to put
your slippers on, and not to keep the bath waiting,
when there's Miss Helen and Miss Mary, as you very
well know, and breakfast coming in five minutes,
which there's sausages this morning, because it's
your birthday, and them all getting cold——"

" Sausages ! "

He was across the floor in a moment, had thrown
off his nightshirt and was in his bath. Sausages !
He was translated into a world of excitement and
splendour. They had sausages so seldom, not always
even on birthdays, and to-day, on a cold morning,
with a crackling fire and marmalade, perhaps—and
then all the presents.

Oh, he was happy. As he rubbed his back with
the towel a wonderful glowing Christian charity
spread from his head to his toes and tingled through
every inch of him. Helen should sit in the chair when
she pleased ; Mary should be allowed to dress and
undress the large woollen dog, known as " Sulks,"
his own especial and beloved property, so often as
she wished ; Jampot should poke the twisted end of
the towel in his ears and brush his hair with the
hard brushes, and he would not say a word. Aunt
Mary should kiss him (as, of course, she would want

to do), and he would not shiver ; he would (bravest deed of all) allow Mary to read " Alice in Wonderland " in her sing-song voice so long as ever she wanted. . . . Sausages ! Sausages !

In his shirt and his short blue trousers, his hair on end, tugging at his braces, he stood in the doorway and shouted :

" Helen, there are sausages—because it's my birthday. Aren't you glad ? "

And even when the only response to his joyous invitation was Helen's voice crossly admonishing the Jampot : " Oh, you do pull so ; you're hurting ! " his charity was not checked.

Then when he stood clothed and of a cheerful mind once more in front of the fire a shyness stole over him. He knew that the moment for Presents was approaching ; he knew that very shortly he would have to kiss and be kissed by a multitude of persons, that he would have to say again and again, " Oh, thank you, thank you so much ! " that he would have his usual consciousness of his inability to thank anybody at all in the way that they expected to be thanked. Helen and Mary never worried about such things. They delighted in kissing and hugging and multitudes of words. If only he might have had his presents by himself and then stolen out and said " Thank you " to the lot of them and have done with it.

He watched the breakfast-table with increasing satisfaction—the large teapot with the red roses, the dark blue porridge plates, the glass jar with the marmalade a rich yellow inside it, the huge loaf with the soft pieces bursting out between the crusty pieces, the solid square of butter, so beautiful a colour and marked with a large cow and a tree on the top (he had seen once in the kitchen the wooden shape with which the cook made this handsome thing). There was also his own silver mug, given him at his christening by Canon Trenchard, his godfather, and his silver spoon, given him on the same occasion by Uncle Samuel. All these things glittered and glowed in the firelight, and a kettle was singing on the hob and Martha the canary was singing in her cage in the window. (No one really knew whether the canary were a lady or a gentleman, but the name had been Martha, after a beloved housemaid, now married to the gardener, and the sex had followed the name.)

There were also all the other familiar nursery things. The hole in the Turkey carpet near the bookcase, the rocking-horse, very shiny where you sit and very Christmas-tree-like as to its tail ; the doll's house, now deserted, because Helen was too old and Mary too clever ; the pictures of " Church on Christmas Morning " (everyone with their mouths very wide open, singing a Christmas hymn, with holly), " Dignity and Impudence," after Landseer, " The Shepherds and the Angels," and " The Charge of the Light Brigade." So packed was the nursery with history for Jeremy that it would have taken quite a week to relate it all. There was the spot where he had bitten the Jampot's fingers, for which deed he had afterwards been slippered by his father ; there the corner where they stood for punishment (he knew exactly how many ships with sails, how many ridges of waves, and how many setting suns there were on that especial piece of corner wallpaper—three ships, twelve ridges, two and a half suns) ; there was the place where he had broken the ink-bottle over his

shoes and the carpet, there by the window, where
Mary had read to him once when he had toothache,
and he had not known whether her reading or the
toothache agonised him the more ; and so on, an
endless sequence of sensational history.

His reminiscences were cut short by the appearance
of Gladys with the porridge.   Gladys, who was only
the between-maid, but was nevertheless stout,
breathless from her climb and the sentiment of the
occasion, produced from a deep pocket a dirty
envelope, which she laid upon the table.

" Many 'appy returns, Master Jeremy," Giggle
. . . " Lord save us if I 'aven't gone and forgotten
they spunes," and she vanished.   The present-giving
had begun.

He had an instant's struggle as to whether it were
better to wait until all the presents had accumulated,
or whether he would take them separately as they
arrived. The dirty envelope lured him. He advanced
towards it and seized it.  He could not read very
easily the sprawling writing on the cover, but he
guessed that it said " From Gladys to Master
Jeremy." Within was a marvellous card, tied
together with glistening cord and shining with all
the colours of the rainbow.  It was apparently a
survival from last Christmas, as there was a church in
snow and a peal of bells ; he was, nevertheless, very
happy to have it.

After this introduction events moved swiftly.
First Helen and Mary appeared, their faces shining
and solemn and mysterious—Helen self-conscious,
and Mary staring through her spectacles like a pro-
found owl.

Because Jeremy had known Mary ever since he

could remember, he was unaware that there was anything very peculiar about her. But in truth she was
a strange-looking child. Very thin, she had a large
head, with big outstanding ears, spectacles, and
yellow hair pulled back and " stringy." Her large
hands were always red, and her forehead was
freckled. She was as plain a child as you were ever
likely to see, but there was character in her mouth
and eyes, and although she was only seven years
old, she could read quite difficult books (she was
engaged at this particular time upon " Ivanhoe "),
and she was a genius at sums.

The passion of her life, as the family were all aware,
was Jeremy, but it was an unfortunate and uncomfortable passion. She bothered and worried him,
she was insanely jealous ; she would sulk for days
did he ever seem to prefer Helen to herself. No one
understood her ; she was considered a " difficult
child," quite unlike any other member of the family,
except possibly Samuel, Mr. Cole's brother-in-law,
who was an unsuccessful painter and therefore
" odd."

As Mary was at present only seven years of age
it would be too much to say that the family was
afraid of her. Aunt Amy's attitude was : " Well,
after all, she's sure to be clever when she grows up,
poor child " ; and although the parishioners of
Mary's father always alluded to her as " the ludicrous Cole child," they told awed little stories about
the infant's mental capacities, and concluded comfortably, " I'm glad Alice (or Jane or Matilda or
Anabel) isn't clever like that. They overwork when
they are young, and then when they grow up——"

Meanwhile Mary led her private life. She attached

herself to no one but Jeremy ; she was delicate and
suffered from perpetual colds ; she therefore spent
much of her time in the nursery reading, her huge
spectacles close to the page, her thin legs like black
sticks stuck up on the fender in front of the fire
or curled up under her on the window-seat.

Very different was Helen. Helen had a mass of
dark black hair, big black eyes, with thick eyelashes,
a thin white neck, little feet, and already an eye to
" effects " in dress. She was charming to strangers,
to the queer curates who haunted the family hall, to
poor people and rich people, to old people and young
people. She was warm-hearted but not impulsive,
intelligent but not clever, sympathetic but not
sentimental, impatient but never uncontrolled.
She liked almost everyone and almost everything,
but no one and nothing mattered to her very deeply ;
she liked going to church, always learnt her Collect
first on Sunday, and gave half her pocket-money to
the morning collection. She was generous but
never extravagant, enjoyed food but was not
greedy. She was quite aware that she was pretty
and might one day be beautiful, and she was glad
of that, but she was never silly about her looks.

When Aunt Amy, who was always silly about
everything, said in her presence to visitors, " Isn't
Helen the loveliest thing you ever saw ? " she
managed by her shy self-confidence to suggest that
she *was* pretty, that Aunt Amy *was* a fool, and life
was altogether very agreeable, but that none of
these things was of any great importance. She was
very good friends with Jeremy, but she played no
part in his life at all. At the same time she often
fought with him, simply from her real deep con-

sciousness of her superiority to him. She valued her authority and asserted it incessantly. That authority had until last year been unchallenged, but Jeremy now was growing. She had, although she did not as yet realize it, a difficult time before her.

Helen and Mary advanced with their presents, laid them on the breakfast-table, and then retreated to watch the effect of it all.

" Shall I now ? " asked Jeremy.

" Yes, now," said Helen and Mary.

There were three parcels, one large and " shoppy," two small and bound with family paper, tied by family hands with family string. He grasped immediately the situation. The shoppy parcel was bought with Mother's money and only " pretended " to be from his sisters ; the two small parcels were the very handiwork of the ladies themselves, the same having been seen by all eyes at work for the last six months, sometimes, indeed, under the cloak of attempted secrecy, but more often—because weariness or ill-temper made them careless—in the full light of day.

His interest was centred almost entirely in the " shoppy " parcel, which by its shape might be " soldiers " ; but he knew the rules of the game, and disregarding the large, ostentatious brown-papered thing, he went magnificently for the two small incoherent bundles.

He opened them. A flat green table-centre with a red pattern of roses, a thick table-napkin ring worked in yellow worsted, these were revealed.

" Oh ! " he cried, " just what I wanted." (Father always said that on *his* birthday).

" Is it ? " said Mary and Helen.

" Mine's the ring," said Mary.  " It's dirty rather, but it would have got dirty, anyway, afterwards." She watched anxiously to see whether he preferred Helen's.

*He* watched them nervously, lest he should be expected to kiss them.  He wiped his mouth with his hand instead, and began rapidly to talk :

" Jampot will know now which mine is.  She's always giving me the wrong one.  I'll have it always, and the green thing too."

" It's for the middle of the table," Helen interrupted.

" Yes, I know," said Jeremy hurriedly.  " I'll always have it too—like Mary's—when I'm grown up and all. . . . I say, shall I open the other one now ? "

" Yes, you can," said Helen and Mary, ceasing to take the central place in the ceremony, spectators now and eagerly excited.

But Mary had a last word.

" You do like mine, don't you ? "

" Of course, like anything."

She wanted to say " Better than Helen's ? " but restrained herself.

" I was ever so long doing it ;  I thought I wouldn't finish it in time."

He saw with terror that she meditated a descent upon him ;  a kiss was in the air.  She moved forward ;  then, to his extreme relief, the door opened, and the elders arriving saved him.

There was Father and Mother, Uncle Samuel and Aunt Amy, all with presents, faces of birthday tolerance and " do-as-you-please-to-day, dear " expressions.

The Rev. Herbert Cole was forty years of age, rector of St. James's, Polchester, during the last ten years, and marked out for greater preferment in the near future.  To be a rector at thirty is unusual, but he had great religious gifts, preached an admirable " as-man-to-man " sermon, and did not believe in thinking about more than he could see.  He was an excellent father in the abstract sense, but the parish absorbed too much of his time to allow of intimacies with anyone.

Mrs. Cole was the most placid lady in Europe. She had a comfortable figure, but was not stout, here a dimple and there a dimple.  Nothing could disturb her.  Children, servants, her husband's sermons, district visiting, her Tuesday " at homes," the butcher, the dean's wife, the wives of the canons, the Polchester climate, bills, clothes, other women's clothes, —over all these rocks of peril in the sea of daily life her barque happily floated.  Some ill-natured people thought her stupid, but in her younger days she had liked Trollope's novels in the *Cornhill*, disapproved placidly of " Jane Eyre " and admired Tennyson, so that she could not be considered unliterary.

She was economical, warm-hearted, loved her children, talked only the gentlest scandal, and was a completely happy woman—all this in the placidest way in the world.

Miss Amy Trefusis, her sister, was very different, being thin both in her figure and her emotions.  She skirted tempestuously over the surface of things, was the most sentimental of human beings, was often in tears over reminiscences of books or the weather, was deeply religious in a superficial way, and really— although she would have been entirely astonished say what he thought of her) and continued to tug at the string. He was given a large pair of scissors. He received (from Father) a silver watch, (from Mother) a paint-box, a dark blue and gold prayer book with a thick squashy leather cover (from Aunt Amy).

He was in an ecstasy. How he had longed for a watch, just such a turnip-shaped one, and a paint-box. What colours he could make! Even Aunt Amy's prayer book was something, with its squashy cover and silk marker (only why did Aunt Amy never give him anything sensible ?).

He stood there, his face flushed, his eyes sparkling, the watch in one hand and the paint-box in the other.

Remarks were heard like : " You mustn't poke it with your finger, Jerry darling, or you'll break the hands off " ; and " I thought he'd better have the square sort, and not the tubes. They're *so* squashy "; and " You'll be able to learn your Collect so easily with that big print, Jerry dear. Very kind of you, Amy."

Meanwhile he was aware that Uncle Samuel had given him nothing. There was a little thick catch of disappointment in his throat, not because he wanted a present, but because he liked Uncle Samuel. Suddenly, from somewhere behind him his uncle said : " Shut your eyes, Jerry. Don't open them until I tell you "—then rather crossly, " No, Amy, leave me alone. I know what I'm about, thank you."

Jeremy shut his eyes tight. He closed them so that the eyelids seemed to turn right inwards and red lights flashed. He stood there for at least a century, all in darkness, no one saying anything save that once Mary cried " Oh ! " and clapped her hands, which same cry excited him to such a pitch that he would have dug his nails into his hands had he not so consistently in the past bitten them that there were no nails with which to dig. He waited. He waited. He waited. He was not eight, he was eighty when at last Uncle Samuel said, " Now you may look."

He opened his eyes and turned ; for a moment the nursery, too, rocked in the unfamiliar light. Then he saw. On the middle of the nursery carpet was a village, a real village, six houses with red roofs, green windows and white porches, a church with a tower and a tiny bell, an orchard with flowers on the fruit trees, a green lawn, a street with a butcher's shop, a post office, and a grocer's. Villagers, Noah, Mrs. Noah and the little Noahs, a field with cows, horses, dogs, a farm with chickens, and even two pigs. . . .

He stood, he stared, he drew a deep breath.

" It comes all the way from Germany," said Aunt Amy, who always made things uninteresting if she possibly could.

There was much delighted talk. Jeremy said nothing. But Uncle Samuel understood.

" Glad you like it," he said, and left the room.

" Aren't you pleased ? " said Helen.

Jeremy still said nothing.

" Sausages. Sausages ! " cried Mary, as Gladys, grinning, entered with a dish of a lovely and pleasant smell.

But Jeremy did not turn. He simply stood there —staring.

the Cathedral, whence one might sometimes see boats on the river, sheep and cows in the meads, and, in their proper season, delight of delights—lambs.

They set out. . . .

Thirty years ago the winter weather in Polchester was wonderful. Now, of course, there are no hard winters, no frost, no snows, no waits, no snow-men, and no skating on the Pol. Then there were all those things. To-day was of a hard, glittering frost ; the sun, like a round, red lacquer tray, fell heavily, slowly through a faint pale sky that was not strong enough to sustain it. The air had the cold, sweet twang of peppermints in the throat. Polchester was a painted town upon a blue screen, the Cathedral towers purple against the sky ; the air was scented with burning leaves, and cries from the town rose up clear and hard, lingering and falling like notes of music. Somewhere they were playing football, and the shouting was distant and regular like the tramp of armed men. " Three " struck the Cathedral clock, as though it were calling " Open Sesame." Other lesser clocks repeated the challenge cry through the town. " Woppley—Woppley—Why ! " sung the man who was selling skins down Orange Street. The sky, turning slowly from blue to gold, shone mysteriously through the glass of the street lamps, and the sun began to wrap itself in tints of purple and crocus and iris. " Woppley—Woppley—Why ! " screamed the skin-man, suddenly appearing at the top of the street.

" Now 'urry, Master Jeremy," said the Jampot, " or we shall never get 'ome this night, and I might have known you'd choose the longest walk possible. Come along, Miss Mary, now—none of that dawd-ling."

Jeremy, in his H.M.S. *Adventure's* cap and rough blue navy coat, felt himself superior to the Jampot, so he only said, " Oh, don't bother, Nurse," and then in the same breath, " I'll run you down the hill, Mary," and before anyone could say a word there they were at the bottom of Orange Street, as though they had fallen into a well. The sun was gone, the golden horizon was gone—only the purple lights began to gather about their feet and climb slowly the high black houses.

Mary liked this, because she now had Jeremy to herself. She began hurriedly, so that she should lose no time :

" Shall I tell you a story, Jeremy ? I've got a new one. Once upon a time there were three little boys, and they lived in a wood, and an old witch ate them, and the Princess who had heaps of jewellery and a white horse and a lovely gold dress came, and it was snowing and the witch——"

This was always Mary's way. She loved to tell Jeremy interesting stories, and he did not mind because he did not listen and could meanwhile think his own thoughts.

His chief decision arrived at as he marched along was that he would keep the village to himself ; no one else should put their fingers into it, arrange the orchard with the coloured trees, decide upon the names of the Noah family, settle the village street in its final order, ring the bell of the church, or milk the cows. He alone would do all these things. And, so considering, he seemed to himself very like God. God, he supposed, could pull Polchester about, root out a house here, another there, knock the Assembly Rooms down and send a thunderbolt on

C

to the apple woman's umbrella. Well, then—so could he with his village. He walked swollen with pride. He arrived at the first Island of Circe, namely, the window of Mr. Thompson, the jeweller in Market Street, pressed his nose to the pane, and refused to listen when the Jampot suggested that he should move forward.

He could see the diamonds like drops of water in the sun, and the pearls like drops of milk, and the rubies like drops of blood, but it was not of diamonds, pearls or rubies that he was thinking—he thought only of his village. He would ring the church bell, and then all the Noah family should start out of the door, down the garden, up the village street. . . . It did not matter if one of the younger Noahs should be lazy and wish to stay at home beneath the flowering trees of the orchard. She would not be allowed. . . . He was as God. . . . He was as God. . . . The butcher should go (if he was not stuck to his shop), and even some of his cows might go. . . . He was as God. . . .

He heard Mary's voice in his ear.

" And after that they all ate chocolates with white cream and red cream, and they sucked it off pins, and there were hard bits and soft bits, and the Princess (she was a frog now. You remember, don't you, Jeremy ? The witch turned her) hotted the oven like cook has, with black doors, and hotted it and hotted it, but suddenly there was a noise——"

And, on the other side, the Jampot's voice : " You naughty boy, stoppin' 'ere for everyone to see, just because it's your birthday, which I wish there wasn't no birthdays, nor there wouldn't be if I had my way."

Jeremy turned from Mr. Thompson's window, a scornful smile on his face.

" I'm bigger'n you, Nurse," he said. " If I said out loud, ' I won't go,' I wouldn't go, and no one could make me."

" Well, come along, then," said Nurse.

" Don't be so stupid, Jerry," said Helen calmly. " If a policeman came and said you had to go home you'd have to go."

" No I wouldn't," said Jeremy.

" Then they'd put you in prison."

" They could."

" They'd hang you, perhaps."

" They could," replied Jeremy.

Farther than this argument cannot go, so Helen shrugged her shoulders and said : " You *are* silly."

And they all moved forward.

He found then that this new sense of God-like power detracted a little from the excitements of the Market Place, although the flower-stall was dazzling with flowers ; there was a new kind of pig that lifted its tail and lowered it again on the toy stall, and the apple-woman was as fat as ever and had thick clumps of yellow bananas hanging most richly around her head. They ascended the High Street and reached the Close. It was half-past three, and the Cathedral bells had begun to ring for evensong All the houses in the Close were painted with a pale yellow light ; across the long green Cathedral lawn thin black shadows like the fingers of giants pointed to the Cathedral door. All was so silent here that the bells danced against the houses and back again, the echoes lingering in the high elms and mingling with the placid cawing of the rooks.

" There's Mrs. Sampson," said Jeremy. " Aunt Amy says she's a wicked woman. Do you think she's a wicked woman, Nurse ? " He gazed at the stout figure with interest. If he were truly God he would turn her into a rabbit. This thought amused him, and he began to laugh.

" You naughty boy ; now come along, do," said the Jampot, who distrusted laughter in Jerry.

" I'll ring the bells when I grow up," he said, " and I'll ring them in the middle of the night, so that everyone will have to go to church when they don't want to. I'll be able to do what I like when I grow up."

" No you won't," said Helen. " Father and Mother can't do what they like."

" Yes, they can," said Jeremy.

" No, they can't," said Helen, " or they would."

" So they do," said Jeremy—" silly."

" Silly yourself," said Helen very calmly, because she knew very well that she was not silly.

" Now, children, stop it, do," said the Jampot.

Jeremy's sense of newly received power reached its climax when they walked round the Close and reached the back of the Cathedral. I know that now, both for Jeremy and me, that prospect has dwindled into its proper grown-up proportions, but how can a man, be he come to three-score and ten and more, ever forget the size, the splendour, the stupendous extravagance of that early vision ?

Jeremy saw that day the old fragment of castle wall, the green expanse falling like a sheeted water-fall from the Cathedral heights, the blue line of river flashing in the evening sun between the bare-boughed trees, the long spaces of black shadow spreading slowly over the colour, as though it were all being rolled up and laid away for another day ; the brown frosty path of the Rope Walk, the farther bank climbing into fields and hedges, ending in the ridge of wood, black against the golden sky. And all so still ! As the children stood there they could catch nestlings' faint cries, stirrings of dead leaves and twigs, as birds and beasts moved to their homes ; the cawing of the rooks about the black branches seemed to promise that this world should be for ever tranquil, for ever cloistered and removed ; the sun, red and flaming above the dark wood, flung white mists hither and thither to veil its departure. The silence deepened, the last light flamed on the river and died upon the hill.

" Now, children, come along do," said the Jampot, who had been held in spite of herself, and would pay for it, she knew, in rheumatism to-morrow. It was then that Jeremy's God-flung sense of power, born from that moment early in the day when he had sat in the wicker chair, reached its climax. He stood there, his legs apart, looking upon the darkening world and felt that he could do anything—anything. . . .

At any rate, there was one thing that he could do, disobey the Jampot.

" I'm not coming," he said, " till I choose."

" You wicked boy ! " she cried, her temper rising with the evening chill, her desire for a cup of hot tea, and an aching longing for a comfortable chair. " When everyone's been so good to you to-day and the things you've been given and all—why, it's a wicked shame."

The Jampot, who was a woman happily without

imagination, saw a naughty small boy spoiled and needing the slipper.

A rook, taking a last look at the world before retiring to rest, watching from his leafless bough, saw a mortal spirit defying the universe, and sympathized with it.

" I shall tell your mother," said the Jampot. " Now come, Master Jeremy, be a good boy."

" Oh, don't bother, Nurse," he answered impatiently. " You're such a fuss."

She realized in that moment that he was suddenly beyond her power, that he would never be within it again. She had nursed him for eight years, she had loved him in her own way ; she, dull perhaps in the ways of the world, but wise in the ways of nurses, ways that are built up of surrender and surrender, gave him, then and there, to the larger life. . . .

" You may behave as you like, Master Jeremy," she said. " It won't be long that I'll have the dealing with you, praise be. You'll be going to school next September, and then we'll see what'll happen to your wicked pride."

" School ! " he turned upon her, his eyes wide and staring.

" School ! " he stared at them all.

The world tumbled from him. In his soul was a confusion of triumph and dismay, of excitement and loneliness, of the sudden falling from him of all old standards, old horizons, of pride and humility. . . . How little now was the Village to him. He looked at them to see whether they could understand. They could not.

Very quietly he followed them home. His birthday had achieved its climax. . . .

# CHAPTER II

## THE FAMILY DOG

### I

THAT winter of Jeremy's eighth birthday was famous for its snow. Glebeshire has never yielded to the wishes of its children in the matter of snowy Christmases, and Polchester has the reputation of muggy warmth and foggy mists, but here was a year when traditions were fulfilled in the most reckless manner, and all the 1892 babies were treated to a present of snow on so fine a scale that certainly for the rest of their days they will go about saying: " Ah, you should see the winters we used to have when we were children. . . ."

The snow began on the very day after Jeremy's birthday, coming down doubtfully, slowly, little grey flakes against a grey sky, then sparkling white, then vanishing flashes of moisture on a wet, unsympathetic soil. That day the snow did not lie, and for a week it did not come again ; then with a whirl it seized the land, and for two days and nights did not loosen its grip. From the nursery windows the children watched it, their noses making little rings on the window-pane, their delighted eyes snatching fascinating glimpses of figures tossed through the storm, cabs beating their way, the rabbit-skin man, the milkman, the postman, brave adventurers all, fighting, as it seemed, for their very lives.

For two days the children did not leave the house, and the natural result of that was that on the second afternoon tempers were like so many dogs, straining, tugging, pulling at their chains.

It could not be denied that Jeremy had been tiresome to everyone since the afternoon when he had heard the news of his going to school next September. It had seemed to him a tremendous event, the Beginning of the End. To the others, who lived in the immediate present, it was a crisis so remote as scarcely to count at all. Mary would have liked to be sentimental about it, but from this she was sternly prevented. There was then nothing more to be said. . . .

Jeremy was suddenly isolated from them all. His destiny was peculiar. They were girls, he was a boy. They understood neither his fears nor his ambitions ; he needed terribly a companion. The snow, shutting them in, laughed at their struggles against monotony. The nursery clock struck three, and they realized that two whole hours must pass before the next meal. Mary, her nose red from pressing on the window-pane, her eyes gazing through her huge spectacles wistfully at Jeremy, longed to suggest that she should read aloud to him. She knew that he hated it ; she pretended to herself that she did not know.

Jeremy stared desperately at Helen, who was sitting, dignified and collected, in the wicker chair hemming a minute handkerchief.

" We might play Pirates," Jeremy said with a little cough, the better to secure her attention. There was no answer.

" Or there's the hut in the wood—if anyone likes it better," he added politely. He did not know what was the matter. Had the Jampot not told him about school he would at this very moment be playing most happily with his village. It spread out there before him on the nursery floor, the Noah family engaged upon tea in the orchard, the butcher staring with fixed gaze from the door of his shop, three cows and a sheep absorbed in the architecture of the church.

He sighed, then said again : " Perhaps Pirates would be better."

Still Helen did not reply. He abandoned the attempted control of his passions.

" It's very rude," he said, " not to answer when gentlemen speak to you."

" I don't see any gentlemen," answered Helen quietly, without raising her eyes, which was, as she knew, a provoking habit.

" Yes, you do," screamed Jeremy. " I'm one."

" You're not," continued Helen ; " you're only eight. Gentlemen must be over twenty like Father or Mr. Jellybrand."

" I hate Mr. Jellybrand and I hate you," replied Jeremy.

" I don't care," said Helen.

" Yes, you do," said Jeremy ; then suddenly, as though even a good quarrel were not worth while on this heavily-burdened afternoon, he said gently : " You might play pirates, Helen. You can be Sir Roger."

" I've got this to finish."

"It's a dirty old thing," continued Jeremy, pursuing an argument, " and it'll be dirtier soon, and the Jampot says you do all the stitches wrong. I wish I was at school."

" I don't know," said Mary, rubbing her nose,
" what it means, but perhaps we'll see presently,
' herself up in w-o-o-l wool.  Alice rubbed her eyes
and looked again she couldn't——' "

" ' Looked again she couldn't ' ? " asked Jeremy.
" It should be, ' she couldn't look again.' "

" Oh, there's a stop," said Mary.  " I didn't see.
After ' again ' there's a stop.  ' She couldn't make
out what had happened at all——' "

" I can't either," said Jeremy crossly.  " It
would be better perhaps if I read it myself."

" It will be all right in a minute," said Mary confidently.  " ' Was she in a shop ?  And was that
really—was it really a ship that was sitting on the
counter ? ' " she finished with a run.

" A what ? " asked Jeremy.

" A ship——"

" A ship !  How could it sit on a counter ? " he
asked.

" Oh no, it's a sheep.  How silly I am ! " Mary
exclaimed.

" You *do* read badly," he agreed frankly.  " I
never can understand nothing."  And it was at that
very moment that he saw the Dog.

2

He had been staring down into the garden with a
gaze half abstracted, half speculative, listening with
one ear to Mary, with the other to the stir of the fire,
the heavy beat of the clock and the rustlings of
Martha the canary.

He watched the snowy expanse of garden, the
black gate, the road beyond.  A vast wave of pale

grey light, the herald of approaching dusk, swept the horizon, the snowy roofs, the streets, and Jeremy felt some contact with the strange air, the mysterious omens that the first snows of the winter spread about the land. He watched as though he were waiting for something to happen.

The creature came up very slowly over the crest of Orange Street. No one else was in sight, no cart, no horse, no weather-beaten wayfarer. At first the dog was only a little black smudge against the snow ; then, as he arrived at the Coles' garden-gate, Jeremy could see him very distinctly. He was, it appeared, quite alone ; he had been, it was evident, badly beaten by the storm. Intended by nature to be a rough and hairy dog, he now appeared before God and men a shivering battered creature, dripping and wind-tossed, bedraggled and bewildered. And yet, even in that first distant glimpse, Jeremy discerned a fine independence. He was a short stumpy dog, in no way designed for dignified attitudes and patronizing superiority ; nevertheless, as he now wandered slowly up the street, his nose was in the air and he said to the whole world : " The storm may have done its best to defeat me—it has failed. I am as I was. I ask charity of no man. I know what is due to me."

It was this that attracted Jeremy ; he had himself felt thus after a slippering from his father, or idiotic punishments from the Jampot, and the uninvited consolations of Mary or Helen upon such occasions had been resented with so fierce a bitterness that his reputation for sulkiness had been soundly established with all his circle.

Mary was reading . . . ! " ' an old Sheep, sitting

in an arm-chair, knitting, and every now and then
leaving off to look at her through a great pair of
spec-t-a-c-les spectacles ! ' "

He touched her arm and whispered :

" I say, Mary, stop a minute—look at that dog
down there."

They both stared down into the garden. The dog
had stopped at the gate ; it sniffed at the bars,
sniffed at the wall beyond, then very slowly but with
real dignity continued its way up the road.

" Poor thing," said Jeremy. " It *is* in a mess."
Then to their astonishment the dog turned back and,
sauntering down the road again as though it had
nothing all day to do but to wander about, and as
though it were not wet, shivering and hungry, it once
more smelt the gate.

" Oh," said Mary and Jeremy together.

" It's like Mother," said Jeremy, " when she's
going to see someone and isn't sure whether it's the
right house."

Then, most marvellous of unexpected climaxes,
the dog suddenly began to squeeze itself between
the bottom bar of the gate and the ground. The
interval was fortunately a large one ; a moment
later the animal was in the Coles' garden.

The motives that led Jeremy to behave as he did
are uncertain. It may have been something to do
with the general boredom of the afternoon, it may
have been that he felt pity for the bedraggled aspect
of the animal—most probable reason of all, was
that devil-may-care independence flung up from the
road, as it were, expressly at himself.

The dog obviously did not feel any great respect
for the Cole household. He wandered about the

garden, sniffing and smelling exactly as though the whole place belonged to him, and a ridiculous stump of tail, unsubdued by the weather, gave him the ludicrous dignity of a Malvolio.

" I'm going down," whispered Jeremy, flinging a curious glance at Helen, who was absorbed in her sewing.

Mary's eyes grew wide with horror and admiration. " You're not going out," she whispered. " In the snow. Oh, Jeremy. They *will* be angry."

" I don't care," whispered Jeremy back again. " They can be."

Indeed, before Mary's frightened whisper he had not intended to do more than creep down into the pantry and watch the dog at close range ; now it was as though Mary had challenged him. He knew that it was the most wicked thing that he could do —to go out into the snow without a coat and in his slippers. He might even, according to Aunt Amy, die of it, but as death at present meant no more to him than a position of importance and a quantity of red-currant jelly and chicken, *that* prospect did not deter him. He left the room so quietly that Helen did not even lift her eyes.

Then upon the landing he waited and listened. The house had all the lighted trembling dusk of the snowy afternoon ; there was no sound save the ticking of the clocks. He might come upon the Jampot at any moment, but this was just the hour when she liked to drink her cup of tea in the kitchen ; he knew from deep and constant study every movement of her day. Fortune favoured him. He reached without trouble the little dark corkscrew servants' staircase. Down this he crept, and found himself beside the little gardener's door. Although here there was only snow-lit dusk, he felt for the handle of the lock, found it, and was, at once, over the steps, into the garden.

Here, with a vengeance, he felt the full romance and danger of his enterprise. It was horribly cold ; he had been in the nursery for two whole days, wrapped up and warm, and now the snowy world seemed to leap up at him and drag him down as though into an icy well. Mysterious shadows hovered over the garden ; the fountain pointed darkly against the sky, and he could feel from the feathery touches upon his face that the snow had begun to fall again.

He moved forward a few steps ; the house was so dark behind him, the world so dim and uncertain in front of him, that for a moment his heart failed him. He might have to search the whole garden for the dog.

Then he heard a sniff, felt something wet against his leg—he had almost stepped upon the animal. He bent down and stroked its wet coat. The dog stood quite still, then moved forward towards the house, sniffed at the steps, at last walked calmly through the open door as though the house belonged to him. Jeremy followed, closed the door behind them ; then there they were in the little dark passage with the boy's heart beating like a drum, his teeth chattering, and a terrible temptation to sneeze hovering around him. Let him reach the nursery and establish the animal there and all might be well, but let them be discovered, cold and shivering, in the passage, and out the dog would be flung. He knew so exactly what would happen. He could hear the voices in the kitchen. He knew that they were sitting warm

there by the fire, but that at any moment the
Jampot might think good to climb the stairs and
see " what mischief they children were up to."
Everything depended upon the dog. Did he bark
or whine, out into the night he must go again,
probably to die in the cold. But Jeremy, the least
sentimental of that most sentimental race the
English, was too intent upon his threatened sneeze
to pay much attention to these awful possibilities.

He took off his slippers and began to climb the
stairs, the dog close behind him, very grave and
dignified, in spite of the little trail of snow and water
that he left in his track. The nursery door was
reached, pushed softly open, and the startled gaze
of Mary and Helen fell wide-eyed upon the
adventurer and his prize.

### 3

The dog went directly to the fire ; there, sitting
in the very middle of the golden cockatoos on the
Turkey rug, he began to lick himself. He did this
by sitting very square on three legs and spreading
out the fourth stiff and erect, as though it had been
not a leg at all but something of wood or iron. The
melted snow poured off him, making a fine little pool
about the golden cockatoos. He must have been a
strange-looking animal at any time, being built
quite square like a toy dog, with a great deal of
hair, very short legs, and a thick stubborn neck ;
his eyes were brown, and now could be seen very
clearly because the hair that usually covered them
was plastered about his face by the snow. In his
normal day his eyes gleamed behind his hair like

D

sunlight in a thick wood.  He wore a little pointed
beard that could only be considered an affectation ;
in one word, if you imagine a ridiculously small
sheep-dog with no legs, a French beard and a stump
of a tail, you have him.  And if you want to know
more than that I can only refer you to the description of his great-great-great grandson " Jacob," described in the Chronicles of the Beaminster Family.

The children meanwhile gazed, and for a long time
no one said a word.  Then Helen said : " Father
*will* be angry."

But she did not mean it.  The three were, by the
entrance of the dog, instantly united into an offensive and defensive alliance.  They knew well that
shortly an attack from the Outside World must be
delivered, and without a word spoken or a look
exchanged they were agreed to defend both themselves and the dog with all the strength in their
power.  They had always wanted a dog ;  they
had been prevented by the stupid and selfish
arguments of uncomprehending elders.

Now this dog was here ;  they would keep him.

" Oh, he's perfectly sweet," suddenly said Helen.

The dog paused for a moment from his ablutions,
raised his eyes, and regarded her with a look of cold
contempt, then returned to his task.

" Don't be so silly," said Jeremy.  " You know
you always hate it when Aunt Amy says things like
that about you."

" Did Nurse see ? " asked Mary.

" No, she didn't," said Jeremy ;  " but she'll be
up in a minute."

" What are you going to do ? " asked Mary, her
mouth wide open.

" Do ? Keep him, of course," said Jeremy
stoutly ; at the same time his heart a little failed him
as he saw the pool of water slowly spreading and em-
bracing one cockatoo after another in its ruinous
flood.

" We ought to wipe him with a towel," said
Jeremy ; " if we could get him dry before Nurse
comes up she mightn't say so much."

But alas, it was too late for any towel ; the door
opened, and the Jampot entered, humming a hymn,
very cheerful and rosy from the kitchen fire and an
abundant series of chronicles of human failings and
misfortunes. The hymn ceased abruptly. She
stayed there where she was, " frozen into an image,"
as she afterwards described. She also said : " You
could 'ave knocked me down with a feather."

The dog did not look at her, but crooked under
him the leg that had been stiff like a ramrod and
spread out another. The children did not speak.

" Well ! " For a moment words failed her ; then
she began, her hands spread out as though she was
addressing a Suffragette meeting in Trafalgar Square.
(She knew, happy woman ! nothing of Suffragettes.)
" Of all the things, and it's you, Master Jeremy, that
'as done it, as anyone might have guessed by the way
you've been be'aving this last fortnight, and what's
come over you is more nor I nor anyone else can tell,
which I was saying only yesterday to your mother
that it's more than one body and pair of hands is up
to the managing of now you've got so wild and
wicked ; and wherever from did you get the dirty
animal dropping water all over the nursery carpet
and smelling awful, I'll be bound, which anyone can
see that's got eyes, and you'd know what your

father will do to you when he knows of it, and so he
shall, as sure as my name is Lizzie Preston. . . .
Go on out, you ugly, dirty animal—ough, you
'orrible creature you. I'll——"

But her advance was stopped. Jeremy stopped it.
Standing in front of the dog, his short thick legs
spread defiantly apart, his fists clenched, he almost
shouted :

" You shan't touch him. . . . No, you shan't. I
don't care. He shan't go out again and die. You're
a cruel, wicked woman."

The Jampot gasped. Never, no, never in all her
long nursing experience had she been so defied, so
insulted.

Her teeth clicked as always when her temper was
roused, the reason being that thirty years ago the
arts and accomplishments of dentistry had not
reached so fine a perfection as to-day can show.

She had, moreover, bought a cheap set. Her
teeth clicked. She began : " The moment your
mother comes I give her notice. To think that all
these years I've slaved and slaved, only to be told
such things by a boy as——"

Then a very dramatic thing occurred. The door
opened, just as it might in the third act of a play by
M. Sardou, and revealed the smiling faces of Mrs.
Cole, Miss Amy Trefusis and the Rev. William Jellybrand, Senior Curate of St. James's, Orange Street.

Mr. Jellybrand had arrived, as he very often did,
to tea. He had expressed a desire, as he very often
did, to see the " dear children." Mrs. Cole, liking to
show her children to visitors, even to such regular
and ordinary ones as Mr. Jellybrand, at once was
eager to gratify his desire.

" We'll catch them just before their tea," she said happily.

There is an unfortunate tendency on the part of our Press and stage to caricature our curates ; this tendency I would willingly avoid.   It should be easy enough to do, as I am writing about Polchester, a town that simply abounds—and also abounded thirty years ago—in curates of the most splendid and manly type.   But, unfortunately, Mr. Jellybrand was not one of these.   I, myself, remember him very well, and can see him now flinging his thin, black, and—as it seemed to me then—gigantic figure up Orange Street, his coat flapping behind him, his enormous boots flapping in front of him, and his huge hands flapping on each side of him like a huge gesticulating crow.

He had, the Polchester people who liked him said, " a rich voice."   The others who did not like him called him " an affected ass."   He ran up and down the scale like this :

| Mrs. |
| dear |
| My |
| Cole. |

and his blue cheeks looked colder than any iceberg. But then I must confess that I am prejudiced.   I did not like him ; no children did.

The Cole children hated him.   Jeremy because he had damp hands, Helen because he never looked at her, Mary because he once said to her, " Little girls must play as well as work, you know."   He always

self-confidence of his heart, had agreed with Miss
Maple, an elderly and bitter spinster, that the next
sewing meeting of the Dorcas Sisterhood should be
held in her house and not at the Rectory. He had
told Mrs. Cole of this on his way upstairs to the
nursery. Now Mrs. Cole liked the Dorcas meetings
at the Rectory ; she liked the cheerful chatter, the
hospitality, the gentle scandal and her own position
as hostess.

She did not like—she never liked—Miss Maple,
who was always pushing herself forward, criticizing
and backbiting. Mr. Jellybrand should not have
settled this without consulting her. He had taken
it for granted that she would agree. He had said :
" I agreed with Miss Maple that it would be better
to have it at her house. I'm sure you will think as I
do." Why should he be sure ? Was he not forgetting his position a little ? . . .

Kindest woman in the world, she had seen with a
strange un-Christian pleasure the dog's advance
upon the black trousers. Then Mr. Jellybrand had
been obviously afraid. He fancied, perhaps, that she
too, had been afraid. He fancied, perhaps, that she
was not mistress in her house, that she could be
brow-beaten by her sister and her nurse.

She smiled at him. " There's no reason to be
afraid, Mr. Jellybrand. . . . He's such a little dog."

Then the dog smiled at her.

" Poor little thing," she said. " He must have
nearly died in the snow."

Thus Miss Maple, bitterest of spinsters, influenced,
all unwitting, the lives not only of a dog and a
curate, but of the entire Cole family, and through
them, of endless generations both of dogs and men

as yet unborn. Miss Maple, sitting in her little yellow-curtained parlour drinking, in jaundiced contentment, her afternoon's cup of tea, was, of course, unaware of this. A good thing that she was unaware—she was quite conceited enough already.

## 4

After that smiling judgment of Mrs. Cole's, affairs were quickly settled.

" Of course it can only be for the night, children. Father will arrange something in the morning. Poor little thing. Where did you find him ? "

" We saw him from the window," said Jeremy quickly, " and he was shivering like anything, so we called him in to warm him."

" My dear Alice, you surely don't mean——" began Aunt Amy, and the Jampot said : " I really think, mum——," and Mr. Jellybrand, in his rich voice, murmured : " Is it quite wise, dear Mrs. Cole, do you think ? "

With thoughts of Miss Maple she smiled upon them all.

" Oh, for one night, I think, we can manage. He seems a clean little dog, and really we can't turn him out into the snow at once. It would be *too* cruel. But mind, children, it's only for one night. He looks a good little dog."

When the " quality " had departed, Jeremy's mind was in a confused condition of horror and delight. Such a victory as he had won over the Jampot, a victory that was a further stage in the fight for independence begun on his birthday, might have very awful qualities. There would begin now one of the

Jampot's sulks—moods well known to the Cole family, and lasting from a day to a week, according to the gravity of the offence. Yes, they had already begun. There she sat in her chair by the fire, sewing, sewing, her fat, roly-poly face carved into a parody of deep displeasure. Life would be very unpleasant now. No tops of eggs, no marmalade on toast, no skins of milk, no stories of " when I was a young girl," no sitting up five minutes " later," no stopping in the market-place for a talk with the banana woman —only stern insistence on every detail of daily life ; swift judgment were anything left undone or done wrong.

Jeremy sighed ; yes, it would be horrid and, for the sake of the world in general, which meant Mary and Helen, he must see what a little diplomacy would do. Kneeling down by the dog, he looked up into her face with the gaze of ingenuous innocence.

" You wouldn't have wanted the poor little dog to have died in the snow, would you, Nurse ? . . . It might, you know. It won't be any trouble, I expect——"

There was no reply. He could hear Mary and Helen drawing in their breaths with excited attention.

" Father always said we might have a dog one day when we were older—and are older now."

Still no word.

" We'll be extra good, Nurse, if you don't mind. Don't you remember once you said you had a dog when you were a little girl, and how you cried when it had its ear bitten off by a nasty big dog, and how your mother said she wouldn't have it fighting round the house, and sent it away, and you cried, and cried, and cried, and how you said that p'r'aps we'll have one one day?—and now we've got one."

He ended triumphantly. She raised her eyes for one moment, stared at them all, bit off a piece of thread, and said in deep, sepulchral tones:

" Either *it* goes, or I go."

The three stared at one another. The Jampot go? Really go? . . . They could hear their hearts thumping one after another. The Jampot go?

" Oh, Nurse, would you really? " whispered Mary. This innocent remark of Mary's conveyed in the tone of it more pleased anticipation than was, perhaps, polite. Certainly the Jampot felt this; a flood of colour rose into her face. Her mouth opened. But what she would have said is uncertain, for at that very moment the drama was further developed by the slow movement of the door, and the revelation of half of Uncle Samuel's body, clothed in its stained blue painting smock, and his ugly fat face clothed in its usual sarcastic smile.

" Excuse me one moment," he said; " I hear you have a dog."

The Jampot rose, as good manners demanded, but said nothing.

" Where is the creature? " he asked.

The new addition to the Cole family had finished his washing; the blazing fire had almost dried him, and his hair stuck out now from his body in little stiff prickles, hedgehog fashion, giving him a truly original appearance. His beard afforded him the air of an ambassador, and his grave, melancholy eyes the absorbed introspection of a Spanish hidalgo; his tail, however, in its upright, stumpy jocularity, betrayed his dignity.

" There he is," said Jeremy, with a glance half of terror, half of delight, at the Jampot. " Isn't he lovely ? "

" Lovely. My word ! " Uncle Samuel's smile broadened. " He's about the most hideous mongrel it's ever been my lot to set eyes on. But he has his points. He despises you all, I'm glad to see."

Jeremy, as usual with Uncle Samuel, was uncertain as to his sincerity.

" He looks a bit funny just now," he explained. " He's been drying on the rug. He'll be all right soon. He wanted to bite Mr. Jellybrand. It *was* funny. Mr. Jellybrand was frightened as anything."

" Yes, that must have been delightful," agreed Uncle Samuel. " What's his name ? "

" We haven't given him one yet. Wouldn't you think of one, Uncle Samuel ? "

The uncle considered the dog. The dog with grave and scornful eyes, considered the uncle.

" Well, if you really ask me," said that gentleman, " if you name him by his character I should say Hamlet would be as good as anything."

" What's Hamlet ? " asked Jeremy.

" He isn't anything just now. But he was a prince who was unhappy because he thought so much about himself."

" Hamlet'll do," said Jeremy comfortably. " I've never heard of a dog called that, but it's easy to say."

" Well, I must go," said Uncle Samuel, making one of his usual sudden departures. " Glad to have seen the animal. Good-bye."

He vanished.

" Hamlet," repeated Jeremy thoughtfully. " I wonder whether he'll like that——"

His attention, however, was caught by the Jampot's sudden outburst.

" All of them," she cried, " supporting you in your wickedness and disobedience. I won't 'ave it nor endure it not a minute longer. They can 'ave my notice this moment, and I won't take it back, not if they ask me on their bended knees—no, I won't—and that's straight."

For an instant she frowned upon them all—then she was gone, the door banging after her.

They gazed at one another.

There was a dreadful silence. Once Mary whispered : " Suppose she really does."

Hamlet only was unmoved.

Ten minutes later, Rose, the housemaid, entered with the tea-things. For a little she was silent. Then the three faces raised to hers compelled her confidence.

" Nurse has been and given notice," she said, " and the Missis has taken it. She's going at the end of the month. She's crying now in the kitchen."

They were alone again. Mary and Helen looked at Jeremy as though waiting to follow his lead. He did not know what to say. There was Tragedy, there was Victory, there was Remorse, there was Triumph. He was sorry, he was glad. His eyes fell upon Hamlet, who was now stretched out upon the rug, his nose between his paws, fast asleep.

Then he looked at his sisters.

" Well," he said slowly, " it's awfully nice to have a dog—anyway."

Such is the true and faithful account of Hamlet's entrance into the train of the Coles.

upon the town walls and hoardings the pictured announcements of the approaching visit to Polchester of Denny's Great Christmas Pantomime " Dick Whittington."   Boxing Night was to see the first performance at our Assembly Rooms, and during every afternoon and evening of the next three weeks this performance was to be repeated.

A pantomime had, I believe, never visited our town before ;  there had, of course, for many years been the Great Christmas Pantomime at the Theatre Royal, Drymouth, but in those days trains were not easy, and if you wished to attend an afternoon performance at the Drymouth Theatre you must rise very early in the morning by the candlelight and return late in the evening, with the cab forgetting to meet you at the station as commanded, and the long walk up Orange Street, and a headache and a bad temper next day.

It happened naturally then that the majority of the Polchester children had never set their inquisitive noses within the doors of a theatre, and although the two eldest daughters of the Dean, aged ten and eleven, had been once to London and to Drury Lane Theatre, their sense of glory and distinction so clouded their powers of accuracy and clarity that we were no nearer, by their help and authority, to the understanding of what a pantomime might really be.

I can myself recall the glory of those " Dick Whittington " pictures.  Just above Martin's the pastrycook's (where they sold lemon biscuits), near the Cathedral, there was a big wooden hoarding, and on to this was pasted a marvellous representation of Dick and his Cat dining with the King of the Zanzibar Islands.   The King, a mulatto, sat with his court in a hall with golden pillars, and the rats were to be seen flying in a confused flood towards the golden gates, whilst Dick, in red plush and diamond buckles, stood in dignified majesty, the Cat at his side. There was another wonderful picture of Dick asleep at the Cross Roads, fairies watching over him, and London Town in a lighted purple distance, and another of the streets of Old London with a comic fat serving man, diamond-paned windows, cobble-stones and high pointing eaves to the houses.

Jeremy saw these pictures for the first time during one of his afternoon walks, and returned home in such a state of choking excitement that he could not drink his tea. As was ever his way he was silent and controlled about the matter, asked very few questions and although he talked to himself a little did not disturb the general peace of the nursery. On Mary and Helen the effect of the posters had been less. Mary was following the adventures of the May family in " The Daisy Chain," and Helen was making necklaces for herself out of a box of beads that had been given her.

When Jeremy said once, " Who was the man in the red trousers with gold on them ? " no one paid any attention save Hamlet, who wagged his tail, looked wise and growled a little.

Who indeed could tell how he ached and longed and desired ? He had a very vague idea as to the nature of a play ; they had often dressed up at home and pretended to be different things and people, and, of course, he knew by heart the whole history of Dick Whittington, but this knowledge and experience did not in the least force him to realize that this performance of Mr. Denny's was simply a

E

larger, more developed "dressing up" and pretending. In some mysterious but nevertheless direct fashion Dick Whittington was coming to Polchester. It was just as he had heard for a long time of the existence of Aunt Emily who lived in Manchester—and then one day she appeared in a black bonnet and a shawl, and gave them wet kisses and sixpence apiece.

Dick Whittington was coming, having perhaps heard that Polchester was a very jolly place. So might come any day Jack of the Beanstalk, Cinderella, Queen Victoria, and God.

There were questions meanwhile that he would like to ask, but he was already a victim to that properly English fear of making a fool of himself, so he asked nothing. He dragged out his toy village and tried to make it a bridge in his imagination between the nursery and Whittington's world. As the village opened a door from the nursery, so might Whittington open a door from the village.

He considered Hamlet and wondered whether he knew anything about it. Hamlet, in spite of his mongrel appearance, was a very clever dog. He had his especial corners in the garden, the kitchen and the nursery. He never misbehaved, was never in the way, and was able to amuse himself for hours together. Although he attached himself quite deliberately to Jeremy, he did this in no sentimental fashion, and in his animosities towards the Jampot, Aunt Amy and the boy who helped with the boots and the knives, he was always restrained and courteous. He did indeed growl at Aunt Amy, but always with such a sense of humour that everyone (except Aunt Amy) was charmed, and he never

actually supported the children in their rebellions
against the Jampot, although you could see that he
liked and approved of such things. The Jampot
hated him with a passion that caused the nursery to
quiver with emotion. Was he not the cause of her
approaching departure, his first appearance having
led her into a tempest of passion that had caused
her to offer a " notice " that she had never for an
instant imagined would be accepted ? Was he
not a devilish dog who, with his quiet movements
and sly expressions, was more than human ?
" Mark my words," she said in the kitchen, " there's
a devil in that there animal, and so they'll find
before they're many years older—'Amlet indeed—
a 'eathenish name and a 'eathenish beast."

Her enemy had discovered that in one corner of
the nursery there were signs and symbols that
witnessed to something in the nature of a mouse
or a rat. That nursery corner became the centre
of all his more adventurous instincts. It happened
to be just the corner where the Jampot kept her
sewing machine, and you would think, if you came
to the nursery as a stranger, and saw him sitting,
his eyes fixed beamingly upon the machine, his tail
erect, his body here and there quivering a little,
that from duties of manly devotion he was protecting the Jampot's property. She knew better ; she
regarded, in some undefined way, this continued
contemplation by him of her possessions as an
ironical insult. She did everything possible to
drive him from the corner ; he inevitably returned,
and as he always delicately stepped aside when she
approached, it could not be said that he was in her
way. Once she struck him ; he looked at her in

such a fashion that " her flesh crept." . . . She never struck him again.

For Jeremy he became more and more of a delight. He understood so much. He sympathized, he congratulated, he sported, always at the right moment. He would sit gravely at Jeremy's feet, his body pressed against Jeremy's leg, one leg stuck out square, his eyes fixed inquisitively upon the nursery scene. He would be motionless ; then suddenly some thought would electrify him—his ears would cock, his eyes shine, his nose quiver, his tail tumble. The crisis would pass ; he would be composed once more. He would slide down to the floor, his whole body collapsing ; his head would rest upon Jeremy's foot ; he would dream of cats, of rats, of birds, of the Jampot, of beef and gravy, of sugar, of being washed, of the dogs' Valhalla, of fire and warmth, of Jeremy, of walks when every piece of flying paper was a challenge, of dogs, dogs that he had known of when he was a puppy, of doing things he shouldn't, of punishment and wisdom, pride and anger, of love-affairs of his youth, of battle, of settling-down, of love-affairs in the future, again of cats and beef, and smells—smells—smells, again of Jeremy, whom he loved. And Jeremy, watching him now, thus sleeping, and thinking of Dick Whittington, wondered why it was that a dog would understand so easily, without explanations, the thoughts and desires he had, and that all grown-up people would not understand, and would demand so many explanations, and would laugh at one, and pity one, and despise one. Why was it ? he asked himself.

" I know," he suddenly cried, turning upon Helen ; " it can be your birthday treat ! "

" What can ? " she asked.

" Why, going to Dick Whittington—all of us."

Helen had, most unfortunately for herself, a birthday only a week after Christmas, the result being that, in her own opinion at any rate, she never received " proper presents " on either of those two great present-giving occasions. She was always allowed, however, a " treat " ; her requests were generally in the nature of food ; once of a ride in the train ; once even a visit to the Polchester Museum. . . . It was difficult in those days to find " treats " in Polchester.

" Oh, do you think they'd let us ? " she said.

" We can try," said Jeremy ; " I heard Aunt Amy say the other day that she didn't think it was right for children to see acting, and mother always does the opposite to what Aunt Amy says, so p'r'aps it will be all right. I wish Hamlet could go," he added.

" Don't be silly ! " said Helen.

" It isn't silly," Jeremy said indignantly. " It's all about a cat, anyway, and he'd love to see all the rats and things. He wouldn't bark if we told him not to, and I held his collar."

" If Aunt Amy sat next him he would," said Mary.

" Oh, bother Aunt Amy," said Jeremy.

After this Helen needed a great deal of urging ; but she heard that Lucy and Angela, the aforesaid daughters of the Dean, were going, and the spirit of rivalry drove her forward.

It happened that the Dean himself one day said something to Mr. Cole about " supporting a very praiseworthy effort. They are presenting, I understand, the proceeds of the first performance to the Cathedral Orphanage."

Helen was surprised at the readiness with which her request was granted.

" We'll all go," said Mr. Cole, in his genial pastoral fashion. " Good for us . . . good for us . . . to see the little ones laugh . . . good for us all."

Only Uncle Samuel said " that nothing would induce him——"

2

I pass swiftly over Christmas Eve, Christmas Day, and the day after, although I should like to linger upon these sumptuous dates. Jeremy had a sumptuous time ; Hamlet had a sumptuous time (a whole sugar rat, plates and plates of bones, and a shoe of Aunt Amy's) ; Mary and Helen had sumptuous times in their own feminine fashion.

Upon the evening of Christmas Eve, when the earth was snow-lit, and the street-lamps sparkled with crystals, and the rime on the doorsteps crackled beneath one's feet, Jeremy accompanied his mother on a present-leaving expedition. The excitement of that ! The wonderful shapes and sizes of the parcels, the mysterious streets, the door-handles and the door-bells, the glittering stars, the maid-servants, the sense of the lighted house, as though you opened a box full of excitements and then hurriedly shut the lid down again. Jeremy trembled and shook, not with cold, but with exalting, com-pletely satisfying happiness.

There followed the Stocking, the Waits, the Carols, the Turkey, the Christmas Cake, the *Tree*, the Presents, Snapdragon, Bed. . . . There followed Headache, Ill-temper, Smacking of Mary, Afternoon Walk, Good Temper again, Complete Weariness,

Hamlet sick on the Golden Cockatoos, Hamlet
Beaten, Five minutes with Mother downstairs,
Bed. . . . Christmas was over.

From that moment of the passing of Boxing Day
it was simply the counting of the minutes to " Dick
Whittington." Six days from Boxing Day. Say
you slept from eight to seven—eleven hours ; that
left thirteen hours ; six thirteen hours was, so
Helen said, seventy-eight. Seventy-eight hours,
and Sunday twice as long as the other days, and
that made thirteen more ; ninety-one, said Helen,
her nose in the air.

The week dragged along, very difficult work for
everybody, and even Hamlet felt the excitement and
watched his corner with the Jampot's sewing
machine in it with more quivering intensity than
ever. The Day Before The Day arrived, the
evening before The Day, the last supper before The
Day, the last bed before The Day. . . . Suddenly,
like a Jack-in-the-box, The Day itself.

Then the awful thing happened.

Jeremy awoke to the consciousness that something terrific was about to occur. He lay for a
minute thinking—then he was up, running about
the nursery floor as though he were a young man in
Mr. Rossetti's poetry shouting : " Helen ! Mary !
Mary ! Helen ! . . . It's Dick Whittington ! Dick
Whittington ! "

On such occasions he lost entirely his natural
reserve and caution. He dressed with immense
speed, as though that would hasten the coming of
the evening. He ran into the nursery, carrying the
black tie that went under his sailor-collar.

He held it out to the Jampot, who eyed him with

disfavour. She was leaving them all in a week and was a strange confusion of sentiment and bad temper, love and hatred, wounded pride and injured dignity.

" Nurse. Please. Fasten it," he said impatiently.

" And that's not the way to speak, Master Jeremy, and well you know it," she said. " 'Ave you cleaned your teeth ? "

" Yes," he answered without hesitation. It was not until the word was spoken that he realized that he had not. He flushed. The Jampot eyed him with a sudden sharp suspicion. He was then and ever afterwards a very bad hand at a lie. . . .

He would have taken the word back, he wanted to take it back—but something held him as though a stronger than he had placed his hand over his mouth. His face flamed.

" You've truly cleaned them ? " she said.

" Yes, truly," he answered, his eyes on the ground. Never was there a more obvious liar in all the world.

She said no more ; he moved to the fireplace. His joy was gone. There was a cold clammy sensation about his heart. Slowly, very slowly, the consciousness stole upon him that he was a liar. He had not thought it a lie when he had first spoken, now he knew.

Still there was time. Had he turned round and spoken, all might still have been well. But now obstinacy held him. He was not going to give the Jampot an opportunity for triumphing over him. After all, he *would* clean them so soon as she went to brush Helen's hair. In a moment what he had said would be true.

But he was miserable. Hamlet came up from the nether regions where he had spent the night, showing his teeth, wagging his tail, and even rolling on the cockatoos. Jeremy paid no attention. The weight in his heart grew heavier and heavier. He watched, from under his eyelids, the Jampot. In a moment she must go into Helen's room. But she did not. She stayed for a little arranging the things on the breakfast table—then suddenly, without a word, she turned into Jeremy's bed-chamber. His heart began to hammer. There was an awful pause; he heard from miles away Mary's voice; " Do do that button, Helen, I can't get it ! " and Helen's " Oh, bother ! "

Then, like Judgment, the Jampot appeared again. She stood in the doorway, looking across at him.

" You 'ave *not* cleaned your teeth, Master Jeremy," she said. " The glass isn't touched, nor your tooth-brush. . . . You wicked, wicked boy. So it's a liar you've become, added on to all your other wickedness."

" I forgot," he muttered sullenly. " I thought I had."

She smiled the smile of approaching triumph.

" No, you did not," she said. " You knew you'd told a lie. It was in your face. All of a piece—all of a piece."

The way she said this, like a pirate counting over his captured treasure, was enraging. Jeremy could feel the wild fury at himself, at her, at the stupid blunder of the whole business rising to his throat.

" If you think I'm going to let this pass you're making a mighty mistake," she continued, " which I wouldn't do not if you paid me all the gold in the kingdom. I mayn't be good enough to keep my place and look after such as you, but anyways I'm able to stop your lying for another week or two. I know my duty even though there's them as thinks I don't."

She positively snorted, and the excitement of her own vindication and the just condemnation of Jeremy was such that her hands trembled.

" I don't care what you do," Jeremy shouted. " You can tell anyone you like. I don't care what you do. You're a beastly woman."

She turned upon him, her face purple. " That's enough, Master Jeremy," she said, her voice low and trembling. " I'm not here to be called names by such as you. You'll be sorry for this before you're much older. . . . You see."

There was then an awful and sickly pause. Jeremy seemed to himself to be sinking lower and lower into a damp clammy depth of degradation. What must this world be that it could change itself so instantly from a place of gay and happy pleasure into a dim groping room of punishment and dismay ?

His feelings were utterly confused. He supposed that he was terribly wicked. But he did not feel wicked. He only felt miserable, sick and defiant. Mary and Helen came in, their eyes open to a crisis, their bodies tuned sympathetically to the atmosphere of sin and crime that they discerned around them.

Then Mr. Cole came in as was his daily habit— for a moment before his breakfast.

" Well, here are you all," he cried. " Ready for to-night ? No breakfast yet ? Why, now . . . ? "

Then perceiving, as all practised fathers instantly must, that the atmosphere was sinful, he changed his voice to that of the Children's Sunday Afternoon Service—a voice well known in his family.

" Please, sir," began the Jampot, " I'm sorry to 'ave to tell you, sir, that Master Jeremy's not been at all good this morning."

" Well, Jeremy," he said, turning to his son, " what is it ? "

Jeremy's face, raised to his father's, was hard and set and sullen.

" I've told a lie," he said ; " I said I'd cleaned my teeth when I hadn't.  Nurse went and looked, and then I called her a beastly woman."

The Jampot's face expressed a grieved and at the same time triumphant confirmation of this.

" You told a lie ? "   Mr. Cole's voice was full of a lingering sorrow.

" Yes," said Jeremy.

" Are you sorry ? "

" I'm sorry that I told a lie, but I'm not sorry I called Nurse a beastly woman."

" Jeremy ! "

" No, I'm not.   She *is* a beastly woman."

Mr. Cole was always at a loss when anyone defied him, even though it were only a small boy of eight. He took refuge now in his ecclesiastical and parental authority.

" I'm very distressed—very distressed indeed.  1 hope that punishment, Jeremy, will show you how wrong you have been.   I'm afraid you cannot come with us to the Pantomime to-night."

At that judgment a quiver for an instant held Jeremy's face, turning it, for that moment, into something shapeless and old. His heart had given a wild leap of terror and dismay. But he showed no further sign. He simply stood there waiting.

Mr. Cole was baffled, as he always was by Jeremy's moods, so he continued :

" And until you've apologized to Nurse for your rudeness you must remain by yourself. I shall forbid your sisters to speak to you. Mary and Helen, you are not to speak to your brother until he has apologized to Nurse."

" Yes, Father," said Helen.

" Oh, Father, mayn't he come to-night ? " said Mary.

" No, Mary, I'm afraid not."

A tear rolled down her cheek. " It won't be any fun without Jeremy," she said. She wished to make the further sacrifice of saying that she would not go unless Jeremy did, but some natural caution restrained her.

Mr. Cole, his face heavy with sorrow, departed.

At the dumb misery of Jeremy's face the Jampot's heart—in reality a kind and even sentimental heart—repented her.

" There, Master Jeremy, you be a good boy all day, and I dare say your father will take you, after all ; and we won't think no more about what you said to me in the 'eat of the moment."

But Jeremy answered nothing ; nor did he respond to the smell of bacon, nor the advances of Hamlet, nor the flood of sunlight that poured into the room from the frosty world outside.

A complete catastrophe. They none of them had wanted to see this thing with the urgent excitement that he had felt. They had not dreamt of it for days

and nights and nights and days, as he had done.
Their whole future existence did not depend upon
their witnessing this, as did his.

During that morning he was a desperate creature,
like something caged and tortured. Do happy
middle-aged philosophers assure us that children are
light-hearted and unfeeling animals ? Let them
realize something of the agony which Jeremy suffered
that day. His whole world had gone.

He was wicked, an outcast ; his word could never
be trusted again ; he would be pointed at as the boy
who told a lie. . . . And he would not meet Dick
Whittington.

The eternity of his punishment hung around his
neck like an iron chain. Childhood's tragedies are
terrible tragedies, because a child has no sense of
time ; a moment's dismay is eternal ; a careless
word from an elder is a lasting judgment ; an
instant's folly is a lifetime's mistake.

The day dragged its weary length along, and he
scarcely moved from his corner by the fire. He did
not attempt conversation with anyone. Once or
twice the Jampot tried to penetrate behind that
little mask of anger and dismay.

" Come, now, things aren't so bad as all that.
You be a good boy, and go and tell your father you're
sorry. . ." or " Well, then, Master Jeremy, there'll be
another time, I dare say, you can go to the the-ayter."

But she found no response. If there was one
thing that she hated, it was sulks. Here they were,
sulks of the worst—and so, like many wiser than
herself, she covered up with a word a situation that
she did not understand, and left it at that.

The evening came on ; the curtains were drawn.

Tea arrived, still Jeremy sat there, not speaking, not raising his eyes, a condemned creature. Mary and Helen and Hamlet had had a wretched day. They all sympathized with him.

The girls went to dress. Seven o'clock struck. They were taken downstairs by Nurse, who had her evening out. Rose, the housemaid, would sit with Master Jeremy.

Doors closed, doors opened, voices echoed, carriage-wheels were heard.

Jeremy and Hamlet were left to themselves. . . .

### 3

The last door had closed, and the sudden sense that everyone had gone and that he might behave now as he pleased, removed the armour in which all day he had encased himself.

He raised his head, looked about the deserted nursery, and then, with the sudden consciousness of that other lighted and busied place where Whittington was pursuing his adventures, he burst into tears. He sobbed, his head down upon his arms, and his body squeezed together so that his knees were close to his nose and his hair in his boots. Hamlet restored him to himself. Instead of assisting his master's grief, as a sentimental dog would have done by sighing or sniffing or howling, he yawned, stretched himself, and rolled on the carpet. He did not believe in giving way to feelings, and he was surprised, and perhaps disappointed, at Jeremy's lack of restraint.

Jeremy felt this, and in a little while sobs came very slowly, and at last were only little shudders, rather pleasant and healthy. He looked about him, rubbed his red nose with a hideously dirty handkerchief, and felt immensely sleepy.

No, he would not cry any more. Rose would shortly appear, and he did not intend to cry before housemaids. Nevertheless, his desolation was supreme. He was a liar. He had told lies before, but they had not been discovered, and so they were scarcely lies. . . . Now, in some strange way, the publication of his lie had shown him what truly impossible things lies were. He had witnessed this effect upon the general public ; he had not believed that he was so wicked. He did not even now feel really wicked, but he saw quite clearly that there was one world for liars and one for truthful men. He wanted, terribly badly, someone to tell him that he was still in the right world. . . .

And then, on the other side, the thought that Mary and Helen were at this very moment witnessing the coloured history of Dick Whittington, the history that he had pursued ceaselessly during all these days and nights—that picture of them all in the lighted theatre—once more nearly overcame him. But he pulled himself together.

He sniffed, left his dirty handkerchief, and went slowly and sorrowfully to drag out his toy village from its corner and see whether anything could be done with it. . . . After all, he was going to school in September. His punishment could not be quite limitless. Hamlet had just shown his approval of this manly conduct by strolling up and sniffing at the Noah family, who were, as usual, on their way to church, when the door suddenly opened, and in came Uncle Samuel.

Jeremy had forgotten his uncle, and now blinked up at him from the floor, where he was squatting, rather ashamed of his swollen eyes and red nose.

Uncle Samuel, however, had no time for details ; he was apparently in a hurry. He did not wear his blue painting-smock, but was in a comparatively clean black suit, and on the back of his head was a squashy brown hat.

" Come on," he said, " or we shall be too late."

Jeremy choked. " Too late ? " he repeated.

" You're coming, aren't you—to the Pantomime ? They sent me back for you."

The room suddenly got on to its legs, like the food and the families during Alice's feast in the " Looking Glass," and swung round, lurching from side to side, and causing the fire to run into the gas and the gas to fly out of the window.

" I—don't—understand," Jeremy stammered.

" Well, if you don't understand in half a shake," said Uncle Samuel, " you won't see any of the show at all. Go on. Wash your face. There are streaks of dirt all down it as though you were a painted Indian ; stick on your cap and coat and boots and come along."

Exactly as one moves in sleep so Jeremy now moved. He had once had a wonderful dream, in which he had been at a meal that included everything that he had most loved—fish-cakes, sausages, ices, strawberry jam, sponge-cake, chocolates, and scrambled eggs—and he had been able to eat, and eat, and had never been satisfied, and had never felt sick—a lovely dream.

He often thought of it. And now in the same bewildering fashion he found his boots and cap and coat, and then, deliberately keeping from him the thought of the Pantomime lest he should suddenly wake up, he said :

" I'm ready, Uncle."

Samuel Trefusis looked at him :

" You're a strange kid," he said ; " you take everything so quietly—but, thank God, I don't understand children."

" There's Hamlet," said Jeremy, wondering whether perhaps the dream would extend to his friend. " I suppose he can't come too."

" No, he certainly can't," said Uncle Samuel grimly.

" And there's Rose. She'll wonder where I've gone."

" I've told her. Don't you worry. What a conscientious infant you are. Just like your father. Anything else ? "

" No," said Jeremy breathlessly, and nearly murdered himself going downstairs because he shut his eyes in order to continue the dream so long as it was possible. Then in the cold night air, grasping his uncle's hand with a feverish hold, he stammered :

" Is it really true ? Are we going—really ? "

" Of course we're going. Come on—step out or you'll miss the Giant."

" But—but—oh ! " he drew a deep breath. ' Then they don't think me a liar any more ? "

" They—who ? "

" Father and Mother and everyone."

" Don't you think about them. You'd better enjoy yourself."

" But you said you wouldn't go to the Pantomime —not for anything ? "

F

strange clothes were standing. In the middle of
the scene was a funny old woman, her hat tumbling
off her head, her shabby skirt dragging, large boots
and a red nose. It was from this strange creature
that the deep ugly voice proceeded. She had, this
old woman, a number of bales of cloth under her
arms, and she tried to carry them all, but one slipped,
and then another, and then another; she bent
to pick them up and her hat fell off; she turned
for her hat and all the bales tumbled together.
Jeremy began to laugh—everyone laughed; the
strange voice came again and again, lamenting,
bewailing, she had secured one bale, a smile of
cautious triumph began to spread over her ugly
face, then the bales all fell again, and once more
she was on her knees. It was then that her voice
or some movement brought to Jeremy's eyes so
vividly the figure of their old gardener, Jordan,
that he turned round to Uncle Samuel, and suddenly
grasping that gentleman's fat thigh, exclaimed
convulsively : " Why, she's a man ! "

What a strange topsy-turvy world this was in
which women were men, and shops turned (as with a
sudden creaking and darkness and clattering did
this one) into gardens by the sea. Jeremy drew
his breath deeply and held on. His mouth was
open and his hair on end. . . .

It is impossible to define exactly Jeremy's ultimate impression as the entertainment proceeded.
Perhaps he had no ultimate impression. It cannot
in reality have been a very wonderful pantomime.
Even at Drury Lane, thirty years back, there were
many things that they did not know, and it is not
likely that a touring company fitted into so inade-

quate an old building as our Assembly Rooms would have provided anything very fine. But Jeremy will never again discover so complete a realization for his illusions. Whatever failures in the presentation there were, he himself made good.

As a finale to the first half of the entertainment there was given Dick's dream at the Cross-Roads. He lay on the hard ground, his head upon his bundle, the cat as large as he watching sympathetically beside him. In the distance were the lights of London, and then, out of the half dusk, fairies glittering with stars and silver danced up and down the dusky road whilst all the London bells rang out " Turn again, Whittington, Lord Mayor of London."

Had Jeremy been of the age and wisdom of Uncle Samuel he would have discovered that Dick was a stout lady and probably the mother of a growing family ; that the fairies knew as much about dancing as the Glebeshire wives sitting on the bench behind ; that the London bells were two hand instruments worked by a youth in shirt sleeves behind the scenes so energetically that the High Road and the painted London blew backwards and forwards in sympathy with his movements. Jeremy, happily, was not so worldly wise as his uncle. This scene created for him then a tradition of imperishable beauty that would never fade again. The world after that night would be a more magical place than it had ever been before. " Turn again, Whittington," continued the education that the Toy Village and Hamlet had already advanced.

When the gas rose once again, sizzling like crackling bacon, he was white with excitement. The only remark that he made was : " It's much better than wife, how they were all swallowed by a whale, cast up by a most lucky chance on the Zanzibars, nearly cooked by the natives, and rescued by the King of the Zanzibars' beautiful daughter, killed all the rats, were given a huge feast, with dance and song, and finally Dick, although tempted by the dusky Princess, refused a large fortune and returned to Alice of Eastcheap, the true lady of his heart. There were, of course, many other things, such as the aspirations and misadventures of Mrs. Fitzwarren, the deep-voiced lady who had already so greatly amused Jeremy. And then there was a Transformation Scene, in which roses turned into tulips and tulips into the Hall of Gold, down whose blazing steps marched stout representatives of all the nations.

It was in the middle of this last thrilling spectacle, when Jeremy's heart was in his mouth and he was so deeply excited that he did not know whether it were he or the lady next to him who was eating peppermints, that his uncle plucked him by the sleeve and said in his ear : " Come on.  It's close on the end. We must go."

Jeremy very reluctantly got up, and stumbled out over knees and legs and exclamations like :

" There's Japan ! "  " No, it ain't ;  it's Chiney ! " " Yon's a fine, hearty young woman ! " and so on. He was dragged through the black curtain, down the stone steps, and into the street.

" But it wasn't the end," he said.

" It will be in one minute," said his uncle.  " And I want us to get home first."

" Why ? " said Jeremy.

" Never you mind.  Come on ;  we'll race it."

They arrived home breathless, and then, once again in the old familiar hall, Uncle Samuel said :

" Now you nip up to the nursery, and then they'll never know you've been out at all."

" Never know ? " said Jeremy. " But you said they'd sent for me."

" Well," said Uncle Samuel, " that wasn't exactly true. As a matter of fact, they don't know you were there."

" Oh ! " said Jeremy, the corner of his mouth turning down. " Then I've told a lie again ! "

" Nonsense ! " said Uncle Samuel impatiently. " It wasn't you ; it was I."

" And doesn't it matter your telling lies ? " asked Jeremy.

The answer to this difficult question was, happily for Uncle Samuel, interrupted by the arrival of the household, who had careered up Orange Street in a cab.

When Mr. and Mrs. Cole saw Jeremy standing in the hall, his great coat still on and his muffler round his neck, there was a fine scene of wonder and amazement.

Uncle Samuel explained. " It was my fault. I told him you'd forgiven him and sent for him to come, after all. He's in an awful state now that you shouldn't forgive him."

Whatever they thought of Uncle Samuel, this was obviously neither the time nor the place to speak out. Mrs. Cole looked at her son. His body defiant, sleepy, excited. His mouth was obstinate, but his eyes appealed to her on the scene of the common marvellous experience that they had just enjoyed.

But Mrs. Cole, with all her placidity, was firm.   The Jampot had to go.

I would like to paint a pleasant picture of the sentiment of the Cole children on this touching occasion ; something, perhaps, in the vein of tragi-comedy with which Mr. Kenneth-Graham embroiders a similar occasion in his famous masterpiece —but in this case there was very little sentiment and no tragedy at all.   They did not think of the event beforehand, and then when it suddenly occurred there was all the excitement of being looked after by Rose, the housemaid, of having a longer time with their mother in the evening, and, best of all, a delightful walk with Aunt Amy, whose virginal peace of mind they attacked from every possible quarter.

The Jampot left in a high state of sulks, declaring to the kitchen that no woman had ever been so unfairly treated ; that her married sister Sarah Francis, of Rafiel, with whom she was now to live, should be told all about it, and that the citizens of Rafiel should be compelled to sympathize.   The children were not unfeeling, but they hated the Jampot's sulks, and while she waited in the nursery, longing for a word or movement of affection, but wearing a face of stony disapproval, they stood awkwardly beholding her, and aching for her to go. She was the more unapproachable in that she wore her Sunday silks and a heavy black bonnet with shiny rattling globes of some dark metal that nodded and becked and bowed like live things.   Hamlet, who had, of course, always hated the Jampot, barked at this bonnet furiously and would have bitten at it had it been within his reach.   She

had meant to leave them all with little sentences
about life and morals, but the noise of the dog, the
indifference of the children, and the general air
of impatience for her departure strangled her
aphorisms.  Poor Jampot !  She was departing to a
married sister who did not want her, and would
often tell her so ; her prospects in life were not
bright, and it is sad to think that no inhabitant of
the Orange Street house felt any sorrow at the sight
of the last gesticulating wave of her black bonnet
as she stepped into the old mouldy Polchester cab.

" The King is dead—long live the King ! "  The
Jampot as a power in the Cole family has ceased to
be.

The day following the Jampot's departure offered
up the news that, for the first time in the history of
the Coles, there was to be a governess.  The word
" Governess " had an awful sound, and the children
trembled with a mixture of delight and terror.
Jeremy pretended indifference.

" It's only another woman," he said.  " She'll be
like the Jampot—only, a lady, so she won't be able
to punish us as the Jampot could."

I expect that Mr. and Mrs. Cole had great difficulty
in finding anyone who would do.  Thirty years ago
governesses were an incapable race, and belonged
too closely either to the Becky Sharp or the Amelia
type to be very satisfactory.  It was then that the
New Woman was bursting upon the scene, but she
was not to be found amongst the governesses.  No
one in Polchester had learnt yet to cycle in rational
costume, it was several years before the publication
of " The Heavenly Twins," and Mr. Trollope's Lilys
and Lucys were still considered the ideal of England's

maidenhood. Mrs. Cole, therefore, had to choose
between idiotic young women and crabbed old
maids, and she finally chose an old maid. I don't
think that Miss Jones was the very best choice
that she could have made, but time was short.
Jeremy, aided by Hamlet, was growing terribly
independent, and Mr. Cole had neither the humour
nor the courage to deal with him. No, Miss Jones
was not ideal, but the Dean had strongly recommended her. It is true that the Dean had never
seen her, but her brother, with whom she had lived
for many years, had once been the Dean's curate.
It was true that he had been a failure as a curate,
but that made the Dean the more anxious to be
kind now to his memory, he—Mr. Jones—having
just died of general bad-temper and selfishness.

Miss Jones, buried during the last twenty years
in the green depths of a Glebeshire valley, found herself now, at the age of fifty, without friends, without
money, without relations. She thought that she
would be a governess.

The Dean recommended her, Mrs. Cole approved
of her birth, education and sobriety, Mr. Cole liked
the severity of her countenance when she came to
call, and she was engaged.

" Jeremy needs a tight hand," said Mr. Cole.
" It's no use having a young girl."

" Miss Jones easily escapes that charge," said
Uncle Samuel, who had met her in the hall.

The children were prepared to be good. Jeremy
felt that it was time to take life seriously. He put
away his toy village, scolded Hamlet for eating
Mary's pincushion, and dragged out his dirty
exercise-book in which he did sums.

" I do hate sums ! " he said, with a sigh, regarding the hideous smudges of thumbs and tears that scored the page. " I shall never understand anything about them."

" I'll help you," said Mary, who was greatly excited at the thought of a governess. " We'll do them together."

" No we won't," said Jeremy, who hated to be dependent. " I'll learn it myself—if only the paper didn't get dirty so quickly."

" Mother says," remarked Helen, " that she's had a very hard life, and no one's ever been kind to her. ' She wants affection,' Mother says."

" I'll give her my napkin-ring that you gave me last Christmas, Mary," said Jeremy. " You don't mind, do you ? It's all dirty now. I hope Hamlet won't bark at her."

Hamlet was worrying Mary's pincushion at the moment, holding it between his paws, his body stretched out in quivering excitement, his short, " snappy " tail, as Uncle Samuel called it, standing up straight in air. He stopped for an instant when he heard his name, and shook one ear.

" Mother says," continued Helen, " that she lived with a brother who never really gave her enough to eat."

Jeremy opened his eyes. This seemed to him a horrible thing.

" She shall have my porridge, if she likes," he said ; " I don't like it very much. And I'll give her that chocolate that Mr. Jellybrand sent us. There's still some, although it's rather damp now, I expect."

" How silly you are ! " said Helen scornfully.

" Of course, Mother will give her anything she wants."

" It isn't silly," said Jeremy. " Perhaps she'll want more than she really wants. I often do."

" Oh, you ! " said Helen.

" And if for ever so long," said Jeremy, " she hasn't had enough to eat, she'll want twice as big meals now as other people—to make up."

" Mother says we've got to remember she's a lady," said Helen.

" What's the difference," asked Jeremy, " between a lady and not a lady ? "

" Oh, you are ! " said Helen. " Why, Aunt Amy's a lady, and Rose isn't."

" Rose is nicer," said Jeremy.

Miss Jones had, I am sorry to say, lied to Mrs. Cole in one particular. She had told her that " she had had to do with children all her life," the fact being that on several occasions some little cousins had come to stay with herself and her brother. On these occasions the little cousins had been so paralysed with terror that discipline had not been difficult. It was from these experiences that Miss Jones flattered herself that " she understood children."

So audacious a self-confidence is doomed to invite the scornful punishment of the gods.

Miss Jones arrived upon a wet January afternoon, one of those Glebeshire days when the town sinks into a bath of mud and mist and all the pipes run water and the eaves drip and horses splash and only ducks are happy. Out of a blurred lamp-lit dusk stumbled Miss Jones's cab, and out of a blurred unlit cab stumbled Miss Jones.

As she stood in the hall trying to look warm and

amiable, Mrs. Cole's heart forsook her. On that earlier day of her visit Miss Jones had looked possible, sitting up in Mrs. Cole's drawing-room, smiling her brightest, because she so desperately needed the situation, and wearing her best dress. Now she was all in pieces ; she had had to leave her little village early in the morning to catch the village bus ; she had waited at wayside stations, as in Glebeshire only one can wait ; the world had dripped upon her head and spattered upon her legs. She had neuralgia and a pain in her back ; she had worn her older dress because, upon such a day, it would not do to travel in her best ; and then, as a climax to everything, she had left her umbrella in the train. How could she do such a thing upon such a day ! Her memory was not her strongest point, poor lady, and it was a good umbrella, and she could not afford to buy another. Perhaps they would find it for her, but it was very unlikely.

She had had it for a numberof years.

She was a little woman, all skin and bone, with dried withered cheeks, a large brown nose and protruding ears. Her face had formed severe lines in self-defence against her brother, but her eyes were mild, and when she smiled her mouth was rather pleasantly pathetic.

" Oh, she'll never do," thought Mrs. Cole, as she looked at her dripping in the hall.

" I can't think how I forgot it," said the poor lady, her mind fixed upon her umbrella. " They said that perhaps they would find it for me, but there was a man in my carriage, I remember, who will most certainly have taken it—and it was a nice one with a silver handle."

G

" Never mind," said Mrs. Cole cheerfully, " I'm
sure they'll find it. You must come up to the nursery—or the schoolroom I suppose we must call it
now ; there's a lovely fire there, and we'll both have
tea with the children to-day, so as to feel at home,
all of us, as quickly as possible."

What Miss Jones wanted was to lie down on a bed
in a dark room and try and conquer her neuralgia.
The thought of a lighted nursery filled her with dismay. However, first impressions are so important.
She pulled herself together.

The children had heard the arrival ; they waited
in a bunch by the fire, their eyes partly fixed on the
door, partly on the strawberry jam that they were
allowed to-day as a treat in the new governess's
honour. Hamlet, his eyes and ears also upon the
door, expecting perhaps a rat, perhaps Aunt Amy,
sat in front of the group, its bodyguard.

" She's in the hall," said Helen, " and now
Mother's saying : ' Do take off your things. You
must be wet,' and now she's saying : ' You'll like to
see the children, I expect,' and now——"

There they were, standing in the doorway, Mrs.
Cole and Miss Jones. There followed a dismal
pause. The children had not expected anyone so
old and so ugly as Miss Jones. Hamlet did not
bark—nothing occurred.

At last Mrs. Cole said : " Now, children, come
and say, ' How do you do ? ' to Miss Jones. This is
Helen, our eldest—this Mary—and this Jeremy."

Miss Jones did a dreadful thing. In her eagerness to be pleasant and friendly she kissed the girls,
and then, before anyone could stop her, kissed
Jeremy. He took it like a man, never turning his

head nor wiping his mouth with his hand afterwards, but she might have seen in his eyes, had she looked, what he felt about it.

She said : " I hope we shall be happy together, dears."

The children said nothing, and presently they all sat down to tea.

**2**

It was unfortunate that there was so little precedent on both sides. Miss Jones had never been a governess before and the children had never had one. Of course, many mistakes were made. Miss Jones had had a true admiration for what she used to call " her brother's indomitable spirit," her name for his selfishness and bad temper. She was herself neither selfish nor bad-tempered, but she was ignorant, nervous, over-anxious, and desperately afraid of losing her situation. She had during so many years lived without affection that the wells of it had dried up within her, and now, without being at all a bad old lady, she was simply preoccupied with the business of managing her neuralgia, living on nothing a week, and building to her deceased brother's memory a monument of heroic character and self-sacrifice.

She was short-sighted and had a perpetual cold ; she was forgetful and careless. She had, nevertheless, a real knowledge of many things, a warm heart somewhere could she be encouraged to look for it again, and a sense of humour buried deep beneath her cares and preoccupations. There were many worse persons in the world than Miss Jones. But most unfortunately, her love for her brother's memory led her to resolve on what she called " firmness."

Mrs. Cole had told her that Jeremy was " getting too much " for his nurse ; she approached Jeremy with exactly the tremors and quaking boldness that she would have summoned to her aid before a bull loose in a field.   She really did look frightening with her large spectacles on the end of her large nose, her mouth firmly set, and a ruler in her hand.

" I insist on absolute obedience," was her motto. Jeremy looked at her but said no word.

It was made clear to them all that the new régime was to be far other than the earlier nursery one. There were to be regular lesson hours—nine to twelve and four to five.   A neat piece of white paper was fastened to the wall with " Monday : Geography 9-10, Arithmetic 10-11," and so on.   A careful graduation of punishments was instituted, copies to be written so many times, standing on a chair, three strokes on the hand with a ruler, and, worst of all, standing in the corner wearing a paper Dunce's cap.   (This last she had read of in books.)

At first Jeremy had every intention of behaving well, in spite of that unfortunate embrace.   He was proud of his advance in life ; he was no longer a baby ; the nursery was now a schoolroom ; he stayed up an hour later at night ; he was to be allowed twopence a week pocket-money ; his whole social status had risen.   He began to read for pleasure, and discovered that it was easier than he had expected, so that he passed quite quickly through " Lottie's Visit to Grandmama " into " Stumps " and out again into " Jackanapes."   He heard some

elder say that the road to a large fortune lay through
" Sums," and, although this seemed to him an extremely mysterious statement, he determined to
give the theory a chance.  In fact, he sat down the
first day at the schoolroom table, Mary and Helen
on each side of him, and Miss Jones facing them,
with fine resolves and high ambitions.  Before him
lay a pure white page, and at the head of this the
noble words in a running hand :

" Slow and steady wins the race."

He grasped his pencil, and Miss Jones, eager to
lose no time in asserting her authority, cried :
" But that's not the way to hold your pencil,
Jeremy, your thumb so, your finger so."

He scowled and found that lifting his thumb over
the pencil was as difficult as lifting Hamlet over a
gate.  He made a bold attempt, but the pencil refused to move.

" Can't hold it that way," he said.

" You must never say, ' can't ' Jeremy," remarked Miss Jones.  " There isn't such a word."

" Oh yes," said Mary eagerly, " there is ; I've
seen it in books."

" You mustn't contradict, Mary," said Miss
Jones.  " I only meant that you must behave as
though there isn't, because nothing is impossible
to one who truly tries."

" My pencil waggles this way," said Jeremy
politely.  " I think I'll hold it the old way, please."

" There's only one way of doing anything," said
Miss Jones, " and that's the right way."

" This is the right way for me," said Jeremy.

" If I say it's not the right way——"

" But it waggles," cried Jeremy.

The discussion was interrupted by a cry from Helen.

"Oh, do look, Miss Jones, Hamlet's got your spectacle-case. He thinks it's a mouse."

There followed general confusion. Miss Jones jumped up, and, with little cries of distress, pursued Hamlet, who hastened into his favourite corner and began to worry the spectacle-case, with one eye on Miss Jones and one on his spoils.

Jeremy hurried up crying: "Put it down, Hamlet, naughty dog, naughty dog," and Mary and Helen laughed with frantic delight.

At last Miss Jones, her face red and her hair in disorder, rescued her property and returned to the table, Hamlet meanwhile wagging his tail, panting and watching for a further game.

"I can't possibly," said Miss Jones, "allow that dog in here during lesson hours. It's impossible."

"Oh, but, Miss Jones——" began Jeremy.

"Not one word," said she; "let us have no more of this. Lead him from the room, Jeremy!"

"But, Miss Jones, he *must* be here. He's learning too. In a day or two he'll be as good as anything, really he will. He's *so* intelligent. He really thought it was his to play with, and he did give it up, didn't he, as soon as I said——"

"Enough," said Miss Jones, "I will listen to no more. I say he is not to remain——"

"But if I promise——" said Jeremy.

Then Miss Jones made a bad mistake. Wearied of the argument, wishing to continue the lesson, and hoping perhaps to please her tormentors, she said meekly: "Well, if he really is good, perhaps——"

From that instant her doom was sealed. The

children exchanged a glance of realization. Jeremy
smiled. The lesson was continued. What possessed Jeremy now? What possesses any child,
naturally perhaps, of a kindly and even sentimental
nature at the sight of something helpless and in its
power? Is there any cruelty in after life like the
cruelty of a small boy, and is there anything more
powerful, more unreasoning, and more malicious
than the calculating tortures that small children
devise for those weaker than themselves? Jeremy
was possessed with a new power.

It was something almost abstract in its manifestations; it was something indecent, sinister, secret,
foreign to his whole nature felt by him now for the
first time, unanalysed, of course, but belonging, had
he known it, to that world of which afterwards he
was often to catch glimpses, that world of shining
white faces in dark streets, of muffled cries from
shuttered windows, of muttered exclamations, half
caught, half understood. He was never again to be
quite free from the neighbourhood of that half-
world; he would never be quite sure of his domi-
nance of it until he died.

He had never felt anything like this power before.
With the Jampot his relations had been quite
simple; he had been rebellious, naughty, disobedient,
and had been punished, and there was an end.
Now there was a game like tracking Red Indians in
the prairie or tigers in the jungle.

He watched Miss Jones and discovered many
things about her. He discovered that when she
made mistakes in the things that she taught them
she was afraid to confess to her mistakes, and so
made them worse and worse. He discovered that

she was very nervous, and that a sudden noise made her jump and turn white and put her hand to her heart. He discovered that she would punish him and then try to please him by saying he need not finish his punishment. He discovered that she would lose things, like her spectacles, her handkerchief, or her purse, and then be afraid to confess that she had lost them and endeavour to proceed without them. He discovered that she hated to hit him on the hand with a ruler (he scarcely felt the strokes). He discovered that when his mother or father was in the room she was terrified lest he should misbehave.

He discovered that she was despised by the servants, who quite openly insulted her.

All these things fed his sense of power. He did not consider her a human being at all ; she was simply something upon which he could exercise his ingenuity and cleverness. Mary followed him in whatever he did ; Helen pretended to be superior, but was not. Yes, Miss Jones was in the hands of her tormentors, and there was no escape for her.

Surely it must have been some outside power that drove Jeremy on. The children called it " teasing Miss Jones," and the aboriginal savagery in their behaviour was as unconscious as their daily speech or fashion of eating their food—some instinct inherited, perhaps, from the days when the gentlemen with the biggest muscles extracted for his daily amusement the teeth and nails of his less happily muscular friends.

There were many games to be played with Miss Jones. She always began her morning with a fine show of authority, accumulated, perhaps, during hours of Spartan resolution whilst the rest of the household slept. "To-morrow I'll see that they do what I tell them——"

"Now, children," she would say, "I'm determined to stand no nonsense this morning. Get out your copy books." Five minutes later would begin: "Oh, Miss Jones, I can't write with this pencil. May I find a better one?" Granted permission, Mary's head and large spectacles would disappear inside the schoolroom cupboard. Soon Jeremy would say very politely: "Miss Jones, I think I know where it is. May I help her to find it?" Then Jeremy's head would disappear. There would follow giggles, whispers, again giggles; then from the cupboard a book tumbles, then another, then another.

Then Miss Jones would say: "Now, Jeremy, come back to the table. You've had quite enough time——" interrupted by a perfect avalanche of books. Mary crying: "Oh, Jeremy!" Jeremy crying: "I didn't; it was you!" Miss Jones: "Now, children——"

Then Jeremy, very politely:

"Please, Miss Jones, may I help Mary to pick the books up? There are rather a lot." Then, both on their knees, more whispers and giggles. Miss Jones, her voice trembling: "Children, I really insist——" And more books dropped, and more whispers and more protests, and so on *ad infinitum*. A beautiful game to be played all the morning.

Or there was the game of not hearing. Miss Jones would say: "And twice two are four." Mary would repeat loudly: "And twice two is five——"

"Four, Mary."

" Oh, I thought you said five."

And then a second later Jeremy would say :

" Did you say four or five, Miss Jones ? "

" I told Mary I said four——"

" Oh, I've written five—and now it's all wrong. Didn't you write five, Mary ? "

" Yes, I've written five.　You did say four, didn't you, Miss Jones."

" Yes—yes.　And three makes——"

" What did you say made five ? " asked Jeremy.

" I didn't say five.　I said four.　Twice two."

" Is that as well as ' add three,' Miss Jones ?　I've got twice two, and then add three, and then twice two——"

" No, no.　I was only telling Jeremy——"

" Please, Miss Jones, would you mind beginning again——"

This is a very unpleasant game for a lady with neuralgia.

Or there is the game of Making a Noise.　At this game, without any earlier training or practice, Jeremy was a perfect master.　The three children would be sitting there very, very quiet, learning the first verse of " Tiger, Tiger, burning bright——" A very gentle creaking sound would break the stillness—a creaking sound that can be made, if you are clever, by rubbing a boot against a boot.　It would not come regularly, but once, twice, thrice, a pause, and then once, twice and another pause.

" Who's making a noise ? "

Dead silence.　A very long pause, and then it would begin again.

" That noise must cease, I say.　Jeremy, what are you doing ? "

He would lift to her then eyes full of meekness and love.

" Nothing, Miss Jones."

Soon it would begin again. Miss Jones would be silent this time, and then Mary would speak.

" Please, would you ask Jeremy not to rub his boots together ?   I can't learn my verse——"

" I didn't know I was," says Jeremy.

Then it would begin again.   Jeremy would say :

" Please, may I take my boots off ? "

" Take your boots off ?   Why ? "

" They will rub together, and I can't stop them, because I don't know when I do it, and it is hard for Mary——"

" Of course not !   I never heard of such a thing. Next time you do it you must stand on your chair."

Soon Jeremy is standing on his chair.   Soon his poetry book drops with a terrible crash to the ground, and five million pins stab Miss Jones's heart.   With white face and trembling hands, she says :

" Go and stand in the corner, Jeremy !   I shall have to speak to your mother ! "

He goes, grinning at Mary, and stands there knowing that his victim is watching the door in an agony lest Mrs. Cole should suddenly come in and inquire what Jeremy had done, and that so the whole story of his insubordination be revealed and Miss Jones lose her situation for incapacity.

How did he discover this final weakness of Miss Jones ?   No one told him ; but he knew, and, as the days passed, rejoiced in his power and his might and his glory.

Then came the climax.   The children were not perfectly sure whether, after all, Miss Jones might not tell their mother. They did not wish this to happen, and so long as this calamity was possible they were not complete masters of the poor lady. Then came a morning when they had been extremely naughty, when every game had been played and every triumph scored. Miss Jones, almost in tears, had threatened four times that the Powers Above should be informed. Suddenly Mrs. Cole entered.

" Well, Miss Jones, how have the children been this morning ? If they've been good I have a little treat to propose."

The children waited, their eyes upon their governess. Her eyes stared back upon her tormentors. Her hands worked together. She struggled. Why not call in Mrs. Cole's authority to her aid ? No ; she knew what it would mean— " I'm very sorry, Miss Jones, but I think a younger governess, perhaps——"

Her throat moved.

" They've been very good this morning, Mrs. Cole."

The eyes of Mary and of Jeremy were alight with triumph.

They had won their final victory.

### 3

I know what Miss Jones suffered during those weeks. She was not an old lady of very great power of resistance, and it must have positively terrified her that these small children should so vindictively hate her. She could not have seen it as anything but hatred, being entirely ignorant of children and

the strange forces to whose power they are subject,
and she must have shivered in her bedroom at the
dreariness and terror of the prospect before her.
Many, many times she must have resolved not to
be beaten, and many many times she must have
admitted herself beaten as badly as anyone can be.

Her life with the people downstairs was not intimate enough, nor were those people themselves
perceptive enough for any realization of what was
occurring to penetrate.

" I hope you're happy with the children, Miss
Jones," once or twice said Mrs. Cole.

" Very, thank you," said Miss Jones.

" They're good children, I think, although parents
are always prejudiced, of course. Jeremy is a little
difficult perhaps. It's so hard to tell what he's really
thinking. You find him a quiet, reserved little
boy ? "

" Very," said Miss Jones.

" In a little while, when you know him better, he
will come out. Only you have to let him take his
time. He doesn't like to be forced——"

" No," said Miss Jones.

Meanwhile, that morning descent into the school
room was real hell for her. She had to summon up
her courage, walking about her bedroom, pressing her
hands together, evoking the memory of her magnificent iron-souled brother, who would, she knew,
despise such tremors. If only she could have discovered some remedy ! But sentiment, attempted
tyranny, anger, contempt, at all these things they
laughed. She could not touch them anywhere.
And she saw Jeremy as a real child of Evil in the
very baldest sense. She could not imagine how

anyone so young could be so cruel, so heartless, so maliciously clever in his elaborate machinations. She regarded him with real horror, and on the occasions when she found him acting kindly towards his sisters or a servant, or when she watched him discoursing solemnly to Hamlet, she was helplessly puzzled, and decided that these better manifestations were simply masks to hide his devilish young heart. She perceived meanwhile the inevitable crisis slowly approaching, when she would be compelled to invite Mrs. Cole's support. That would mean her dismissal and a hopeless future. There was no one to whom she might turn. She had not a relation, not a friend —too late to make friends now.

She could see nothing in front of her at all.

The crisis did come, but not as she expected it.

There arrived a morning when the dark mist outside and badly made porridge inside tempted the children to their very worst. Miss Jones had had a wakeful night struggling with neuralgia and her own hesitating spirit. The children had lost even their customary half humorous, half contemptuous reserve. They let themselves appear for what they were—infant savages discontented with food, weather and education.

I will not detail the incidents of that morning. The episodes that were on other mornings games were to-day tortures. There was the Torture of Losing Things, the Torture of Not Hearing, the Torture of Many Noises, the Torture of Sudden Alarm, the Torture of Outright Defiance, the Torture of Expressed Contempt. When twelve struck and the children were free, Miss Jones was not far from a nervous panic that can be called,

without any exaggeration, incipient madness. The
neuralgia tore at her brain, her own self-contempt
tore at her heart, her baffled impotence bewildered
and blinded her. She did not leave the schoolroom
with the children, but went to the broad window-sill
and sat there looking into the dreary prospect.
Then suddenly for no reason except general weakness
and physical and spiritual collapse she began to cry.

Jeremy was considered to have a cold, and was,
therefore, not permitted to accompany his mother
and sisters on an exciting shopping expedition,
which would certainly lead as far as old Poole's
the bookseller, and might even extend to Martins',
the pastrycook, who made lemon biscuits next door
to the Cathedral. He was, therefore, in a very
bad temper indeed when he returned sulkily to the
schoolroom. He stood for a moment there unaware
that there was anybody in the room, hesitating
as to whether he should continue " A Flat Iron
for a Farthing," or hunt up Hamlet. Suddenly
he heard the sound of sobbing. He turned and saw
Miss Jones.

He would have fled had flight been in any way
possible, but she had looked up and seen him, and her
sudden arrested sniff held them both there as though
by some third invisible power. He saw that she was
crying ; he saw her red nose, mottled cheeks, untidy
hair. It was the most awful moment of his young
life. He had never seen a grown-up person cry
before ; he had no idea that they ever did cry.
He had, indeed, never realized that grown-up persons
had any active histories at all, any histories in the
sense in which he and Mary had them. They were
all a background, simply a background that blew

backwards and forwards like tapestry according to one's need of them. His torture of Miss Jones had been founded on no sort of realization of her as a human being; she had been a silly old woman, of course, but just as the battered weather-beaten Aunt Sally in the garden was a silly old woman.

Her crying horrified, terrified, and disgusted him. It was all so dreary, the horrible weather outside, the beginning of a cold in his head, the schoolroom fire almost out, everyone's bad temper, including his own, and this sudden horrible jumping-to-life of a grown-up human being. She, meanwhile, was too deeply involved now in the waters of her affliction to care very deeply who saw her or what anyone said to her. She did feel dimly that she ought not to be crying in front of a small boy of eight years old, and that it would be better to hide herself in her bedroom, but she did not mind—she *could* not mind—her neuralgia was too bad.

"It's the neuralgia in my head," she said in a muffled confused voice. That he could understand. He also had pains in his head. He drew closer to her, flinging a longing backward look at the door. She went on in convulsed tones:

"It's the pain—awake all night, and the lessons. I can't make them attend; they learn nothing. They're not afraid of me—they hate me. I've never really known children before——"

He did not know what to say. Had it been Mary or Helen the formula would have been simple. He moved his legs restlessly one against the other.

Miss Jones went on:

"And now, of course, I must go. It's quite impossible for me to stay when I manage so badly——"

She looked up and suddenly realized that it was truly Jeremy. "You're only a little boy, but you know very well that I can't manage you. And then where am I to go to? No one will take me after I've been such a failure."

The colour stole into his cheeks. He was immensely proud. No grown-up person had ever before spoken to him as though he was himself a grown-up person—always laughing at him like Uncle Samuel, or talking down to him like Aunt Amy, or despising him like Mr. Jellybrand. But Miss Jones appealed to him simply as one grown-up to another. Unfortunately he did not in the least know what to say. The only thing he could think of at the moment was: "You can have my handkerchief, if you like. It's pretty clean——"

But she went on: "If my brother had been alive he would have advised me. He was a splendid man. He rowed in his college boat when he was at Cambridge, but that, of course, was forty years ago. He could keep children in order. I thought it would be so easy. Perhaps if my health had been better it wouldn't have been so hard."

"Do your pains come often?" asked Jeremy.

"Yes. They're very bad."

"I have them too," said Jeremy. "It's generally, I expect, because I eat too much—at least, the Jampot used to say so. They're in my head sometimes, too. And then I'm really sick. Do you feel sick?"

Miss Jones began to pull herself together. She wiped her eyes and patted her hair.

"It's my neuralgia," she said again. "It's from my eyes partly, I expect."

H

" It's better to be sick," continued Jeremy, " if you can be——"

She flung him then a desperate look, as though she were really an animal at bay.

" You see, I can't go away," she said. " I've nowhere to go to. I've no friends, nor relations, and no one will take me for their children if Mrs. Cole says I can't keep order."

" Then I suppose you'd go to the workhouse," continued Jeremy, pursuing her case with excited interest. " That's what the Jampot always used to say, that one day she'd end in the workhouse ; and that's a horrible place, *she* said, where there was nothing but porridge to eat, and sometimes they took all your clothes off and scrubbed your back with that hard yellow soap they wash Hamlet with."

His eyes grew wide with the horrible picture.

" Oh, Miss Jones, you mustn't go there ! "

" Would you mind," she said, " just getting me some water from the jug over there ? There's a glass there."

Still proud of the level to which he had been raised, but puzzled beyond any words as to this new realization of Miss Jones, he fetched her the water ; then, standing quite close to her, he said :

" You must stay with us, always."

She looked up at him, and they exchanged a glance. With that glance Miss Jones learnt more about children than she had ever learnt before—more, indeed, than most people learn in all their normal lives.

" I can't stay," she said, and she even smiled a little, " if you're always naughty."

" We won't be naughty any more." He sighed.
" It was great fun, of course, but we won't do it any
more. We never knew you minded."

" Never knew I minded ? "

" At least, we never thought about you at all.
Helen did sometimes. She said you had a headache
when you were very yellow in the morning, but I
said it was only because you were old. But we'll
be good now. I'll tell them to——"

Then he added : " But you won't go away now
even if we're not *always* good ? We won't always
be, I suppose ; and I'm going to school in September,
and it will be better then, I expect. I'm too old,
*really*, to learn with girls now."

She wanted terribly to kiss him, and, had she
done so, the whole good work of the last quarter of
an hour would have been undone. He was aware
of her temptation ; he felt it in the air. She saw
the warning in his eyes. The moment passed.

" You won't go away, will you ? " he said again.

" Not if you're good," she said.


### 4

Half an hour later, when Mary and Helen returned
from their walk, they were addressed by Jeremy.

" She was crying because we'd been so naughty,
and she had pains in her head, and her brother was
dead. Her brother was very strong, and he used to
row in a boat forty years ago. She told me all about
it, just as though I'd been Aunt Amy or Mother.
And she says that if we go on being naughty she'll go
away, and no one else will have her, because they'll
hear about our having been naughty. And I told

her about the workhouse and the porridge and the
yellow soap that the Jampot told us of, and it would
be awful if she went there because of us, wouldn't
it ? "

" Awful," said Mary.

But Helen said :   " She wouldn't go there.   She'd
take a little house, like Miss Dobell, and have tea-
parties on Thursdays—somewhere near the Cathedral."

" No, she wouldn't ! " said Jeremy excitedly.
" How could she take a little house if she hadn't any
money ?   She told me she hadn't, and no friends,
nor nobody, and she cried like anything——" He
paused for breath, then concluded :  " So we've
got to be good now, and learn sums, and not make
her jump.   Really and truly, we must."

" I always thought you were very silly to make so
much noise," said Helen in a superior fashion.
" You and Mary—babies ! "

" We're not babies," shouted Jeremy.

" Yes, you are."

" No, we're not."

Miss Jones was no longer the subject of the conversation.

That same day it happened that rumours were
brought to Mrs. Cole through Rose, the housemaid,
or some other medium for the first time, of Miss
Jones's incapacity.

That evening Jeremy was spending his last half-
hour before bedtime in his mother's room happily in
a corner with his toy village.   He suddenly heard his
mother say to Aunt Amy :

" I'm afraid Miss Jones won't do.   I thought she
was managing the children, but now I hear that she

can't keep order at all. I'm sorry—it's so difficult to get anyone."

Jeremy sprang up from the floor, startling the ladies, who had forgotten that he was there.

" She's all right," he cried. " Really she is, Mother. We're going to be as good as anything, really we are. You won't send her away, will you ? "

" My dear Jeremy," his mother said, " I'd forgotten you were there. Rose says you don't do anything Miss Jones tells you."

" Rose is silly," he answered. " She doesn't know anything about it. But you will keep her, won't you, Mother ? "

" I don't know—if she can't manage you——"

" But she *can* manage us. We'll be good as anything. I promise. You will keep her, won't you, Mother ? "

" Really, Jeremy," said Aunt Amy, " to bother your mother so! And it's nearly time you went to bed."

He brushed her aside. " You *will* keep her, Mother, won't you ? "

" It depends, dear," said Mrs. Cole, laughing. " You see——"

" No—we'll be bad with everyone else," he cried. " We will, really—everyone else. And we'll be good with Miss Jones."

" Well, so long as you're good, dear," she said, " I'd no idea you liked her so much."

" Oh, she's all right," he said. " But it isn't that——" Then he stopped ; he couldn't explain —especially with that idiot Aunt Amy there, who'd only laugh at him, or kiss him, or something else horrible.

Afterwards, as he went slowly up to bed, he
stopped for a moment in the dark passage thinking.
The whole house was silent about him, only the
clocks whispering.

What a tiresome bother Aunt Amy was ! How he
wished that she were dead ! And what a bore it
would be being good now with Miss Jones. At the
same time, the renewed consciousness of her personal
drama most strangely moved him—her brother who
rowed, her neuralgia, her lack of relations. Perhaps
Aunt Amy also had an exciting history ! Perhaps
she also cried !

The world seemed to be suddenly filled with
pressing, thronging figures, all with businesses of
their own.

It was very odd.

He pushed back the schoolroom door and blinked
at the sudden light.

# CHAPTER V

## I

VERY few matter-of-fact citizens of the present-
day world will understand the part that the
sea used to play in our young lives thirty years ago
in Polchester.

It is very easy to look at the map and say that
the sea is a considerable distance from Polchester,
and that even if you stood on the highest ridge of the
highest corn-field above the town you would not be
able to catch the faintest glimpse of it. That may be
true, although I myself can never be completely
assured, possessing so vividly as I do a memory of a
day when I stood with my nurse at the edge of
Merazion Woods and, gazing out to the horizon, saw
a fleet of ships full-sail upon the bluest of seas, and
would not be persuaded that it was merely wrack of
clouds. That may be or no ; the fact remains that
Polchester sniffed the sea from afar, was caught with
sea breezes and bathed in reflected sea-lights ; again
and again of an evening the Cathedral sailed on dust
and shadow towards the horizon, a great white ghost
of a galleon, and the young citizens of the town with
wondering eyes watched it go. But there were more
positive influences than mere cloud and light. We
had, in the lower part of our town, sailors, quite a
number of them. There were the old white-bearded

107

ones who would sit upon tubs and tell smuggling
tales ; these haunted the River Pol, fished in it,
ferried people across it, and let out boats for hire.
There were younger sailors who, tired of the still
life of their little villages and dreading the real
hard work of a life at sea, lurched and slouched by
the Pol's river bed, fishing a little, sleeping, eating
and drinking a great deal.

And there were the true sailors, passing through
perhaps on their way to Drymouth to join their
ships, staying in the town for a day or two to visit
their relations, or simply stopping for an hour or so
to gaze open-mouthed at the Cathedral and the
Market Place and the Canons and the old women.
These men had sometimes gold rings in their ears, and
their faces were often coloured a dark rich brown,
and they carried bundles across their backs all in
the traditional style.

Then there were influences more subtle than either
clouds or men. There were the influences of the
places that we had ourselves seen in our summer
holidays—Rafiel and St. Lowe, Marion Bay or Borhaze—and, on the other coast, Newbock with its
vast stretch of yellow sand, St. Borse with its wild
seas and giant Borse Head, or St. Nails-in-Cove with
its coloured rocks and sparkling shells. Every child
had his own place ; my place was, like Jeremy's,
Rafiel, and a better, more beautiful place, in the
whole world, you will not find. And each place has
its own legend : at Rafiel the Gold-laced Pirates,
and the Turnip-Field ; at Polwint the Giant Excise
Man ; at Borhaze the Smugglers of Trezent Rock ;
at St. Borse the wreck of " The Golden Galleon "
in the year 1563, with its wonderful treasure ;

and at St. Maitsin Cove the famous Witch of St.
Maitsin Church Town who turned men's bones into
water and filled St. Maitsin Church with snakes.
Back from one summer holiday, treasuring these
stories together with our collections of shells and
seaweed and dried flowers, we came, and so the tales
settled in Polchester streets and crept into the heart
of the Polchester cobbles and haunted the Polchester
corners by the fire, and even invaded with their
romantic, peering, mischievous faces the solemn
aisles of the Cathedral itself.

The sea was at the heart of all of them, and whenever a sea-breeze blew down the street carrying with
it wisps of straw from the field, or dandelion seeds,
or smell of sea-pinks, we children lifted our noses
and sniffed and sniffed and saw the waves curl in
across the shore, or breakers burst upon the rock, and
whispered to one another of the Smugglers of Trezent
or the Gold-laced Pirates of Rafiel.

But I think that none of us adored the sea as
Jeremy did. From that first moment when, as a
small baby, he had been held up in Rafiel Cove to
see the tops of the waves catch the morning light
as they rolled over to shore, he had adored it. He
had never felt any fear of it ; he had been able to
swim since he could remember, and he simply lived
for those days at the end of July when they would
all, in a frantic hurry and confusion, take the train
for Rafiel and arrive at Cow Farm in the evening,
with the roar of the sea coming across the quiet
fields to mingle with the lowing of the cows and the
bleating of the sheep. He had in his bedroom a
wonderful collection of dusty and sticky sea-shells,
and these he would turn over and over, letting

them run through his fingers as a miser counts his gold.

Let him catch the faintest glimpse of a shadow of a sailor in the street and he was after it, and he had once, when he was only four or five, been caught by the terrified Jampot, only just in time, walking away confidently down the Market Place, his hand in the huge grasp of a villainous-looking mariner. He was exceedingly happy in his home, but he did often wonder whether he would not run away to sea ; of course, he was going to be a sailor, but it seemed so long to wait until he was thirteen or fourteen, and there was the sea all the time rolling in and out and inviting him to come.

Mrs. Cole warned Miss Jones of this taste of Jeremy's : " Never let him speak to a sailor, Miss Jones. There are some horrible men in the town, and Jeremy simply is not to be trusted when sailors are concerned."

Miss Jones, however, could not be always on her guard, and Fate is stronger than any governess. . . .

**2**

Early in February there came one of those hints of spring that in Glebeshire more than in any other place in the world thrill and stir the heart. Generally they give very little in actual reward, and are followed by weeks of hail and sleet and wind, but for that reason alone their burning promise is beyond all other promises beguiling. Jeremy got up one morning to feel that somewhere behind the thick wet mists of the early hours there was a blazing sun. After breakfast, opening the window and

leaning out, he could see the leaves of the garden
still shining with their early glitter and the earth
channelled into fissures and breaks, dark and
hard under the silver-threaded frost; beneath the
rind of the soil he could feel the pushing, heaving
life struggling to answer the call of the sun above it.
Far down the road towards the Orchards a dim veil
of gold was spreading behind the walls of mist;
the sparrows on the almond tree near his window
chattered like the girls of the High School, and blue
shadows stole into the dim grey sky, just as light
breaks upon an early morning sea; the air was warm
behind the outer wall of the frosty morning, and the
faint gold of the first crocus beneath the garden wall
near the pantry door, where always the first crocuses
came, caught his eye. Even as he watched the sun
burst the mist, the trees changed from dim grey to
sharp black, the blue flooded the sky, and the
Cathedral beyond the trees shone like a house of
crystal.

All this meant spring, and spring meant hunting
for snowdrops in the Meads. Jeremy informed Miss
Jones, and Miss Jones was, of course, agreeable.
They would walk that way after luncheon.

The Meads fall in a broad green slope from the old
Cathedral battlement down to the River Pol. Their
long stretches of meadow are scattered with trees,
some of the oldest oaks in Glebeshire, and they are
finally bounded by the winding path of the Rope
Walk that skirts the river bank. Along the Rope
Walk in March and April the daffodils first, and the
primroses afterwards, are so thick that, from the
Cathedral walls, the Rope Walk looks as though it
wandered between pools and lakes of gold. In

the Orchards on the hill also they run like
rivers.

Upon this afternoon there were only the trees,
faintly pink, along the river and the wide unbroken
carpet of green.  Miss Jones walked up and down
the Rope Walk, whilst Mary told her an endless and
exceedingly confused story that had begun more than
a week ago and had reached by now such a state of
" To be continued in our next " that Miss Jones had
only the vaguest idea of what it was all about.  Her
mind therefore wandered, as indeed, did always the
minds of Mary's audiences, and Mary never noticed
but stared with the rapt gaze of the creator through
her enormous glasses, out into an enchanted world of
golden princesses, white elephants and ropes and
ropes of rubies.  Miss Jones meanwhile thought of
her young days, her illnesses and a certain hat that
she had seen in Thornley's windows in the High
Street.   Jeremy, attended by Hamlet, hunted
amongst the trees for snowdrops.

Hamlet had been worried ever since he could
remember by a theory about rabbits.  He had been
told, of course, about rabbits by his parents, and it
had even been suggested to him that he would be a
mighty hunter of the same when he grew to a certain
age.  He had now reached that age, but never a
rabbit as yet had he encountered.  He might even
have concluded that the whole Rabbit story was a
myth and a legend were it not that certain scents
and odours were for ever tantalizing his nose that
could, his instinct told him, mean Rabbit and only
Rabbit   These scents met him at the most tantalizing times, pulling him this way and that, exciting
the wildest hopes in him, afterwards condemned to

sterility ; as ghosts haunt the convinced and trusting spiritualist, so did rabbits haunt Hamlet. He dreamt of Rabbits at night, he tasted Rabbits in his food, he saw them scale the air and swim the stream —now, he was close on their trail, now he had them round that tree, up that hill, down that hole . . . sitting tranquilly in front of the schoolroom fire he would scent them ; always they eluded him, laughed at him, mocked him with their stumpy tails. They were rapidly becoming the obsession of his nights and days.

Upon this afternoon the air was full of Rabbit. The Meads seemed to breathe Rabbit. He left his master, rushed hither and thither, barked and whined, scratched the soil, ran round the trees, lay cautiously motionless waiting for his foes, and now and then sat and laughed at himself for a ludicrous rabbit-bemused idiot. He had a delightful afternoon. . . .

Jeremy then was left entirely to himself and wandered about, looking for snowdrops under the trees, talking to himself, lost in a chain of ideas that included food and the sea and catapults and a sore finger and what school would be like and whether he could knock down the Dean's youngest, Ernest, whom he hated without knowing why.

He was lost in these thoughts, and had indeed wandered almost into the little wood that lies at the foot of the Orchards, when he heard a deep rich voice say :

" I suppose you 'aven't such a thing as a match upon you anywhere, young gentleman ? "

He liked to be asked for a match, a manly thing to be supposed to possess, but of course he hadn't

one, owing to the stupidity of elderly relations, so
he looked up and said politely : " No, I'm afraid I
haven't." Then how his heart whacked beneath
his waistcoat ! There, standing in front of him,
was the very figure of his dreams ! Looking down
upon Jeremy was a gentleman of middle-age whom
experienced men of the world would have most
certainly described as " seedy."

Jeremy did not see his " seediness." He saw first
his face, which was of a deep brown copper colour,
turning here and there to a handsome purple ; ill-
shaved, perhaps, but with a fine round nose and a
large smiling mouth. He saw black curling hair and
a yachting cap, faded this last and the white of it a
dirty grey but set on jauntily at a magnificent angle.
He saw a suit of dark navy blue, this again faded,
spotted too with many stains, ragged at the trouser-
ends and even torn in one place above the elbow,
fitting also so closely to the figure that it must have
been at bursting point. He saw round the neck a
dark navy handkerchief, and down the front of the
coat brass buttons that shook and trembled as their
owner's chest heaved.

And what a chest ! Jeremy had never conceived
that any human being could be so thick and so broad.
The back, spreading to the farthest limits of the
shiny seams of the coat, was like a wall. The thighs
were pillows, the arms bolsters, and yet not fat,
mind you, simply muscle, all of it. One could see
in a minute that it was all muscle, the chest thrust
forward, the legs spread wide, the bull-neck bursting
the handkerchief, everything that Jeremy himself
most wished to be. A sailor, a monument of
strength, with the scent of his " shag " strong enough

to smell a mile away, and—yes, most marvellous of all, gold rings in his ears! His chest would be tattooed probably, and perhaps his legs also!

There on the back of his hand, was a blue anchor. . . . Jeremy looked up and trembled lest the vision should fade, then flung a hurried look around him to see whether Miss Jones were near. No one was about. He was alone with the desire of his life.

" I'm so sorry I haven't a match," he said. " I'm not allowed to have them, you know."

" No, I suppose not," said the vision. " Just my blamed luck. There I am with hundreds of pounds lying around my room at 'ome careless as you please, and then held up for a bloomin' match. What's gold to a man like me? But a match . . . there you are . . . that's life."

He looked at Jeremy with great interest; he took in, as Jeremy realized, every detail of his personal appearance.

" I like boys," he said. " 'Ad two myself—'ealthy little nippers they was. Both dead—'ere to-day and gone to-morrer, as you might say. Got your nurse 'anging around anywhere? "

" Nurse? " said Jeremy indignantly. " I don't have a nurse. I'm much too old! There is a governess, but she's over there talking to Mary. She's my sister—but they won't bother yet—not till the Cathedral bell begins."

" No intention of 'urting your feelings, young fellow my lad. Didn't think you'd want a nurse of course—big chap like you. Thought you might 'ave a baby brother or such. No offence—I suppose you 'aven't begun to smoke yet. Can't offer you some tobacco."

Jeremy coloured. The man was laughing at him.

" I'm eight if you want to know," he said, " and I'm going to school in September."

" School ! " said the mariner, sniffing contemptuously. " I don't think much of school if you ask me. Now I never went to school, and I can't see that I'm much the worse for it not 'aving been there. Contrariwise—I've seen many a fine promising lad spoiled by too much schoolin'. Be a man of the world, I say ; that's the direction you want to sail in."

" Did you really never go to school ? " asked Jeremy.

" Not I ! " replied the sailor. " Flung out at the age of six, I was, turned into a boat sailing to the West Indies and left to shift for myself—and 'ere I am to-day a Captain of as fine a craft as you're ever likely to see, with gold in 'er lockers and peacocks in the 'old—all in a manner of speaking, you know."

Jeremy's eyes glittered ; his face was flushed a brilliant red. Hamlet had returned from his rabbit hunting and sat with his tongue out and a wild adventurous eye glittering up at his master from behind his hair, yet he was not noticed.

" You were very lucky," he said devoutly, then he went on hurriedly : " Would you mind—you see, Miss Jones may come at any moment—would you mind——" he choked.

" Would I mind what," asked the Captain.

" Would you mind telling me ? Are you tattooed on your body, snakes and ships and things, like a gardener we had once ? He had a sea-serpent all down his back. He showed me one day."

The Captain smiled proudly.

" Tattooed ! Talk of tattooing ! I'll show yer— and it isn't everybody I'd do it for neither. But I've taken a fancy to you, like my own young nipper what died."

With an air of vast ceremony, as though he were throwing open the door to all the universe, he slowly unwound from about his neck the dark blue hand- kerchief, unbuttoned his coat, then a grimy shirt and displayed a wall of deep brown chest. This fine ex- panse had no hair upon it, but was illuminated with a superb picture of a ship in full sail against a setting sun, all worked in the most handsome of blue tattoo. Jeremy gasped. He had never dreamed that such things could be. He ventured to touch the ship with his finger, and he could feel the Captain's manly heart thumping like a muffled hammer beneath the skin.

" There's Queen Victoria on my right thigh and Nelson on my left, and the battle of Trafalgar on the middle of my back. P'raps I'll show 'em you one day. It wouldn't be decent exactly 'ere—too public. But one day you come to my little place and I'll show 'em you."

" Will you really ? " said Jeremy. " Didn't it hurt terribly ? "

" Hurt ! " said the Captain. " I should just think it did. I 'ad to put cotton wool behind my teeth to prevent myself from screaming. But that's nothing. What do you say to being tortured by the Carribees natives every day after breakfast for three 'ole months. A tooth out a day——"

" But your teeth are all there," said Jeremy.

" False," said the Captain. " Every one of 'em.

1

And the things they'll do to your toenails—it 'ud make your 'air creep on your 'ead to listen to the things I could tell you——"

" Oh, it's awful ! " said Jeremy. " And where is your ship now ? "

" Ah, my ship ! " the Captain replied, winking in the most mysterious fashion ; " it would be telling to say where that is. I can trust you, I know ; I'm a great judge o' character, I am, but not even with my own mother, gone to glory now twenty years and as holy a soul as ever breathed, I wouldn't trust even 'er with the secret."

" Why is it a secret ? " asked Jeremy breathlessly.

" Treasure," said the Captain, dropping his voice. " Treasure, nothing less nor more. Between you and me there's enough gold on that there ship to satisfy the Prime Minister 'imself, to say nothing of the jewels—rubies, pearls, diamonds. My word, if you could see them diamonds. I'm looking about me now for an extra man or two, and then I'm off again —silent come, silent go's my motto——"

" I suppose you don't happen to want a cabin-boy ? " gasped Jeremy, his voice choked in his throat.

" Well, now, that's a funny thing," said the Captain. " It's one of the very things. But I'm afraid you're a bit young. Yet, I don't know. We might——"

He broke off, suddenly lifted his finger to his lip, whispered :

" Keep your eyes open. I'll be around again," and had vanished.

Directly after Jeremy heard Miss Jones's unwel-

come voice : " Why, Jeremy, we couldn't find you
anywhere. It's turning cold—tea-time——"

With a thump and a thud and a bang he fell back
into the homely world.

### 3

Jeremy was a perfectly normal little boy, and
I defy anyone to have discovered in him at
this stage in his progress, those strange morbidities
and irregular instincts that were found in such unhappy human beings as Dostoieffsky's young hero
in " *Podrostok*," or the unpleasant son and heir of
Jude and Sue. Nevertheless, eight years old is not
too early for stranger impulses and wilder dreams
than most parents even conceive of, and the fortnight that followed Jeremy's meeting with the Sea-
Captain was as peculiar and fantastic a fortnight as
he was ever, in all his later life, to know.

For he was haunted—really haunted in the good
old solid practical meaning of the term—haunted
with the haunting that pursued Sintram and many
another famous hero. And he was haunted not only
by the Sea-Captain, but by a thousand things that
attended in that hero's company. He was haunted
by a picture—whence it had come to him he did not
know—of a dead-white high road, dropping over the
hill into shadow, the light fading around it, black,
heavy hedges on every side of it. From below the
hill came the pounding of the sea, exactly as he had
heard it so many times on the hill above Rafiel, and
he knew, although his eyes could not catch it, that
in the valley round the head of the road was the fishing village with the lights just coming in the windows

and beyond the village the sloping shingly Cove. But he could see only the dead-white road, and upon this his eyes were always fixed as though he were expecting someone. And he could smell the sea-pinks and the grass damp with evening dew, and the cold dust of the road, and the sea-smell in the wind. And he waited, knowing that the time would come when he would be told to descend the hill, pass through the village, and step out, under the heavy grey clouds, upon the little shingly beach. He was aware then that out at sea a dark, black ship was riding, slipping a little with the tide, one light gleaming and swinging against the pale glow of the dusky horizon. The church clock struck four below the hill ; he was still on the high road waiting, his eyes straining for figures. . . . He was prepared for some journey, because he had at his feet a bundle. And he knew that he ought not to be there. He knew that something awful was about to happen and that, when it had occurred, he would be committed always to something or someone. . . . A little cold breeze then would rise in the hedges, and against the silence that followed the chiming of the clock he could hear first the bleating of a sheep, then a sudden pounding of the sea as though the breakers responded to the sudden rising of the wind, then the hoofs of a horse, clear and hard upon the road. . . . At that moment the picture clouded and was dim. Had this been a dream ? Was it simply a confusion of summer visits to Rafiel, stories told him by Mary, pictures in books (a fine illustrated edition of " Redgauntlet " had been a treasure to him since he was a baby), the exciting figure of the Captain, and the beginning of spring ? And yet the

vision was so vividly detailed that it was precisely
like a remembered event. He had always seen
things in pictures ; punishment meant standing in
the corner counting the ships on the wallpaper ;
summer holidays meant the deep green meadows of
Cow Farm, or a purple pool under an afternoon sun ;
religion meant walking up the great wide aisle of the
Cathedral in creaking boots and clean underclothes,
and so on. It was nothing new for him to make a
picture, and to let that picture stand for a whole
complex phase of life. But this ? What had it
to do with the Sea-Captain, and why was it, as he
knew in his heart that it was, wicked and wrong and
furtive ? For this had begun as a high adventurous
romance. There had been nothing wrong in that
first talk in the Meads, when the Captain had shown
him the tattooes. The wickedness of it had
developed partly with his growing longing to see
the Captain again, partly with the meeting that
actually followed and partly with the sense that
grew and grew as the days passed that the Captain
was always watching him.

The Captain, during these weeks, seemed to be
everywhere. Never was there an afternoon that
Jeremy walked out with Miss Jones and his sisters
that he did not appear. It was not very difficult to
snatch a conversation with him. Because the
beauty of the spring weather continued, the children
went every day for a walk in the Meads, and on at
least three separate occasions Jeremy and the
Captain enjoyed quite long conversations together.
These were, none of them, so good as that first one
had been. The Captain was not so genial, nor so
light-hearted ; it seemed that he had something

you come to my little place I'll teach yer a thing or
two "—and Jeremy would wonder for hours what
this little place would be like and what the Captain
would teach him.   Meanwhile, he saw him everywhere, even when he was not there—behind lamp-
posts, at street corners, behind the old woman's
umbrella in the Market Place, peering round the
statues in the Cathedral, jerking up his head from
behind chimney pots, looking through the nursery
windows just when dusk was coming on, in the passages, under stairs, out in the dark garden—and
always behind him that horrid dream of the dead-
white road and the shingly Cove. . . . Yes, poor
Jeremy was truly haunted.

4

That Miss Jones suspected nothing of these meetings must be attributed partly to that lady's habit of
wrapping herself in her own thoughts on her walks
abroad, and partly to her natural short-sightedness.
Once Mary said that she had noticed " a horrid man
with a red face " staring at them ; but Miss Jones,
although she was not a vain woman, thought it
nevertheless quite natural men should stare, and
fancied more frequently that they did so than was
strictly the truth.

Jeremy, meanwhile, was occupied now with the
thought as to what he would do did the Captain
really want him to go away with him.   He discussed
it with himself, but he did not doubt what he would
do ; he would go.   And he would go, he knew, with
fear and dread, and with a longing to stay and be
warm in the schoolroom, and have jam for tea, and

half an hour before bedtime downstairs, and Yorkshire pudding on Sundays.   But the Captain could
make him do anything. . . . Yes, the Captain could
make him do anything. . . .

His afternoon walks were now prolonged agonies.
He would turn his head at every movement, would
stare into dark corners, would start at the sound of
steps.   His sleep now was broken with horrid
dreams, and he would jump up and cry out ; and
one night he actually dreamt of his dead-white road
and the sounds that came up from below the hill, the
bell and the sea, and the distant rattle of little carts.

Then the Captain drew near to the very house
itself.   He haunted Orange Street, could be seen
lounging against a lamp-post opposite the High
School, looked once into the very garden of the Coles,
Jeremy watching him with beating heart from the
schoolroom window.   It was incredible to Jeremy
that no one else of the house perceived him ; but
no one ever mentioned him, and this made it appear
all the more a dream, as though the Captain were
invisible to everyone save himself.   He began to
hate him even more than he feared him, and yet
with that hatred the pleasure and excitement
remained.   I remember how, years ago in Polchester,
when I could not have been more than six years old,
I myself was haunted with exactly that same mixture
of pleasure and horror by the figure of a hunch-
backed pedlar who used to come to our town.   Many
years after I heard that he had been hanged for the
murder of some wretched woman who had accompanied him on some of his journeys.   I was not
surprised ; but when I heard the story I felt then
again the old thrill of mingled pleasure and fear.

One windy afternoon, near dusk, when they were returning from their walk, Jeremy suddenly heard the voice in his ear :

" I may be coming to visit yer one o' these nights. Keep yer eyes open and yer tongue quiet if I do."

Jeremy saw the figures of Miss Jones and his sisters pass round the corner of the road.

" What for ? " he gasped.

The Captain's figure seemed to swell gigantic against the white light of the fading sky.   The wind whistled about their ears.

" Just to visit yer, that's all.   'Cause I've taken a fancy to yer." The Captain chuckled and had vanished. . . .

Jeremy flung one glance at the grey desolate road behind him, then ran for his life to join the others.

What, after that, did he expect ?  He did not know.  Only the Captain was drawing closer, and closer, and closer.

He could feel now always his hot breath upon his ear.

Two days after the whispered dialogue in the road, that first promise of spring broke down into a tempest of wind and rain.  The Coles' house in Orange Street, although it looked, with its stout, white stone, strong enough, was old and shaky. Now, in the storm, it shook and wheezed and rattled in every one of its joints. Jeremy, at ordinary times, loved the sound of the wind about the house, when he himself was safe and warm and cosy ; but this was now another affair.  Lying in his bed he could hear the screams down the chimney, then the tug at his window-pane, the rattling clutch upon the wood, then the sweep under the bed and the rush up

the wallpaper, until at last from behind some badly
defended spot where the paper was thin, there would
come a wailing, whistling screech as though someone
were being murdered in the next room. On other
days Jeremy, when he heard this screech, shivered
with a cosy, creeping thrill ; but now he put his
head under the bedclothes, shut his eyes very tight,
and tried not to see the Captain with his ugly nose
and tiny gimlet eyes.

He would be half asleep.

" Come," said the Captain from the window, " the
boat is waiting ! You promised, you know. Come
just as you are—no time to dress," and poor Jeremy
would feel the great, heavy hand upon his shoulder
and wake shivering and shaking from head to
foot.

On the third day following his last interview with
the Captain he went to bed a little reassured and
comforted. Perhaps the Captain had gone away.
For three days he had seen and heard nothing of him
at all.

That was a night of rain—rain that slashed and
whipped the house as though it would batter it to
the ground. The rain would come with a wild fury
upon the panes, trembling with its excited anger,
would crash against the glass, then fall back and
hang waiting for a further attack ; next the results
of the first attack would slip and slide like the crawling of a thousand snakes, then fall and drop slowly
and heavily as though every drop were foretelling
some awful peril. Jeremy lay and listened ; but
he resolved that to-night he would not be frightened,
would not think of the Captain.

He said the Lord's Prayer five times, then counted

sheep jumping over the gate, a safe solution for sleep-
less hours. He saw the sheep—first one a very fat
one, then one a very thin one ; but the gate stood
at the bottom of a little hill, so that it was very difficult for the poor creatures, who jumped and slipped
back on the incline. Then a lot of sheep insisted on
jumping together, and he could hardly count them—
forty-five, forty-six, forty-seven, forty-eight. . . .
He was asleep.

After a long long time of soundlessness, of lying
upon a sea that was like a bed of down, and looking
up, happily into clear blue light, he was once more
conscious of the rain. Yes, there it was with its
sweeping rush, its smash upon the pane, its with-
drawal, its trickling patter and heavy drops, as
though it were striking time. Yes, that was the
rain and that—What was that ?

He was wide awake, lying back against his pillow,
but his eyes staring in front of them till they burnt.
The house was absolutely dark, absolutely silent, but
between the attacks of the rain there was a sound,
something that had not to do with the house nor
with the weather. He strained his ears, sitting
up in bed, his hands clutching the bed-clothes. He
heard it quite clearly now. Someone was moving
in the nursery.

With that the whole of his brain was awake and
he knew quite clearly, beyond a shadow of any
doubt, what had happened ; the Captain had come
to fetch him. With that knowledge an icy despair
gripped him. He did not want to go. Oh, he did
not want to go ! He was trembling from head to
foot so that the bed shook beneath him, his breath
came in little hot gasping pants, and his eyes

were wide with terror. He was helpless. The Captain would only say " Come," and go he must, leave his warm house and his parents whom he· loved and Mary and Helen and Hamlet, yes, and even Miss Jones. He would be dragged down the long white road, through the lighted village, out on to the shiny beach, in a boat out to the dark ship —and then he would be alone with the Captain, alone in the dark ship, with the Captain's heavy hand upon his shoulder, his mouth smiling, his great legs drawing him in as a spider draws a fly into its web, and everyone asleep, only the stars and the dark water. He tried to say the Lord's Prayer again, but the words would not come. The sweat began to trickle down his nose. . . .

Then he heard in the next room some movement against a piece of furniture and a voice muttering. That decided him : better to go and face it than to wait there, so, as though he were moving in his sleep, he got out of bed, crossed the floor and entered the schoolroom.

The first sound that he heard was the ticking of the old nursery clock, a strange familiar voice in this awful world, then suddenly, although the room was in black darkness, he himself was staring into blazing light.

He started back and uttered a little cry, but even as he did so that well-remembered hand was upon his shoulder and the well-known voice in his ear :

" Move an inch, utter a sound, and I blow yer brains out, yer——" the voice, very low, faded into the dark. He was staring into a lantern, and above the lantern was the dark body of the Captain. Then as he looked up he was indeed near his last moment, for had he not been a brave boy, old for his years, and determined, he would have cried out with a scream that would have raised the house.

The Captain had no face. . . . The Captain had no face. . . . Only out of a deep darkness those little eyes glittered like candle-points. Jeremy uttered no sound.

Then catching the Captain's coat because he trembled so, he said : " I'm coming at once—but don't wake Mary and Helen. They'd be frightened. May I get a coat, because it's raining ? "

" Coming ! " whispered the Captain, his voice coming from that space in the air where were his eyes. " You move one inch from 'ere or utter one sound and I do yer in, yer——   I'm watching yer, mind ! "

The lantern light suddenly vanished. The room was black. There was no sound but the ticking of the clock, and now the rain, which had seemed to stop during this terrible dialogue, beat with friendly comfort once more upon the pane. Jeremy stood there, his body held together as though in an iron case, scarcely breathing. There was no more sound at all. Quite clearly now Mary's snores could be heard coming from her room.

Jeremy had only one thought—only one thought in all the world. The Captain did not want him. The Captain had gone and not taken him with him. He was safe ; he was freed ; the terror was over and he was at liberty.

At last he moved back to his room. He got into bed again. He was terribly cold, and little spasms of shivers seized him, but he did not care. The Captain was gone, and he had not taken him with him. . . .

But Mrs. Cole, with all her placidity, was firm. The Jampot had to go.

I would like to paint a pleasant picture of the sentiment of the Cole children on this touching occasion; something, perhaps, in the vein of tragi-comedy with which Mr. Kenneth-Graham embroiders a similar occasion in his famous masterpiece—but in this case there was very little sentiment and no tragedy at all. They did not think of the event beforehand, and then when it suddenly occurred there was all the excitement of being looked after by Rose, the housemaid, of having a longer time with their mother in the evening, and, best of all, a delightful walk with Aunt Amy, whose virginal peace of mind they attacked from every possible quarter.

The Jampot left in a high state of sulks, declaring to the kitchen that no woman had ever been so unfairly treated; that her married sister Sarah Francis, of Rafiel, with whom she was now to live, should be told all about it, and that the citizens of Rafiel should be compelled to sympathize. The children were not unfeeling, but they hated the Jampot's sulks, and while she waited in the nursery, longing for a word or movement of affection, they stood awkwardly beholding her, and aching for her to go. She was the more unapproachable in that she wore her Sunday silks and a heavy black bonnet with shiny rattling globes of some dark metal that nodded and becked and bowed like live things. Hamlet, who had, of course, always hated the Jampot, barked at this bonnet furiously and would have bitten at it had it been within his reach. She

## 5

whether he slept or no, but
in the room, the bath-water
was singing and Hamlet was
r. He jumped out of bed
he heard Rose's voice from

verything, 'e 'as. All the
plate what was give to
e Society, and Master
t 'is christening and all
—and the gold clock out
mess! Why, I says to
ore mess, I say, not if
Grease everywhere,
all the drawers open
. Thank 'Eaven 'e
Real gold they was
Cook ever so many
man! She'd 'ave
st 'em. . . . And
ryone sleepin' all
oes it! I thank
died of fright—
e knew a 'ouse

not care. As
his hand he

was gone!
en him, and

home breathless, and then, once
miliar hall, Uncle Samuel said :
p to the nursery, and then they'll
been out at all."
said Jeremy. " But you said

e Samuel, " that wasn't exactly
fact, they don't know you were

y, the corner of his mouth
I've told a lie again ! "
Uncle Samuel impatiently.
."

r your telling lies ? " asked

ult question was, happily
ted by the arrival of the
d up Orange Street in a

aw Jeremy standing in
and his muffler round
scene of wonder and

It was my fault. I
nd sent for him to
ful state now that

le Samuel, this was
he place to speak
son. His body
h was obstinate,
he scene of the
t they had just

---

## CHAPTER VI

### FAMILY PRIDE

#### I

I AM afraid that too great a part of this book is about old maids, but it is hard for anyone who knows only the thriving bustling world of to-day to realize how largely we children were hemmed in and surrounded by a proper phalanx of elderly single ladies and clergymen. I don't believe that we were any the worse for that, and to such heroines as Miss Jane Maple, Miss Mary Trefusis and old Miss Jessamin Trenchard I here publicly acknowledge a deep and lasting debt—but it did make our life a little monotonous, a little unadventurous, a little circumscribed—and because I am determined to give the whole truth and nothing but the truth about the year of Jeremy's life that I am describing, this book will also, I am afraid, be a little circumscribed, a little unadventurous.

The elderly lady who most thoroughly circumscribed Jeremy was, of course—putting Miss Jones, who was a governess and therefore did not count, aside—Aunt Amy.

Now Aunt Amy was probably the most conceited woman in Polchester. There is of course ordinary human conceit, of which every living being has his or her share. I am not speaking of that ; Miss Amy Trefusis might be said to be fanatically conceited.

132

Although she was now a really plain elderly woman it is possible that when she was a little girl she was pretty. In any case, it is certain that she was spoiled when she was a little girl, and because she was delicate and selfish she received a good deal more attention and obedience from weak and vacillating elders than she deserved.

After her growing up she had a year or two of moderate looks and she received, during this period, several proposals ; these she refused because they were not good enough and something better must be coming very shortly, but what really came very shortly was middle-age, and it came of course entirely unperceived by the lady. She dressed and behaved as though she were still twenty, although her brother Samuel tried to laugh her out of such absurdities. But no sister ever pays attention to a brother on such matters, and Aunt Amy wore coloured ribbons and went to balls and made eyes behind her fan for season after season. Then as time passed she was compelled by her mirror to realize that she was not quite so young as she had once been, so she hurriedly invented a thrilling past history for herself, alluding to affair after affair that had come to nothing only because she herself had ruthlessly slain them, and dressing herself more reasonably, but with little signs and hints, in the shape of chains and coloured bows and rings, that she could still be young if she so pleased, and that she was open to offers, although she could not promise them much encouragement. She liked the society of Canons, and was to be seen a great deal with old Canon Borlase, who was as great a flirt as he was an egoist, so that it did not matter to him in

J

the least with whom he flirted, and sat at the feet of old Canon Morphew, who was so crazy about the discoveries that he had made in the life of Ezekiel that it was quite immaterial to him to whom he explained them.

She descended from these clerical flights into the bosom of family life with some natural discontent. Her brother Samuel she had always disliked because he laughed at her ; her sister she did not care for because she was very innocently, poor lady, flaunting her superior married state ; and her brother-in-law she did not like because he always behaved as though she were one of a vast public of elderly ladies who were useful for helping in clerical displays, but were otherwise non-existent. Then she hated children, so that she really often wondered why she continued to live with her brother-in-law, but it was cheap, comfortable and safe, and although she assured herself and everyone else that there were countless homes wildly eager to receive her, it was perhaps just as well not to put their eagerness too abruptly to the test.

There had been war between her and Jeremy since Jeremy's birth, but it had been war of a rather mild and inoffensive character, consisting largely in Jeremy on his side putting out his tongue at her when she could not see him, and she on her side sending him to wash his ears when they really did not require to be washed. She had felt always in Jeremy an obstinate dislike of her, and as he had seemed to her neither a very clever nor intelligent child she had consoled herself very easily with the thought that he did not like her simply because he was stupid. So it had been until this year, and then suddenly they had been flung into sharper opposition.  It was hard to say what had brought this about, but it was perhaps that Jeremy had sprung suddenly from the unconscious indifference of a young child into the active participation of a growing boy.  Whatever the truth might have been, the coming of Hamlet had drawn their attitudes into positive conflict.

Aunt Amy had felt from the first that Hamlet laughed at her.  Had you asked her to state, as a part of her general experience, that she really believed that dogs could laugh at human beings she would indignantly have repudiated any idea so fantastic, nevertheless, unanalysed and unconfronted, that was her conviction.  The dog laughed at her, he insulted her by walking into her bedroom with his muddy feet and then pretending that he hadn't known that it was her bedroom, regarding her through his hair with an ironical and malicious glance, barking suddenly when she made some statement as though he enjoyed immensely an excellent joke, but, above all, despising her, she felt, so that the wall of illusion that she had built around herself had been pulled down by at least one creature, more human, she knew, in spite of herself, than many human beings.  Therefore, she hated Hamlet, and scarcely a day passed that she did not try to have him flung from the house, or at least kept in the kitchen offices.

Hamlet had, however, won the hearts of the family; it was, indeed, Aunt Amy alone to whom he had not thought it worth while to pay court.  To her alone he would not come when she called, by her alone he would not be cajoled, even though she offered him sugary tea, his deadliest temptation.  No, he sat and looked at her through his hair, his fiery eye glinting, his peaked beard ironically humorous, his leg stuck out from his body, a pointing signal of derision.

She resolved to wait for an opportunity when she might conquer Hamlet and Jeremy together, but her power in the house was slight, so long as Mr. and Mrs. Cole were there. " If I only had the children to myself," she would say, " I would improve their manners in many ways. Poor Alice——! " Then suddenly she did have them. At the beginning of May Mr. Cole was summoned to take a mission to the seamen of Drymouth, and Mrs. Cole, who had relations in Drymouth, accompanied him. They would be absent from Polchester a whole week.

" Oh, won't Aunt Amy be a nuisance," said Jeremy, realizing the situation. Then turning to Mary he added : " We'll pretend to do what she tells us and not do it really. That's much the easiest."

A week is a short time, especially at the beginning of a shining and burning May, but Aunt Amy did her best not only with the children but with the servants, and even old Jordan, the gardener, who had been with the Cole family for twenty years. During that short week the cook, the parlourmaid, Rose, the housemaid, and the boot-boy all gave notice, and Mrs. Cole was only able to keep them (on her return) by raising the wages of all of them. Jordan, who was an old man with a long white beard, said to her when she advised him to plant pinks where he had planted tulips and tulips where he had planted pinks, and further inquired why the cauliflower that he sent in was so poor and the cabbages so small : " Leave things alone, Miss,

Nature's wiser than we be, not but what you mayn't mean well, but fussin's never done any good where Nature's concerned, nor never will "; and when she said that he was very rude to her, he shook his head and answered :

" Maybe yes, and maybe no. What's rude to one ain't rude to another "—out of which answer she could make nothing at all.

In the schoolroom she sustained complete defeat. At the very outset she was baffled by Miss Jones. She had always despised Miss Jones as a poor unfortunate female who was forced to teach children in her old age because she must earn her living—a stupid, sentimental, cowed, old woman at whom the children laughed. She found now that the children instead of laughing at her laughed with her, formed a phalanx of protection around her and refused to be disobedient. Miss Jones herself was discovered to have a dry, rather caustic, sense of humour that Aunt Amy felt to be impertinence, but could not penetrate.

" And is that really how you teach them history, Miss Jones ? Not quite the simplest way, surely. . . . I remember an excellent governess whom we once had—— "

" Perhaps," said Miss Jones, gently, " you would give them a history lesson yourself, Miss Trefusis. I would be so glad to pick up any little hints—— "

" I have, of course, no time," said Aunt Amy hurriedly, " but, speaking generally, I am afraid I can't approve altogether of your system."

" It isn't very good, I'm afraid," said Miss Jones weakly. " The children would be glad, I know, to have a few hints from you if you could spare a moment—— "

Jeremy, who was listening, giggled, tried to turn the giggle into a sneeze and choked.

" Jeremy ! " said Aunt Amy severely.

" Oh, do look, Aunt Amy ! " cried Mary, always Jeremy's faithful ally, " all your hairpins are dropping out ! "

She devoted herself then to Jeremy and worried him in every possible way, and after two days of this he hated her with a deep and bitter hatred, very different from that earlier teasing of Miss Jones. That had sprung from a sudden delicious discovery of power, and had been directed against no one. This was a real personal hatred that children of a less solid and tenacious temperament than Jeremy would have been incapable of feeling.

He did not laugh at her, he did not tease her, he no longer put out his tongue at her.   He was older than that now—he was simply reserved and silent, watching her with his large eyes, his square body set, and resolved as though he knew that his moment would come.

Her experience with him was baffling.   She punished him, petted him, she ignored him, she stormed at him ;  it seemed that she would do any-thing could she only win from him an acknowledg-ment of her power, her capability.  But she could not. He only said : " Yes, Aunt Amy." " No Aunt Amy."

She burst out :  " You're a sullen, wicked little boy, Jeremy.   Do you know what happens to little boys who sulk ? "

" No, Aunt Amy."

" They grow into cross, bad-tempered men whom nobody likes and nobody trusts.   Do you want to be like that when you're a man ? "

" I don't care."

" You know what happened to ' Don't Care.' I shall have to punish you if you're rude to me."

" What have I done that's rude ? "

" You mustn't speak to me like that. Is that the way you speak to your mother ? "

" No, Aunt Amy."

" Well, then, if you don't speak to your mother like that, you mustn't speak to me like that, either."

" Well, then. . . ."

This hatred was quite new to him. He had once, years ago, hated a black-faced doll that had been given to him. He had not known why he had hated it, but there it had been. He had thrown it out of the window, and the gardener had found it and brought it into the house again, battered and bruised, but still alive, with its horrid red smile, and this had terrified him. . . . He had begun to burn it, and the nurse had caught him and slapped him. He had begun to cut it with scissors, and when the sawdust flowed he was more terrified than ever. But that doll was quite different from Aunt Amy. He was not terrified of her at all. He hated her. Hated the fringe of her black hair, the heavy eye-lashes, the thin down on her upper lip, the way that the gold cross fell up and down on her breast, her thin, blue-veined hands, her black shoes. She was his first enemy, and he waited, as an ambush hides and watches, for his opportunity. . . .

2

One of our nicest old maids, Miss Maddison, gave
every year what she called her "early summer
party." This was different from all our other
parties, because it occurred neither in the summer
nor in the winter, but always during those wonderful
days when the spring first began to fade into the
high bright colours, the dry warmth, the deep green
shadows of the heat of the year. It was early in
May that Miss Maddison had her party, and we
played games on her little sloping green lawn, and
peered over her pink-brick wall down on to the
brown roofs of the houses below the Close, and had
a tremendous tea of every kind of cake and every
kind of jam in her wainscotted dining-room that
looked out through its tall open windows on to the
garden.

Those old houses that run in a half-moon round
the Close, and face the green sward and the great
western door of the Cathedral, are the very heart of
Polchester. Walking down the cobbled street, one
may still to-day look through the open door, down
the dusky line of the little hall, out into the swimming colour of the garden beyond. In these little
gardens, what did not grow? Hollyhocks, pinks,
tulips, nasturtiums, pansies, lilies of the valley, roses,
honeysuckle, sweet williams, stocks—I remember
them all at their different seasons in that muddled,
absurd profusion. I can smell them now, can see
them in their fluttering colours, the great grey wall
of the Cathedral, with its high carved door and
watching saints behind me, the sun beating on to the

cobbles, the muffled beat of the summer day, the
sleepy noises of the town, the pigeons cutting the
thin, papery blue into arcs and curves and
circles, the little lattice-windowed houses, with
crooked chimneys and shining doors, smiling down
upon me. I can smell, too, that especial smell that
belonged to those summer hours, a smell of dried
blotting-paper, of corn and poppies from the fields,
of cobble-stones and new-baked bread and lemonade ;
and behind the warmth and colour the cool note of
the Cathedral bell echoed through the town, down
the High Street, over the meads, across the river,
out into the heart of the dark woods and the long
spaces of the summer fields. I can see myself, too,
toiling up the High Street, my cap on the back of
my head, little beads of perspiration on my forehead, and my eyes always gazing into the air, so
that I stumbled over the cobbles and knocked
against doorsteps. All these things had to do with
Miss Maddison's party, and it was always her party
that marked the beginning of them for us ; she
waited for the fine weather, and so soon as it came
the invitations were sent out, the flower-beds were
trimmed, the little wooden seats under the mulberry
tree were cleaned, and Poupée, the black poodle, was
clipped.

It happened this year that Miss Maddison gave
her party during the very week that Mr. and Mrs.
Cole went to Drymouth. She sent out her invitations only three days before the great event, because
the summer had come with so fine a rush. " Master
Jeremy and the Misses Cole. . . . Would they give
Miss Maddison the pleasure . . . ? " Yes, of course
they would. Aunt Amy would take them.

On the morning of the great day Jeremy poured the contents of his watering-can upon Aunt Amy's head. It was a most unfortunate accident, arranged obviously by a malignant fate. Jeremy had been presented with a pot of pinks, and these, every morning, he most faithfully watered. He had a bright-red watering-can, bought with his own money, and, because it held more water than the pinks needed, he was in the daily habit of emptying the remnant in a glittering shower out of the pantry window on to the bed nearest the garden wall. Upon this morning someone called him ; he turned his head ; the water still flowed, and Aunt Amy, hatless and defenceless, received it as it tumbled with that sudden rush which always seizes a watering-can when at its last gasp. Jeremy was banished into his bedroom, where he employed the sunny morning in drawing pictures of Aunt Amy as a witch upon the wall-paper. For doing this he was caned by Aunt Amy herself with a ruler, and at the end of the operation he laughed and said she hadn't hurt him at all. In return for this impertinence he was robbed, at luncheon, of his pudding—which was, of course, on that very day, marmalade pudding —and then, Mary being discovered putting some of hers into a piece of paper, to be delivered to him in due course, they were both stood in different corners of the room " until you say you're sorry."

When the jingle arrived at three o'clock they had still not made this acknowledgment, and Jeremy said he never would, " not if he lived till he was ninety-nine."

At quarter-past three Jeremy might have been seen sitting up very straight in the jingle, his face crimson from washing and temper. He was wearing his new sailor suit, which tickled him and was hot and sticky ; he sat there devoting the whole of his energies to the business of hating Aunt Amy. . . .

As I have said, he had never hated anyone before and he was surprised at the glow of virtuous triumph that this new emotion spread over his body. He positively loved to hate Aunt Amy, and as Parkes, the pony, slowly toiled up the hill to the Cathedral, he sat stiff and proud with an almost humorous anger. Then, as they turned over the hot shining cobbles into the Close and saw the green trees swimming in the sun, he turned his mind to the party. What games would they play ? Who would be there ? What would there be for tea ? He felt creeping over him the stiff shyness that always comes when one is approaching a party, and he wished that the first handshaking and the first plunge into the stares of the critical guests might be over. But he did not really care. His hatred of Aunt Amy braced him up ; when one was capable of so fine and manly an emotion as this hatred, one need not bother about fellow-guests. Then the jingle stopped outside a house immediately opposite the great west-end door of the Cathedral ; in the little hall Miss Maddison was standing, and from the glittering garden behind her the sun struck through the house into the shadowed street.

Jeremy's public manners were, when he pleased, quite beautiful—" the true old-fashioned courtesy," gushing friends of the Cole family used to say. He was preparing to be very polite now, when suddenly the voice of the Dean's Ernest ordering people about in the garden struck upon his ear. He had not seen

the Dean's Ernest for nearly three months, for the
very good reason that that gentleman had been ex-
periencing his first term at his private school. Last
year young Ernest and Jeremy had been, on the
whole, friendly, although Ernest, who was nine,
and strong for his age, had always patronized. And
now ? Jeremy longed to inform his friend that he
also shortly would proceed to school, that in another
six months' time there would be practically no
difference between them. Nevertheless, at the
present moment there was a difference. . . . Ernest
had a whole term to his credit.

New arrivals gently insinuated the Cole family
into the garden. Helen, proud and cold, Mary, blinking and nervous, stood pressed close together whilst
other little girls stared and giggled, moved forward
and then backward again, until suddenly Canon
Lasker's Emily, who was fifteen and had such long
legs that she was known as the " Giraffe," came up
and said : " Isn't it hot ! Do you play croquet ?
Please—do ! I'll have—the—blue ball. . . ." And
the Coles were initiated.

Meanwhile, Aunt Amy had said : " Now, Jeremy,
dear, run about and make friends." Which so
deeply infuriated him that he choked. Oh ! sup-
posing the Dean's Ernest had heard her ! . . .

And he had ! A mocking voice behind him said :
" Now, Jeremy, dear——"

Jeremy turned round and beheld the Dean's
Ernest mockingly waiting his retort. And he could
not retort. No words would come, and he could only
stand there, his cheeks flushed, aware that Ernest
had grown and grown during those three months,
that he wore a straw hat with a black-and-red ribbon

upon it, that round his long ugly neck was a stiff white collar, and that across his waistcoat was festooned a thick silver watch-chain.

" Hallo ! " said Jeremy.

" Hallo ! " said the new Ernest scornfully

A long pause.

Then Ernest, turning on his heel, said to someone behind him : " Let's get away from all these girls ! "

The tears burnt in Jeremy's eyes, hot and salt. He clenched his fists and gazed upon a garden that swam in a mist of tears and sunlight. He felt a sudden strange impulse of family affection. He would like to have gathered behind him his father and mother, Mary, Helen, Hamlet, Uncle Samuel— yes, and even Aunt Amy, and to have advanced not only upon Ernest, but upon the whole Dean's family. It would have given him great pleasure to have set his teeth into the fat legs of the Dean himself ; he would gladly have torn the hat from the head of Mrs. Dean. . . . Upon Ernest there was no torture he would not employ.

He would get even ; he resolved that before he left that house he would have his revenge.

Kind Miss Maddison, tripping along and seeing him as a pathetic little boy in a sailor suit without guile or malice, swept him into an " I spy " party composed for the most part of small girls who fell down and cried and said they would go home.

Jeremy, hiding behind a tree, watched the thin back of Ernest as it lifted itself autocratically above two small boys who looked up to him with saucer-eyes. Ernest was obviously talking about his school. Jeremy, lost in the contemplation of his vengeance, forgot his game, and was taken prisoner with the greatest of ease. He did not care. The afternoon was spoilt for him. He was not even hungry. Why could he not go to school to-morrow, and then challenge Ernest to combat? But he might challenge Ernest without going to school. . . . He had never fought a real fight, but the sight of his enemy's thin peaky body was encouraging.

" Now, Jeremy, dear," said Miss Maddison, " it's your turn to hide. . . ."

Soon they all went in to tea. Everyone was thoroughly at home by this time, and screamed and shouted quite in the most natural manner in the world. The long table stretched down the whole room, almost from wall to wall; the sunlight played in pools and splashes upon the carpet and the flowers and the pictures. There was every sort of thing to eat—thin bread-and-butter rolled up into little curly sandwiches, little cakes and big cakes, seed and sugar cakes, and, of course, saffron buns, jam in little shining dishes, and hot buttered toast so buttery that it dripped on to your fingers.

Jeremy sat next to Mary, and behind him hovered Aunt Amy. Only half an hour ago how this would have angered him! To have her interfering with him, saying: " Not two at a time, Jeremy," or " Pass the little girl the sugar, Jeremy—remember your manners," or " Not so big a piece, Jeremy." But now—he did not know. . . . She was one of the family, and he felt as though the Dean's Ernest had scorned her as well as himself. Also Mary. He felt kind to Mary, and when she whispered, " Are you enjoying it, Jeremy ? " he answered " Yes ; are you ? " Not because he was really enjoying it, but because he knew that she wanted him to say that.

He could see Ernest from where he sat, and he knew that Ernest was laughing at him. He remembered that he had given Ernest three splendid marbles, just before his departure to school, as a keepsake. How he wished that he had kept them! He would never give Ernest anything again except blows. Mary might be tiresome sometimes, but she *was* his sister, and he greatly preferred her as a girl to Ernest's sisters. He could see them now, greedy, ugly things. . . .

"Now, Jeremy, wipe your mouth," said Aunt Amy. He obeyed at once.

### 3

Tea over, they all trooped out into the garden again. The evening light now painted upon the little green lawn strange trembling shadows of purple and grey ; the old red garden wall seemed to have crept forward, as though it would protect the house and the garden from the night ; and a sky of the faintest blue seemed, with gentle approval, to bless the quiet town fading into dusk beneath it. Over the centre of the lawn the sun was still shining, and there it was warm and light. But from every side the shadows stealthily crept forward. A group of children played against the golden colour, their white dresses patterns that formed figures and broke and formed again. The Cathedral bell was ringing for Evensong, and its notes stole about the garden, and in and out amongst the children, as though some guardian spirit watching over their safety counted their numbers.

Jeremy, feeling rather neglected and miserable,

stood in the shadow near the oak on the farther side
of the lawn. He did not want to play with those
little girls, and yet he was hurt because he had not
been asked. The party had been a most miserable
failure, and a year ago it would have been such a
success. He did not know that he was standing
now, in the middle of his eighth year, at the parting
of the ways ; that only yesterday he had been a
baby, and that he would never be a baby again.
He did not feel his independence—he felt only
inclined to tears and a longing, that he would never,
never confess, even to himself, that someone should
come and comfort him ! Nevertheless, even at this
very moment, although he did not know it, he, a free,
independent man, was facing the world for the first
time on his own legs. His mother might have
realized it had she been there—but she was not.
Mary, however, was there, and in the very middle of
her game, searching for him, as she was always
doing, she found him desolate under the shadow of
the oak. She slipped away, and, coming up to him
with the shyness and fear that she always had when
she approached him, because she loved him so much
and he could so easily hurt her, said :

" Aren't you coming to play, Jeremy ? "

" I don't care," he answered gruffly.

" It isn't any fun without you." She paused and
added : " Would you mind if I stayed here too ? "

" I'd rather you played," he said ; and yet he was
comforted by her, determined, as he was, that she
should never know it !

" I'd rather stay," she said, and then gazed, with
that melancholy stare through her large spectacles
that always irritated Jeremy, out across the garden.

" I'm all right," he said again ; " only my stocking tickles, and I can't get at it—it's the back of my
leg. I say, Mary, don't you hate the Dean's
Ernest ? "

" Yes, I do," she answered fervently, although she
had not thought about him at all—enough for her
that Jeremy should hate him ! Then she gasped :
" Here he comes——"

He was walking towards them with a swagger
of his long yellow neck and his thin leggy body
that Jeremy found especially offensive. Jeremy
" bristled," and Mary was conscious of that bristling.

" Hallo ! " said Ernest.

" Hallo ! " said Jeremy.

" What rot these silly games are ! " said Ernest.
" Why can't they have something decent, like
cricket ? "

Jeremy had never played cricket, so he said
nothing. " At our school," said Ernest, " we're
very good at cricket. We win all our matches
always——"

" I don't care about your school," said Jeremy,
breathing through his nose.

The Dean's Ernest was obviously surprised by
this ; he had not expected it. His pale neck began
to flush.

" Look here, young Cole," he said, " none of your
cheek."

This was a new dialect to Jeremy, who had no
friends who went to school. All he said, however,
breathing more fiercely than before, was : " I don't
care——"

" Oh, don't you ? " said Ernest. " Now, look
here——" Then he paused, apparently uncertain,

K

for a moment, of his courage. The sight of Mary's timorous anxiety, however, reassured him, and he continued : " It's all right for you, this sort of thing. You ought to be in the nursery with your old podge-faced nurse. Kids like you oughtn't to be allowed out of their prams."

" I don't care," said Jeremy again, seeing in front of him the whole family of the Reverend Dean. " Your school isn't much anyway, I expect, and I'm going to school in September, and I'll wear just the same things as you do and——"

He wanted to comment upon the plain features of Ernest's sisters, but his gentlemanly courtesy restrained him. He paused for breath, and Ernest seized his advantage.

" You have to have an old aunt to look after you anyway—an ugly old aunt. I wouldn't have an old aunt always hanging over me—' Now, Jeremy dear ' —' Blow your nose, Jeremy dear '—' Wipe your feet, Jeremy dear.' Look at the things she wears and the way she walks. If I did have to have an aunt always I'd have a decent one, not an old clothes bag."

What happened to Jeremy at the moment ? Did he recollect that only a few hours before he had been hating Aunt Amy with a fine frenzy of hatred ? For nearly a week he had been chafing under her restraint, combating her commands, defying her orders. He had been seeing her as everything that the Dean's Ernest had but now been calling her. Now he only saw her as someone to be defended, someone who was his, someone even who depended on him for support. He would have challenged a whole world of Deans in her defence.

He said something, but no one could hear his words ; then he sprang upon the startled Ernest.

It was not a very distinguished combat ; it was Jeremy's first battle, and he knew at that time nothing of the science of fighting. The Dean's Ernest in spite of his term at school, also knew nothing—and the Dean's Ernest was a coward. . . .

It lasted but a short while, for Mary, after the first pause of horrified amazement (aware only that Ernest was twice as big as her Jeremy), ran to appeal to authority. Jeremy himself was aware of neither time nor prudence. He realized immediately that Ernest was a coward, and this realization filled him with joy and happiness. He had seized Ernest by his long yellow neck, and, with his other hand, he struck at his eyes and cheeks and nose. He did not secure much purchase for his blows because their bodies were very close against one another, but he felt the soft flesh yield and suddenly something wet against his hand which must, he knew, be blood. And all the time he was thinking to himself : " I'll teach him to say things about Aunt Amy ! Aunt Amy's mine ! I'll teach him ! He shan't touch Aunt Amy ! . . ."

Ernest meanwhile kicked and kicked hard ; he also tried to bite Jeremy's hand and also to pull his hair. But his own terror handicapped him ; every inch of his body was alarmed, and that alarm prevented the freedom of his limbs. Then when he felt the blood from his nose trickle on to his cheek his resistance was at an end ; panic flooded over him like water. He broke away and flung himself howling on to the ground, kicking his legs and screaming : " It isn't fair ! He's bitten me ! Take him away ! "

Jeremy himself was no beautiful sight. His hair was wild, his white navy collar crumpled and soiled, the buttons of his tunic torn, his stocking down, and his legs already displaying purple bruises. But he did not care ; he was well now ; he was no longer unhappy.

He had beaten Ernest and he was a man ; he had risen victorious from his first fight, and Authority might storm as it pleased. Authority soon arrived, and there were, of course, many cries and exclamations. Ernest was led away still howling ; Jeremy, stubborn, obstinate, and silent, was also led away. . . . A disgraceful incident.

Aunt Amy, of course, was disgusted. Couldn't leave the boy alone one minute but he must misbehave himself, upset the party, be the little ruffian that he always was. She had always said that his mother spoiled him, and here were the fruits of that foolishness. How could she ever say enough to Miss Maddison ? Her delightful party completely ruined ! . . . Shocking ! . . . Shocking ! . . . Too terrible ! . . . And Ernest, such a quiet, well-behaved little boy as a rule. It must have been Jeremy who . . .

While they were waiting in the decent dusk of Miss Maddison's sitting-room for a cleaned and chastened Jeremy, Mary touched her Aunt's arm and whispered in her nervous voice :

" Aunt Amy—Jeremy hit Ernest because he said rude things about you."

" About me ! Nonsense, child."

" No, but it was, really. Ernest said horrid things about you, and then Jeremy hit him."

" About me ? What things ? "

" That you were ugly," eagerly continued Mary—
never a tactful child, and intent now only upon
Jeremy's reputation—" and wore ugly clothes and
horrid things. He did really. I heard it all."

Aunt Amy was deeply moved. Her conceit, her
abnormal all-embracing conceit was wounded—yes,
even by so insignificant a creature as the Dean's
Ernest, but she was also unexpectedly touched. She
would have greatly preferred not to be touched, but
there it was, she could not help herself. She did not
know that, in all her life before, anyone had ever
fought for her, and that now of all champions in the
world fate should have chosen Jeremy, who was, she
had supposed, her enemy—never her defender !

And that horrid child of the Dean—she had always
disliked him, with his long yellow neck and watery
eyes ! How dared he say such things about her !
He had always been rude to her. She remembered
once——

Jeremy arrived ; washed, brushed, and obstinate.
He would, of course, be scolded to within an inch of
his life, and he did not care. He had seen the Dean's
Ernest howling and kicking on the ground ; he had
soiled his straw hat for him, dirtied his stiff white
collar for him, and made his nose bleed. He glared
at his aunt (one eye was rapidly disappearing beneath a blue bruise), and he was proud, triumphant,
and very tired.

Farewells were made—again many apologies—
" Nothing, I assure you, nothing. Boys will be
boys, I know," from Miss Maddison.

Then they were seated in the jingle, Jeremy next
to Aunt Amy, awaiting his scolding. It did not
come. Aunt Amy tried ; she knew what she should

say.  She should be very angry, disgusted, ashamed.
She could not be any of these things.  That horrid
boy had insulted her.  She was touched and proud
as she had never been touched and proud in her life
before.

Jeremy waited, and then as nothing came his
weariness grew upon him.  As the old fat pony
jogged along, as the evening colours of street and sky
danced before him, sleep came nearer and nearer.

He nodded, recovered, nodded and nodded again.
His body pressed closer to Aunt Amy's, leaned
against her.  His head rested upon her shoulder.

After a moment's pause she put her arm round
him—so, holding him, she stared, defiantly and
crossly, upon the world

# CHAPTER VII

## RELIGION

### I

ALWAYS in after years Jeremy remembered that party of Miss Maddison's, not because it had been there that he had won his first fight, but for the deeper reason that from that day his life received a new colour, woven into the texture of it ; even now when he thinks of those hours that followed Miss Maddison's party he catches his breath and glances around him to see whether everything is safe. The children, on arriving home that evening, found that their father and mother had already returned from Drymouth. Jeremy, sleepy though he was, rushed to his mother, held her hand, explained his black eye, and then suddenly, in a way that he had, fell asleep, there as he was, and had to be carried up to bed.

When he awoke next morning his first thought was of his mother. He did not know why ; she was so definitely part of the background of his daily life that he felt too sure of her continual and abiding presence to need deliberate thought of her. But this morning he wanted to get up quickly and find her. Perhaps her absence had made him feel more insecure, but there had also been something that night, something in her face, something in the touch of her hand.

And the other thing that he realized was that summer had truly come. He knew at once that hot smell that pressed even through the closed window-panes of his room ; the bars and squares of light on the floor when he jumped out of bed and stood upon them seemed to burn the soles of his feet, and the rays of light on the ceiling quivered as only summer sunlight can quiver. The two windows of his bed-room looked back behind Polchester over fields and hedges to a dim purple line of wood. A tiny stream ran through the first two fields, and this little river was shining now with a white hot light that had yet the breeze of the morning ruffling it. He ran to his window and opened it. Beyond the wall that bordered their house was a little brown path, and down this path, even as he watched, a company of cows were slowly wandering along. Already they were flapping their ears lazily in anticipation of the flies, and the boy who was driving them was whistling as one only whistles on a summer morning. He could see the buttercups, too, in the nearest field ; they seemed to have sprung to life in the space of a night. Someone was pulling the rope of a well somewhere and someone else was pouring water out upon some stone court. Even as he watched, a bee came blundering up to his window, hesitated for a moment, and then went whirring off again, and through all the sun and glitter and the sparkle of the little river there was a scent of pinks, and mignonette, and even, although it could not really be so, of the gorse. The sky was a pale white blue, so pale that it was scarcely any colour at all, and a few puffs of clouds, dead white like the purest smoke, hovered in dancing procession, above the purple wood. The sun burnt upon his bare feet and his head and his hands.

This coming of summer meant so much more to him than merely the immediate joy of it—it meant Rafiel and Cow Farm and the Cove and green pools with crabs in them, and shrimping and paddling and riding home in the evening on haycarts, and drinking milk out of tin cans, and cows and small pigs, and peeling sticks and apples, and collecting shells, and fishermen's nets, and sandwiches, and saffron buns mixed with sand, and hot ginger beer, and one's ears peeling with the sun, and church on Sunday with the Rafiel sheep cropping the grass just outside the church door, and Dick Marriott, the fisherman, and slipping along over the green water, trailing one's fingers in the water, in his boat, and fishy smells by the sea-wall, and red masses of dog-fish on the pier, and the still cool feel of the farmhouse sheets just after getting into bed—all these things and a thousand more the coming of summer meant to Jeremy.

But this morning he did not feel his customary joy. Closing his window and dressing slowly, he wondered what was the matter. What could it be ? It was not his eye—certainly it was a funny colour this morning and it hurt when you touched it, but he was proud of that. No, it was not his eye. And it was not the dog, who came into his room, after scratching on the door, and made his usual morning pretence of having come for any other purpose than to see his friend and master, first looking under the bed, then going up to the window pretending to gaze out of it (which he could not do), barking, then rolling on a square of sunlit carpet, and, after that, lying on his back, his legs out stiff, his ridiculous " Imperial " pointed and ironical, then suddenly turning, with a twist on his legs, rushing at last up to Jeremy, barking at him, laughing at him, licking him, and even biting his stockings—last of all seizing a bedroom slipper and rushing wildly into the schoolroom with it.

No, there was nothing the matter with Hamlet. Nor was there anything the matter with Miss Jones, free, happily, from her customary neuralgia, and delighted with the new number of the *Church Times*. Nor was it the breakfast, which to-day included bacon and strawberry jam. Nor, finally, was it Mary or Helen, who, pleased with the summer weather (and Mary additionally pleased with the virtues of Lance as minutely recorded in the second volume of " The Pillars of the House "), were both in the most amiable of tempers. No, it must be something inside Jeremy himself.

He waited until the end of breakfast to ask his question :

" Can I go and see Mother, Miss Jones ? "

Mary and Helen looked across at him inquisitively.

" What do you want to see your mother for now, Jeremy ? You always see her at twelve o'clock." Miss Jones pushed her spectacles lower upon her nose and continued her reading.

" I want to."

" Well, you can't now."

" Why not ? "

" Because I say not—that's enough."

But Jeremy was gentle to-day. He got off his chair, went round to Miss Jones's chair, and, looking up at her out of his bruised eye, said in the most touching voice :

" But, please, Miss Jones, I want to. I really do."

Then she said what he had known all the time was
coming : " I'm afraid you won't see your mother
to-day, dear. She's not well. She's in bed."

" Why ? Is she ill ? "

" She's tired after her journey yesterday, I
expect."

He said no more.

He tried during the whole of that day not to think
of his mother, and he found that, for the first time
in his life, he could do nothing else but think of her.
During the morning he sat very silently over his
lessons, did all that he was told, did not once kick
Mary under the table, nor ask Miss Jones to sharpen
his pencil, nor make faces at Hamlet. Once or twice,
in a way that he had, he leaned his head on his hand
as though he were an ancient professor with a whole
library of great works behind him, and when Miss
Jones asked him whether he had a headache he said
" No, thank you," instead of seizing on the wonderful
opportunity of release that such a question offered
him. When they all went out for a walk in the
afternoon, he sprang for a moment into something
of his natural vivacity. They came upon a thin, ill-
shaven tramp dressed as a sailor, with a patch over
one eye, producing terrible discordance from a fiddle.
This individual held in one hand a black tin cup,
and at his side crouched a mongrel terrier, whose
beaten and dishevelled appearance created at once
hopes in the breast of the flamboyant Hamlet. This
couple were posted just outside Mr. Poole's second-
hand bookshop, close to the " 2d." box, and for a
moment Jeremy was enthralled. He wanted to give
the hero his week's penny, and upon finding that his
week's penny was not, owing to sweet purchases on

the previous day, he began elaborate bargainings with Miss Jones as to the forestalling of future pennies. Meanwhile, Hamlet leapt, with every sign of joyful expectation, upon the pauper dog ; the blind sailor began to hit wildly about with his stick, Mr. Poole's "2d." box was upset, and the sailor's black patch fell off, revealing him as the possessor of two beautiful eyes, just like any other gentleman, and a fine, vigorous stock of the best Glebeshire profanities. Mr. Poole, an irascible old man, himself came out, a policeman approached, two old ladies from the Close, well known to Jeremy, were shocked by the tramp, and the Cathedral bell, as though it had just awoken up to its real responsibilities, suddenly began to ring.

All this was, of course, delightful to Jeremy, and offered so many possible veins of interest that he could have stayed there for hours. He wanted very badly to ask the sailor why he covered up a perfectly wholesome eye with a black patch, and he would have liked to see what Hamlet could do in the direction of eating up the scattered remnants of Mr. Poole's "2d." box ; but he was dragged away by the agitated hand of Miss Jones, having to console himself finally with a wink from the august policeman, who, known throughout Polchester as Tom Noddy, was a kindly soul, and liked gentlemanly little boys, but persecuted the street sort.

For a moment this exciting adventure carried him away, and he even listened for a minute or two to Mary, who, seizing her opportunity, began hurriedly : " Once upon a time there lived a sailor, very thin, and he never washed, and he had a dog and a violin——" But soon he remembered, and sighed

and said : " Oh bother, Mary ! " and then walked on
by himself. And still, all through that hot afternoon, when even the Rope Walk did not offer any
shade, and when the Pol was of so clear a colour that
you could see trout and emerald stones and golden
sand as under glass, and when Hamlet was compelled
to run ahead and find a piece of shade and lie there
stretched, panting, with his tongue out, until they
came up to him—even all these signs of a true and
marvellous summer did not relieve Jeremy of his
burden. Something horrible was going to happen.
He knew it with such certainty that he wondered
how Mary and Helen could be so gaily light-hearted,
and despised them for their carelessness. This
was connected in some way with the hot weather ; he
felt as though, were a cold breeze suddenly to come,
and rain to fall, he would be happy again. There
had been once a boy, older than he, called Johnny
Bain, a fat, plump boy, who had lived next door to
the Coles. Whenever he had the opportunity he
bullied Jeremy, pinching his arms, putting pins into
his legs, and shouting suddenly into his ears.
Jeremy, who had feared Johnny Bain, had always
" felt " the stout youth's arrival before he appeared.
The sky had seemed to darken, the air to thicken,
the birds to gather in the " rooky " wood.

He had trembled and shaken, his teeth had chattered and his throat grown dry for no reason at all.
As he had once felt about Johnny Bain so now he
felt about life in general. Something horrible was
going to happen. . . . Something to do with
Mother. . . . As he came up the road to their house
his heart beat so that he could not hear his own steps.

Jeremy sat there whilst the dusk fell and all the beautiful lights were drawn from the sky and the rooks went to bed. Rose came to draw the curtains, and then he left his window-seat, dragged out his toy village and pretended to play with it. He looked at his sisters. They seemed quite tranquil. Helen was sewing, and Mary deep in " The Pillars of the House." The clock ticked. Hamlet, lost in sleep, snored and sputtered ; the whole world pursued its ordinary way. Only in himself something was changed ; he was unhappy, and he could not account for his unhappiness. It should have been because his mother was ill, and yet she had been ill before, and he had been only disturbed for a moment. After all, grown-up people always got well. There had been Aunt Amy, who had had measles, and the wife of the Dean, who had had something, and even the Bishop once. . . . But now he was frightened. There was some perception, coming to him now for the first time in his life, that this world was not absolutely stable—that people left it, people came into it, that there was change and danger and something stronger. . . . Gradually this perception was approaching him as though it had been some dark figure who had entered the house, and now, with muffled step and veiled face, was slowly climbing the stairs towards him. He only knew that his mother could not go ; she could not go. She was part of his life, and she would always be so. Why, now, when he thought of it, he could do nothing without his mother ; every day he must tell her what he had done and what he was going to do, must show her what he had acquired and must explain to her what he had lost, must go to her when he was hurt and when he was frightened and when he was glad. . . . And of all these things he had never even thought until now.

As he sat there the house seemed to grow ever quieter and quieter about him. He felt as though he would have liked to have gone to the schoolroom door and listened. It was terrible imagining the house behind the door—quite silent—so that the clocks had stopped, and no one walked upon the stairs and no one laughed down in the pantry. He wished that they would make more noise in the schoolroom. He upset the church and the orchard and Mrs. Noah.

But the silence after the noise was worse than ever.

Soon Miss Jones took the two girls away to her room to fit on some clothes, an operation which Helen adored and Mary hated. Jeremy was left alone, and he was, at once, terribly frightened. He knew that it was of no use to be frightened, and he tried to go on with his game, putting the church with the apple trees around it, and the Noah family all sleeping under the trees, but at every moment something compelled him to raise his head and see that no one was there, and he felt so small and so lonely that he would like to have hidden under something.

Then when he thought of his mother all alone and the house so quiet around her and no one able to go to her, he felt so miserable that he turned round from his village and stared desolately into the fireplace. The thought of his new sister came to him, but was dismissed impatiently. He did not want a new sister—Mary and Helen were trouble enough as it was—and he felt, with an old weary

L

air, that it was time, indeed, that he was off to
school. Nothing was the same. Always new
people. Never any peace. . . .

He was startled by the sound of the opening door,
and, turning, saw his father. His father and he
were never very easy together. Mr. Cole had very
little time for the individual, being engaged in
saving souls in the mass, and his cheery, good-
tempered Christianity had a strange, startling
fashion of proving unavailing before some single
human case.

He did not understand children except when they
were placed in masses before him. His own children, having been named, on their arrival, " Gifts
from God," had kept much of that incorporeal
atmosphere throughout their growing years.

But to-night he was a different man. As he
looked at his small son across the schoolroom floor
there was terror in his eyes. Nothing could have
been easier or more simple than his lifelong assump-
tion that, because God was in His heaven all was
right with the world. He had given thanks every
evening for the blessings that he had received and
every morning for the blessings that he was going to
receive, and he had had no reason to complain. He
had the wife, the children, the work that he deserved,
and his life had been so hemmed in with security
that he had had no difficulty in assuring his congregation on every possible occasion that God was
good and far-seeing, and that " not one sparrow . . ."

And now he was threatened—threatened most
desperately. Mrs. Cole was so ill that it was doubtful
whether she would live through the night. He was
completely helpless. He had turned from one side to

another, simply demanding an assurance from someone or something that she could not be taken from him. No one could give him that assurance. Life without her would be impossible ; he would not know what to do about the simplest matter. Life without her . . . oh ! but it was incredible !

Like a blind man he had groped his way up to the schoolroom. He did not want to see the children, nor Miss Jones, but he must be moving, must be doing something that would break in upon that terrible ominous pause that the whole world seemed to him, at this moment, to be making.

Then he saw Jeremy. He said :

" Oh ! Where's Miss Jones ? "

" She's in the next room," said Jeremy, looking at his father.

" Oh ! " He began to walk up and down the schoolroom. Jeremy left his toy village and stood up.

" Is Mother better, Father ? "

He stopped in his walk and looked at the boy as though he were trying to recollect who he was.

" No . . . No—that is—No, my boy, I'm afraid not."

" Is she very bad, Father—like the Dean's wife when she had fever ? "

His father didn't answer. He walked to the end of the room, then turned suddenly as though he had seen something there that terrified him, and hurried from the room.

Jeremy, suddenly left alone, had a desperate impulse to scream that someone must come, that he was frightened, that something horrible was in the house. He stood up, staring at the closed door, his face white, his eyes large and full of fear. Then he flung himself down by Hamlet, and taking him by the neck, whispered :

" I'm frightened ! I'm frightened ! Bark or something ! . . . There's someone here ! "

### 3

Next morning Mrs. Cole was still alive. There had been no change during the night ; to-day, the doctor said, would be the critical day. To-day was Sunday, and Mr. Cole took his morning service at the church as usual. He had been up all night ; he looked haggard and pale, still wearing that expression as of a man lost in a world that he had always trusted. But he would not fail in his duty. " When two or three are gathered together in My name . . ." Perhaps God would hear him.

It was a day of wonderful heat for May. No one had ever remembered so hot a day at so early a time of year. The windows of the church were open, but no breeze blew through the aisles. The relentless blazing blue of the sky penetrated into the cool shadows of the church, and it was as though the congregation sat there under shimmering glass. The waves of light shifted, rose and fell above the bonnets and hats and bare heads, and all the little choir boys fell asleep during the sermon.

The Cole family did not fall asleep. They sat with pale faces and stiff backs staring at their father and thinking about their mother. Mary and Helen were frightened ; the house was so strange, everyone spoke in whispers, and, on the way into church, many ladies had asked them how their mother was.

They felt important as well as sad. But Jeremy did not feel important. He had not heard the ladies and their questions—he would not have cared if he had. People had always called him " a queer little boy," simply because he was independent and thought more than he spoke. Nevertheless, he had always in reality been normal enough until now. To-day he was really " queer," was conscious for the first time of the existence of a world whose adjacence to the real world was, in after days, to trouble him so often and to complicate life for him so grievously. The terror that had come down upon him when his father had left him seemed to-day utterly to soak through into the very heart of him. His mother was going to die unless something or somebody saved her. What was dying ? Going away, he had always been told, with a golden harp, to sing hymns in a foreign country. But to-day the picture would not form so easily. There was silence and darkness and confusion about this Death. His mother was going, against her will, and no one could tell him whither she was going. If he could only stop her dying, force God to leave her alone, to leave her with them all as she had been before. . . .

He fixed his eyes upon his father, who climbed slowly into his pulpit and gave out the text of his sermon. To-day he would talk about the sacrifice of Isaac. " Abraham, as his hearers would remember " . . . and so on.

Jeremy listened, and gradually there grew before his eyes the figure of a strange and terrible God. This was no new figure. He had never thought directly about God, but for a very long time now

he had had Him in the background of his life as
Polchester Town Hall was in the background.
But now he definitely and actively figured to himself this God, this God Who was taking his mother
away and was intending apparently to put her into
some dark place where she would know nobody.
It must be some horrible place, because his father
looked so frightened, which he would not look if his
mother was simply going, with a golden harp, to
sing hymns. Jeremy had always heard that this
God was loving and kind and tender, but the figure
whom his father was now drawing for the benefit
of the congregation was none of these things.

Mr. Cole spoke of a God just and terrible, but a
God Who apparently for the merest fancy put His
faithful servant to terrible anguish and distress, and
then for another fancy, as light as the first, spared
him his sorrow. Mr. Cole emphasized the necessity
for obedience, the need for a willing surrender of
anything that may be dear to us, " because the love
of God must be greater than anything that holds us
here on earth." But Jeremy did not listen to these
remarks ; his mind was filled with this picture of a
vast shadowy figure, seated in the sky, his white
beard flowing beneath eyes that frowned from dark
rocky eyebrows out upon people like Jeremy who,
although doing their best, were nevertheless at the
mercy of any whim that He might have. This
terrible figure was the author of the hot day, author
of the silent house, and the shimmering darkened
church, author of the decision to take his mother
away from all that she loved and put her somewhere
where she would be alone and cold and silent—
" simply because He wishes . . ."

"From this beautiful passage," concluded Mr. Cole, "we learn that God is just and merciful, but that He demands our obedience. We must be ready at any instant to give up what we love most and best. . . ."

Afterwards they all trooped out into the sunshine.

## 4

There was a horrible Sunday dinner when—the silence and the roast beef and Yorkshire pudding and the dining-room quivering with heat, emphasized every minute of the solemn ticking clock—Mary suddenly burst into tears, choked over a glass of water, and was led from the room. Jeremy ate his beef and rice pudding in silence, except that once or twice in a low, hoarse voice whispered: "Pass the mustard, please," or "Pass the salt, please." Miss Jones, watching his white face and the tremble of his upper lip, longed to say something to comfort him, but wisely held her peace.

After dinner Jeremy collected Hamlet and went to the conservatory. This, like so many other English conservatories, was a desolate and desperate little place, where boxes of sand, dry corded-looking bulbs, and an unhappy plant or two languished, forgotten and forlorn. It had been inherited with the house many years ago, and, at first, the Coles had had the ambition to make it blaze with colour, to grow there the most marvellous grapes, the richest tomatoes, and even—although it was a little out of place in the house of a clergyman of the Church of England—the most sinister of orchids. Very quickly the little conservatory had been abandoned ;

the heating apparatus had failed, the plants had refused to grow, the tomatoes never appeared, the bulbs would not burst into colour.

For Jeremy the place had had always an indescribable fascination. When he was very young there had been absolute trust that things would grow ; that every kind of wonder might spring before one's eyes at any moment of the day. Then, when no wonder came, there had been the thrill of the empty boxes of earth ; the probing with one's fingers to see what the funny-looking bulbs would be, and watching the fronds of the pale vine. Afterwards, there was another fascination—the fascination of some strange and sinister atmosphere that he was much too young to define. The place, he knew, was different from the rest of the house. It projected, conventionally enough, from the drawing-room ; but the heavy door with thick windows of red glass shut it off from the whole world. Its rather dirty and obscure windows looked over the same country that Jeremy's bedroom window commanded. It also caught all the sun, so that in the summer it was terribly hot. But Jeremy loved the heat. He was discovered once by the scandalized Jampot quite naked dancing on the wooden boards, his face and hands black with grime. No one could ever understand "what he saw in the dirty place," and at one time he had been forbidden to go there. Then he had cried and stamped and shouted, so that he had been allowed to return. Amongst the things that he saw there were the reflections that the outside world made upon the glass ; it would be stained, sometimes, with a strange, green reflection of the fields beyond the wall ; sometimes it would catch the blue of the sky, or the red and gold of the setting sun ; sometimes it would be grey with waving shadows across its surface, as though one were under water. Through the dirty windows the country, on fine days, shone like distant tapestry, and in the glass that covered the farther side of the place strange reflections were caught : of cows, horses, walls, and trees—as though in a kind of magic mirror.

Another thing that Jeremy felt there, was that he was in a glass cage swinging over the whole world. If one shut one's eyes one could easily fancy that one was swinging out—swinging—swinging, and that, suddenly perhaps, the cage would be detached from the house and go sailing, like a magic carpet, to Arabia and Persia, and anywhere you pleased to command.

To-day the glass burnt like fire, and the green fields came floating up to be transfigured there like running water. The house was utterly still ; the red glass door shut off the world. Jeremy sat, his arms tightly round Hamlet's neck, on the dirty floor, a strange mixture of misery, weariness, fright, and anger. There was already in him a strain of impatience, so that he could not bear simply to sit down and bewail something as, for instance, both his sisters were doing at this moment. He must act. They could not be happy without their mother ; he himself wanted her so badly that even now, there in the flaming conservatory, if he had allowed himself to do such a thing, he would have sat and cried and cried and cried. But he was not going to cry. Mary and Helen could cry —they were girls ; he was going to do something.

As he sat there, getting hotter and hotter, there grew, larger and larger before his eyes, the figure of Terrible God. That image of Someone of a vast size sitting in the red-hot sky, his white beard flowing, his eyes frowning, grew ever more and more awful. Jeremy stared up into the glass, his eyes blinking, the sweat beginning to pour down his nose, and yet his body shivering with terror. But he had strung himself up to meet Him. Somehow he was going to save his mother and hinder her departure. At an instant, inside him, he was crying : " I want my mother ! I want my mother ! " like a little boy who had been left in the street, and at the other, " You shan't have her ! You shan't have her ! " as though someone were trying to steal his Toy-Village or Hamlet away from him. His sleepy, bemused, heated brain wandered, in dazed fashion, back to his father's sermon of that morning. Abraham and Isaac ! Abraham and Isaac !

Abraham and Isaac ! Suddenly, as though through the flaming glass something had been flung to him, an idea came. Perhaps God, that huge, ugly God was teasing the Coles just as once He had teased Abraham. Perhaps He wished to see whether they were truly obedient as the Jampot had sometimes wished in the old days. He was only, it might be, pretending. Perhaps He was demanding that one of them should give up something—something of great value. Even Jeremy, himself ! . . .

If he had to sacrifice something to save his mother, what would be the hardest sacrifice ? Would it be his Toy-Village, or Mary or Helen, or his soldiers, or his paint-box, or his gold fish that he had in a bowl, or—— No, of course, he had known from the first what would be hardest—it would, of course, be Hamlet.

At this stage in his thinking he removed his arm from Hamlet's neck and looked at the animal. At the same moment the light that had filled the glasshouse with a fiery radiance that burnt to the very heart of the place was clouded. Above, in the sky, black, smoky clouds, rolling in fold after fold, as though some demon were flinging them out across the sky as one flings a carpet, piled up and up, each one darker than the last. The light vanished; the conservatory was filled with a thick, murky glow, and far across the fields, from the heart of the black wood, came the low rumble of thunder. But Jeremy did not hear that; he was busy with his thoughts. He stared at the dog, who was lying stretched out on the dirty floor, his nose between his toes. It cannot truthfully be said that the resolve that was forming in Jeremy's head had its birth in any fine, noble idealisms. It was as though some bully, seizing his best marbles, had said: "I'll give you these back if you hand over this week's pocket-money!" His attitude to the bully could not truthfully be described as one of homage or reverence; rather was it one of anger and impotent rebellion.

He loved Hamlet, and he loved his mother more than Hamlet; but he was not moved by sentiment. Grimly, his legs apart, his eyes shut tight, as they were when he said his prayers, he made his challenge.

"I'll give you Hamlet if you don't take Mother——" A pause. "Only I can't cut Hamlet's throat. But I could lose him, if that would

do. . . . Only you must take him now—I couldn't
do it to-morrow." His voice began to tremble.
He was frightened. He could feel behind his closed
eyes that the darkness had gathered. The place
seemed to be filled with smoke, and the house was
so terribly still!

He said again: " You can take Hamlet. He's
my best thing. You can—You can——"

There followed then, with the promptitude of a
most admirably managed theatrical climax, a peal
of thunder that seemed to strike the house with the
iron hand of a giant. Two more came, and then,
for a second, a silence, more deadly than all the
earlier havoc.

Jeremy felt that God had leapt upon him. He
opened his eyes, turned as though to run, and then
saw, with a freezing check upon the very beat of his
heart, that Hamlet was gone.


5

There was no Hamlet!

In that second of frantic unreasoning terror he
received a conviction of God that no rationalistic
training in later years was able to remove.

There was no Hamlet!—only the dusky dirty
place with a black torrent-driven world beyond it.
With a rush as of a thousand whips slashing the air
the rain came down upon the glass. Jeremy
turned, crying " Mother! Mother! I want
Mother! " and flung himself at the red glass doors;
fumbling in his terror for the handle, he felt as though
the end of the world had come; such a panic had
seized him as only belongs to the most desperate

of nightmares. God had answered him. Hamlet was gone and in a moment Jeremy himself might be seized. . . .

He felt frantically for the door ; he beat upon the glass. He cried " Mother ! Mother ! Mother ! "

He had found the door, but just as he turned the handle he was aware of a new sound, heard distantly, through the rain. Looking back he saw, from behind a rampart of dusty flower-pots, first a head, then a rough tousled body, then a tail that might be recognized amongst all the tails of Christendom.

Hamlet (who had trained himself to meet with a fine natural show of bravery every possible violence save only thunder) crept ashamed, dirty and smiling towards his master.

God had only played His trick—Abraham and Isaac after all.

Then with a fine sense of victory and defiance Jeremy turned back, looked up at the slashing rain, gazed out upon the black country, at last seized Hamlet and dragging him out by his hind-legs, knelt there in the dust and suffered himself to be licked until his face was as though a snail had crossed over it.

The thunder passed. Blue pushed up into the grey. A cool air blew through the world.

Nevertheless, deep in his heart, the terror remained. In that moment he had met God face to face ; he had delivered his first challenge.

P.S.—To the incredulous and cynical of heart authoritative evidence can be shown to prove that it was on the evening of that Sunday that Mrs. Cole turned the corner towards recovery.

# CHAPTER VIII

## TO COW FARM!

### I

THIS next episode in Jeremy's year has, be it thoroughly understood, no plot nor climax to it—it is simply the chronicle of an Odyssey. Nor can it be said to have been anything but a very ordinary Odyssey to the outside observer, who, if he be a parent, will tell you that going to the seaside with the family is the most bothering thing in the world, and if he is a bachelor or old maid will tell you that being in the same carriage with other people's children who are going to the sea is an abominable business and the Law ought to have something to say to it.

All through May, June and July Mrs. Cole slowly pulled back to something like her natural health. The new infant, Barbara by name, was as strong as a pony, and kicked and screamed and roared so that the house was quite a new place. Her arrival had done a great deal for Helen, whose gaze had hitherto been concentrated entirely upon herself; now she suddenly discovered a new element in life, and it was found that she was " ideal with a baby " and " a great help to nurse." This made her more human, and Barbara, realizing as babies always do who understands and who does not, would behave with Helen when she would behave with no one else. Mary could not be expected to transfer

her allegiance from Jeremy, and then Barbara was
frightened at her spectacles; Jeremy, having
Hamlet, did not need a baby!

There came a fine hot morning towards the end
of July when Miss Jones said, suddenly, in the middle
of the history lesson: "Saturday week we go to
Rafiel." Jeremy choked, kicked Mary under the
table, and was generally impossible during the rest
of the morning. It was Miss Jones's fault; she
should have chosen her occasion more carefully.
Before the evening Jeremy was standing in the corner
for drawing on his bedroom wall-paper enormous
figures in the blackest of black lead. These were
to mark the days that remained before Saturday
week, and it was, Jeremy maintained, a perfectly
natural thing to do and didn't hurt the old wall-
paper, which was dirty enough anyway, and Mother
had said, long ago, he should have a new one.

Meanwhile, impossible to describe what Jeremy
felt about it. Each year Cow Farm and Rafiel had
grown more wonderful; this was now the fifth that
would welcome them there. At first the horizon
had been limited by physical incapacity, then the
third year had been rainy, and the fourth—ah, the
fourth! There had been very little the matter
with that! But this would be better yet. For
one thing, there had never been such a summer as
this year was providing—a little rain at night, a
little breeze at the hottest hour of the day—everything arranged on purpose for Jeremy's comfort.
And then, although he did not know it, this was
to be truly the wonderful summer for him, because
after this he would be a schoolboy, and, as is well
known, schoolboys believe in nothing save what

they can see with their own eyes and are told by other boys physically stronger than themselves.

Five or six days before the great departure he began to worry himself about his box. Two years ago he had been given a little imitation green canvas luggage box exactly like his father's, except that this one was light enough to carry in one's hand. Jeremy adored this box and would have taken it out with him, had he been permitted, on all his walks, but he had a way of filling it with heavy stones and then asking Miss Jones to carry it for him ; it had therefore been forbidden.

But he would, of course, take it with him to Cow Farm, and it should contain all the things that he loved best. At first " all the things that he loved best " had not seemed so very numerous. There would, first of all, of course, be the Hottentot, a black and battered clown for whom he had long ceased to feel any affection, but he was compelled by an irritating sense of loyalty to include it in the party just as his mother might include some tiresome old maid " because she had nowhere to go to, poor thing." After the Hottentot there would be his paint-box, after the paint-box a blue writing-case, after the writing-case the family photographs (Father, Mother, Mary and Helen), after the photographs a toy pistol, after the pistol Hamlet's ball (a wasted affair rendered by now shapeless and incoherent), after the ball " Alice in Wonderland " (Mary's copy, but she didn't know), after " Alice " " Herr Baby," after " Herr Baby " the Prayer Book that Aunt Amy gave him last birthday, after the Prayer Book some dried flowers which were to be presented to Mrs. Monk, the lady of Cow Farm

(this might be called carrying coals to Newcastle),
after the flowers a Bible, after the Bible four walnuts
(very dry and hard ones), after the walnuts some
transfer papers, after the transfer papers six marbles
—the box was full and more than full, and he had not
included the hammer and nails that Uncle Samuel
had once given him, nor the cigarette-case (innocent
now of cigarettes, and transformed first into a home
for walking snails, second a grave for dead butter-
flies, third a mouse-trap), nor the butterfly net, nor
" Struwwelpeter," nor the picture of Queen Victoria
cut from the chocolate-box, nor—most impossible
omission of all—the toy village. The toy village !
What must he do about that ? Obviously impossible to take it all—and yet some of it he must
have. Mr. and Mrs. Noah and the church, perhaps
—or no, Mrs. Monk would want to see the garden—
it would never do not to show her the orchard with
the apple-trees, and then the youngest Miss Noah !
She had always seemed to Jeremy so attractive with
her straight blue gown and hard red cheeks. He
must show *her* to Mrs. Monk. And the butcher's shop,
and then the sheep, and the dogs and the cows !

He was truly in despair. He sat on the schoolroom floor with his possessions all around him. Only
Helen was in the room, and he knew that it would be
no use to appeal to her—she had become so much
more conceited since Barbara's arrival—and yet he
must appeal to somebody, so he said to her very
politely :

" Please, Helen, I've got my box and so many
things to put into it and it's nearly Saturday already
—and I want to show the Noahs to Mrs. Monk."

This would have been a difficult sentence for the

M

most clear-headed person to unravel, and Helen was, at that moment, trying to write a letter to an aunt whom she had never seen and for whom she had no sort of affection, so she answered him rather roughly :

" Oh, don't bother with your box, Jeremy. Can't you see I'm busy ? "

" You may be busy," said Jeremy, rising indignantly to his feet, " but I'm busy too, and my business is just as good as yours with your silly old letter."

" Oh, *don't bother !* " said Helen, whereupon Jeremy crept behind her and pinched her stocking. A battle followed, too commonplace in its details to demand description here. It need only be said that Hamlet joined in it and ran away with Helen's letter, which had blown to the ground during the struggle, and that he ate it, in his corner, with great satisfaction. Then, when they were at their angriest, Helen suddenly began to laugh, which she did sometimes, to her own intense annoyance, when she terribly wanted to be enraged, then Jeremy laughed too, and Hamlet yielded up fragments of the letter—so that all was well.

But the problem of the box was not solved—and, in the end, the only part of the toy village that Mrs. Monk ever saw was the youngest Miss Noah and one apple-tree for her to sit under.

2

The ritual of the journey to Cow Farm was, by this time, of course, firmly established, and the first part of the ritual was that one should wake up at three in the morning. This year, however, for some strange mysterious reason Jeremy overslept himself and did not wake up until eight o'clock, to find then that everyone was already busy packing and brushing and rushing about, and that all his own most sacred preparations must be squeezed into no time at all if he were to be ready. Old Tom Collins's bus came along at twelve o'clock to catch the one o'clock train, so that Jeremy might be considered to have the whole morning for his labours, but that was not going to be enough for him unless he was very careful. Grown-up people had such a way of suddenly catching on to you and washing your ears, or making you brush your teeth, or sitting you down in a corner with a book, that circumnavigating them and outplotting them needed as much nerve and enterprise as tracking Red Indians. When things were fined down to the most naked accuracy he had apparently only two " jobs : " one to accustom Hamlet to walking with a " lead," the other to close the green box ; but of course Mary would want advice, and there would, in all probability, be a dispute or two about property that would take up the time.

It was indeed an eventful morning. Trouble began with Mary suddenly discovering that she had lost her copy of " Alice in Wonderland " and rushing to Jeremy's box and upsetting all Jeremy's things to see whether it were there. Jeremy objected to this with an indignation that was scarcely in the sequel justified, because Mary found the book jammed against the paint-box and a dry walnut nestling in its centre. She cried and protested and then suddenly, with the disgusting sentimentality that was so characteristic of her, abandoned her position altogether and said that Jeremy could have it, and then cried again because he said he didn't want it.

Then Jeremy had to put everything back into the box again, and in the middle of this Hamlet ran off with the red-cheeked Miss Noah between his teeth and began to lick the blue off her dress, looking up at the assembled company between every lick with a smile of the loveliest satisfaction. Then, when the box was almost closed, it was discovered by a shocked and virtuous Helen that Jeremy had left out his Bible.

" There'll be one there," said Jeremy in an angry whisper, hoping to escape the attention of Miss Jones.

" What's that, Jeremy dear ? " said Miss Jones.

" Oh, fancy, Miss Jones ! " said Helen. " He's taking all his dirty old toys and even his old clown and he's leaving out his Bible."

" I'm not ! " cried Jeremy, taking it and trying to squeeze it down between three walnuts and the toy pistol.

" Oh, Jeremy dear, that's not the way to treat your Bible. I'll get you some paper to wrap it up in, and you'd better take the things out again and put it in at the bottom of the box." Yes, obviously he would not be ready in time.

The matter of Hamlet and the " lead " was also very exhausting. Hamlet had never, in all his days, been tied to anyone or anything. Of course no one could tell what had been his history before he came strolling on to the Cole horizon, and it may be that once as a very small puppy he *had* been tied on to something. On the whole, that is probable, his pro-

tests on this occasion being of a kind so vehement as
to argue some reminiscences behind them. Mrs.
Cole had bought a beautiful " lead " of black
leather ; of course he had already a collar studded
with little silver nails, and the point was very simply
to fasten the " lead " on to the collar.  Jeremy had
been promised that he should conduct Hamlet, and
it had seemed, when the promise had been made, as
though it would be a very simple thing to carry out.
Hamlet no sooner saw the cord than he began his
ingenious protests, sitting up and smiling at it,
suddenly darting at the recumbent Miss Noah and
rushing round the room with her, finally catching
the " lead " itself in his teeth and hiding with it
under Miss Jones's skirt.

The result was that Tom Collins's bus arrived when
no one in the schoolroom was in the least prepared
for it.  Then what confusion there was ! Mrs. Cole,
looking strange in her hat and veil, as though she
were dressed up for a play, came urging them to
hurry, " because Father was waiting." Then
Hamlet tied himself and his " lead " round the leg
of the table ; then Mary said in her most tiresome
manner, apropos of nothing at all, " You *do* love me,
Jeremy, don't you ? " just at the moment when he
was trying to unlace Hamlet, and her lip began to
tremble when he said " Oh, don't bother," so that
he was compelled to add " Of course I do ; " then
father came running up the stairs with " Really,
this is too disgraceful.  We shall miss that train ! "

Then Uncle Samuel appeared, looking so queer
that Jeremy was compelled to stare at him.  Jeremy
had seen very little of Uncle Samuel during these
last months.  He had hoped, after that wonderful

adventure of the Christmas Pantomime, that they were going to be friends, but it had not been so. He had been away somewhere, in some strange place, painting, and then, on his return, he had hid himself and his odd affairs away in some corner of the house where no one saw him. He had had *his* life and Jeremy had had *his*.

Nevertheless Jeremy was delighted to see him. It would be fun to have him at Cow Farm with his squashy brown hat, his fat cheeks, his blue painting smock, and his short legs with huge boots. He was different, in some way, from all the rest of the world, and Jeremy, even at that early stage of his education, already perceived that he could learn more from Uncle Samuel than from any other member of the family.

Now he put his head in through the door and said : " Well, you kids, aren't you ready ? It's time ! " Then, seeing Miss Jones, he said : " Good morning," and bolted like a rabbit. Even then Jeremy noticed that he had paint in his fingers, and that two of his waistcoat buttons were unfastened.

Then down in the hall what confusion there was ! Boxes here, there and everywhere. Mother, Father, Aunt Amy, Uncle Samuel, and, most interesting of all, Barbara and the new nurse. The new nurse was called Mrs. Patcham, and she was stout, red-cheeked and smiling. The bundle in white called Barbara was, most happily, sleeping ; but Hamlet barked at Mrs. Patcham, and that woke Barbara, who began to cry. Then Collins came in with his coat off, and the muscles swelling on his shoulders, and handled the boxes as though they were paper, and the cook, and Rose, and William, the handy-boy, and old

Jordan, the gardener, and Mrs. Preston, a lady from two doors down, who sometimes came in to help, all began to bob and smile, and Father said : " Now, my dear. Now, my dear," and Hamlet wound himself and his lead round everything that he could see, and Helen fussed and said : " Now, Jeremy," and Miss Jones said : " Now, children," and last of all Collins said : " Now, mum ; now, sir," and then they all were bundled into the bus, with the cart and the luggage coming along behind.

The drive through the streets was, of course, as lovely as it could be ; not in the least because anyone could see anything—that was hindered by the fact that the windows of the bus were so old that they were crusted with a kind of glassy mildew, and no amount of rubbing on the window-panes provided one with a view—but because the inside of the bus was inevitably connected with adventure—partly through its motion, partly through its noise, and partly through its lovely smell. These were, of course, Jeremy's views, and it can't definitely be asserted that all grown-up people shared them. But whenever Jeremy had ridden in that bus he had always been on his way to something delightful. The motion, therefore, rejoiced his heart, although the violence of it was such that everyone was thrown against everyone else, so that Uncle Samuel was suddenly hurled against the bonnet of Miss Jones, and Helen struck Aunt Amy in the chest, and Jeremy himself dived into his sister Barbara. As to the smell, it was that lovely well-known one that has in it mice and straw, wet umbrellas and whisky, goloshes and candle-grease, dust and green paint ! Jeremy loved it, and sniffed

on this occasion so often that Miss Jones told him
to blow his nose. As to the noise, who is there
who does not remember that rattle and clatter, that
sudden, deafening report as of the firing of a hundred
firearms, the sudden pause when every bolt and bar
and hinge sighs and moans like the wind or a
stormy sea, and then that sudden scream of the
clattering windows, when it is as though a frenzied
cook, having received notice to leave, was breaking
every scrap of china in the kitchen ? Who does
not know that last maddened roar as the vehicle
stumbles across the last piece of cobbled road—a
roar that drowns, with a savage and determined
triumph, all those last directions not to forget this,
that, and the other ; all those inquiries as to
whether this, that, and the other had been remembered ? Cobbles are gone now, and old buses sleep
in deserted courts, and Collins, alas ! is not. His
youngest son has a motor-garage, and Polchester
has asphalt—*sic transit gloria mundi*.

Jeremy, clutching his green box with one hand and
Hamlet's lead with the other, was in an ecstasy of
happiness. The louder the noise, the rocking
motion, the stronger the smell, the better. " Isn't
it lovely ? " he murmured to Miss Jones during one
of the pauses.

It may be that it was at this moment that Uncle
Samuel finally made up his mind about Jeremy. In
spite of his dislike, even hatred of children, he had
been coming slowly, during the last two years, to an
affection for, and interest in, his nephew that was
something quite new to his cynical, egoistic nature.
It had leapt into activity at Christmas time, then had
died again. Now as, flung first into his sister's bony

arms, then on to the terrified spectacles of his niece
Mary, he tried to recover himself, he was caught and
held by that picture of his small nephew, seated,
solid and square, in his blue sailor suit, his bare knees
swinging, his hand clutching his precious box with
an energy that defied Fate itself to take it from him,
his mouth set, his eyes staring, radiant with joy, in
front of him.

On arrival at the station it was found that the one
o'clock to Liskane was " just about due," so that
there was no time to be lost. They had to rush
along under the great iron dome, passing by the
main line, disregarding the tempestuous express
from Truxe that drew up, as it were disdainfully,
just as they passed, and finding the modest side line
to Liskane and St. Lowe. Here there was every kind
of excitement for Jeremy. Anyone who has any
kind of passion for observation must have discovered
long ago that a side line has ever so much more
charm and appeal about it than a main line. A
main line is scornful of the station in whose heart
it consents for a moment to linger, its eyes are
staring forward towards the vast cities who are
impatiently awaiting it ; but a side line has its very
home here. So much gossip passes from day to
day above its rails (and gossip that has for its cir-
cumference five green fields, a country road, and a
babbling brook), that it knows all its passengers
by heart.

To the people who travel on a side line, the train
itself is still something of a wonder. How much
more was that true thirty years ago. On this
especial line there were only two stations—Liskane
and St. Lowe, and, of a certainty, these stations

would not even now be in existence were it not that
St. Lowe was a fishing centre of very great importance. The little district that comprehended St.
Lowe, Garth in Roselands, Stoep in Roselands,
Lucent-Polwint, Rafiel, and all the smaller hamlets
around them, was fed by this line; but, even so,
the little train was never crowded. Tourists did
not, and even now do not, go to Polwint and St.
Lowe because " they smell so fishy," nor to Rafiel
" because it's too far from the railway," nor to
the Roseland valleys " because there's nothing to
see there." May these reasons hold good for many
years to come!

To-day there were three farmers in brown leggings,
with pipes, and thick knotted walking-sticks, two or
three women with baskets, and a child or so, and an
amiable, absent-minded clergyman in a black cloth
so faded that it was now green, reading *The Times*,
and shaking his head over it as he stumbled up and
down the platform. One of the farmers had a large
woolly sheep-dog, who, of course, excited Hamlet to
a frenzy. Jeremy, therefore, had his time fully
occupied in checking this; but he had, nevertheless,
the opportunity to observe how one of the farmers
puffed the smoke out of his cheeks as though he
were an engine; how one of the women, with a
back as broad as a wall, had red stockings; and
how the clergyman nearly fell on to the railway-
line every time he turned round, and only saved
himself from disaster by a miracle. The train
arriving at last, they all climbed into it, and then
had to wait for a hot, grilling half-hour whilst the
engine made up its mind that it was worth its while
to take all the trouble to start off again.

"An hour late, upon my word," said Mr. Cole
angrily, when at last, with a snore and a heave, and
a grunt and a scream, they started. "It's really too
bad. I shall have to complain," which, as everyone
present knew, he had not the slightest intention of
doing. In Jeremy's carriage there were his father,
his mother, Uncle Samuel, himself, Mary, and, of
course, Hamlet. Hamlet had never been in a train
before, and his terror at the way that the ground
quivered under him was pitiful to see. He lay first
under the seat, trying to hold himself tightly
together, then, when that failed, he made startled
frenzied leaps on to laps (the lead had been removed
for the time), finally he cowered up into the corner
behind Uncle Samuel, who seemed to understand
his case and sympathized with it. Whenever the
train stopped (which, being a Glebeshire train, it
did continually), he recovered at once his *savoir-
faire*, asserted his dignity, gazed through the
windows at the fields and cows as though he owned
them all, and barked with the friendly greeting of
comrade to comrade whenever he saw another dog.

The next thing that occupied Jeremy's attention
was lunch. Many people despise sandwiches and
milk out of beer-bottles and bananas and seed-cake.
Jeremy, of course, did not. He loved anything
eaten out of paper, from ice-cream sold by the
Barney man in Polchester Square (only once did he
secure some) down to the frills that there are round
the tail of any self-respecting ham. But the paper
on this journey to Rafiel! There was nothing in
the world to touch it. In the first place you spread
newspaper on your knees, then there was paper
under the sandwiches (chicken), and more paper

under the sandwiches (beef), and still more under
the sandwiches (egg) ; there was paper round the
seed-cake, and, most wonderful of all, paper round
the jam-puffs. Jam-puffs with strawberry jam
eaten in the odour of ginger-beer and eggshells ! Is
it possible for life at its very best to hold more ?
He kept his jam-puff so long as he could until, at
last, Mr. Cole said : " Now, my boy ! Finish it up
—finish it up. Paper out of the window—all
neat and tidy ; that's right ! " speaking in that
voice which Jeremy hated, because it was used, so
especially, when cod-liver oil had to be taken. He
swallowed his puff in a gulp, and then gazed out of
the window lamenting its disappearance.

" Did you like it ? " whispered Mary hoarsely.

" You've got some jam on the side of your nose,"
said Jeremy.

He was sitting next to his father, who had the
corner seat, and he now devoted all his energies to
prevent himself from falling asleep against his
father's leg. But the ginger-beer, the glazed and
shining fields beyond the window, the little blobs of
sunlight that danced upon the floor of the carriage,
the scents of food and flowers, and the hot breeze,
the hum of the train, and the dancing of the tele-
graph wires—all these things were against him. His
head began to nod and then to jump back with a
sudden terrible spring as though an evil demon
pulled it with a rope from behind, the carriage
swelled like a balloon, then dwindled into a thin,
straight line. The strangest things happened to
his friends and relations. His mother, who was
reading *The Church Family Newspaper*, developed
two faces and a nose like a post, and Uncle Samuel,

who had, in harsh reality, two chins, seemed to be all folds and creases like a balloon when it is shivering down into collapse. Jeremy fought with these fantasies ; the lines on the newspaper doubled and redoubled, vanished and sprang to life again. He said : " I will not," and, instantly, his head on the soft part of his father's thigh, was asleep.

### 3

In his dreams he was riding on a cloud all pink and gold, and behind came a row of shining, white clouds fluffy like bales of wool wrapped round lighted lanterns.

His cloud rose and fell, rose and fell, and a voice said in his ear : " All is well ! All is well ! You can go on like this for ever. There will be jam-puffs soon, and ice-cream, and fish-cakes, and you can go to China this way whenever you like."

And he said : " Can't I take Hamlet with me ? "

And the voice answered : " Hamlet is with you already," and there, behold, was Hamlet sitting on the pink cloud with a stiff gold collar round his neck, wagging his tail. And then the voice shouted so loudly that Jeremy jumped off the pink cloud in his astonishment : " Liskane ! Liskane ! Liskane ! " and Jeremy jumped and fell and fell—right into his father's lap, with someone crying in his ear : " Wake up, Jeremy ! We're there ! We're there ! "

His first thought was for his green box, which was, he found, safely and securely in his hand. Then for Hamlet, who was, he saw with horror, already upon the platform, the lead trailing behind him like a neglected conscience, his burning eyes piercing his

He wasn't speaking to Jeremy, but to himself. However, Jeremy said : " Did you see Jim, Uncle ?"

" No, I did not."

" He's fatter and redder than last year."

" I shouldn't wonder."

" Are you going to paint, Uncle ? "

" I am."

" What ? "

" Oh, just lines and circles."

Jeremy paused, standing for a moment, and looked puzzled. Then he said :

" Do you like babies, Uncle Samuel ? "

" No, I do not."

" Not even Barbara ? "

" No—certainly not."

" I don't, too. . . . Why don't you paint cows and houses like other people, Uncle Samuel ? I heard Father say once that he never knew what your pictures meant."

" That's why I paint them."

" Why ? "

" So that your father shan't know what they mean."

Although he did not understand this any more than he understood his uncle, Jeremy was pleased with this conversation. It had been, somehow, in tone with the place and the hour ; it had conveyed to him in some strange fashion that his uncle cared for all of this rather as he himself cared. Oh ! he liked Uncle Samuel !

He had hoped that he might have sat on the box next to Jim, but that place was now piled up with luggage, so he was squeezed in between his mother and Mrs. Patcham, with Hamlet, very uncomfort-

able, between his knees. They drove off down the
high road ; the hot smell of the grass came to his
nostrils, the sun blazed down upon them, turning
the path before them into gleaming steel, and the
high Glebeshire hedges, covered with thin powder,
rose on both sides above them, breaking once and
again to show the folding valleys, and the faint blue
hills, and the heavy, dark trees with their thick
black shadows staining the grass.

The cows were clustered sleeping wherever they
could find shadow ; faintly sheep-bells tinkled in the
distance, and, now and then a stream, like broken
glass, floated, cried, and was gone. They drove into
a dark wood, and the sun scattered through the trees
in pieces of gold and shadowy streams of arrowed
light. The birds were singing, and whenever the
hoofs of the horses and the wheels turned on to soft
moss or lines of grass, in the sudden silence the air
was filled with birds' voices. That proved that it
must now be turning to the evening of the day ; the
sun was not very high above the wood, and the sea
of blue was invaded by a high galleon of cloud that
hovered with spreading sail, catching gold into its
heart as it moved.

They left the wood, crossed the River Garth, and
came out on to moorland. Here, for the first time,
Jeremy smelt the sea ; the lanes had been hot, but
here the wind blew across the moor, with the smell
of sea-pinks and sea-gulls in it. The grass was short
and rough ; the soil was sand. On the horizon was
the grey, melancholy tower of a deserted mine.
Some bird flew with swiftly driving wings, crying as
it went. The smell of the moor was as fresh as
though the foot of man had never crossed it—

N

deserted, but not alone; bare, but not empty; uninhabited, but peopled; silent, but full of voices.

Jeremy's excitement grew. He knew now how every line of the road would be. They left the moor and were on the road leading to Rafiel. These were the days before they built the road from Liskane wide enough for motor-cars and other horrible inventions. Thirty years ago the way was so narrow that the briers and ferns brushed your face as you passed, and you could reach out your hand and pluck snapdragons and dandelions and foxgloves. Many roads twisted in and out upon one another; the corners were so sharp that sometimes the wagonette seemed to hang upon one wheel as it turned. Still no sight of the sea, but the smell of it now was everywhere, and sometimes at a sudden bend there would come a faint beat, beat upon the ear with something rhyming and measured in it, like the murmur of a sleeping giant.

They came to the bend where the hill suddenly dips at a fearful angle down into Rafiel. Here they turned to the right, deep between hedges again, then through a little copse, and then, as though with a whisk of the finger, right on to Cow Farm itself.

It was an old square house, deep red brick, with crooked chimneys, and a stone court in front of it. To either side of the court there were barns. Behind the house thick trees, clouded with green, showed. In the middle of the court was a pump, and all about the flagged stones pigeons were delicately walking. As they drove up, the pigeons rose in a wheeling flight against the sky now staining faintly with amber; dogs rushed barking from the barns; a hay-cart turned the corner, its wheels creaking, and four little children perched high on the top of the hay. Then the hall-door opened, and behold Mrs. Monk, Mr. Monk, and, clustering shyly behind, the little Monks.

In the scene that followed Jeremy was forgotten. He did not know what it was that made him hang behind the others, but he stood beside the wagonette, bent down and released Hamlet, and then waited, hiding under the shadow of the cart.   His happiness was almost intolerable ; he could not speak, he could not move, and in the heart of his happiness there was a strange unhappiness that he had never known before.   The loneliness that he had felt at Liskane Station was intensified, so that he felt like a stranger, who was seeing his father, or his mother, or aunt, or sisters for the first time.   Everything about him emphasized the loneliness :  the slow evening light that was stealing into the sky, the sound of some machine in the farmhouse turning with a melancholy rhythmic whine, a voice calling in the fields, the rumble of the sea, the twittering of birds in the garden trees, the bark of a dog far, far away, and, through them all, the sense that the world was sinking down into silence, and that all the sounds were slipping away, like visitors hurrying from the park before the gates are shut ; he stood there, listening, caught into a life that was utterly his own and had no share with any other.   He looked around and saw that they were all going into the house, that Jim and Mr. Monk were busy with the boxes, and that no one was aware of him.   He knew what he wanted.

He slipped across the court and dropped into the black cavernous hole of the farther barn.   At first the darkness stopped him ;  but he knew his way, found the steps that led up to the loft, and was soon perched high behind a little square window that was now blue and gold against the velvety blackness behind him. This was his favourite spot in all the farm. Here, all the year, they stored the apples, and the smell of the fruit was thick in the air, sweet and strong, clinging about every fibre of the place, so that you could not disturb a strand nor a stone without sending some new drift of the scent up against your nostrils. All the year after his first visit Jeremy had been longing to smell that smell again, and now he knelt up against the window, drinking it in. With his eyes he searched the horizon. From here you could see the garden with the sun-dial, the fields beyond, the sudden dip with the trees at the edge of it bent crossways by the wind, and there, in such a cup as one's hands might form, just beyond, was the sea. . . .

He stared as though his eyes would start from his head. Behind him was the cloudy smoke of the apple-scent ; in front of him the sun was sinking towards the dark elms. Soon the trees would catch the sun and hide it ; the galleon cloud that had been over them as they drove was now banked in red and gold across the horizon ; birds slowly fled to their homes.

He heard someone call, " Jeremy ! Jeremy ! " With a last gaze he saw the blue cup turn to gold, the sun reached the tops of the elms ; the fields were lit with the glitter of shining glass, then, even as he watched, they were purple, then grey, then dim like smoke.

Again the voice called " Jeremy ! " He slipped from the window, found the little stair, ran across the dusky court and entered the house.

# CHAPTER IX

## THE AWAKENING OF CHARLOTTE

### I

TOWARDS the end of the first fortnight's stay at Cow Farm it was announced that very shortly there would be a picnic at Rafiel Cove.

Jeremy had been waiting for this proclamation; once or twice he had asked whether they were going to the Cove and had been told " not to bother," " all in good time," and other ridiculous elderly finalities, but he knew that the day must come, as it had always come every year. The picnic at Rafiel was always the central event of the summer.

And he had this year another reason for excited anticipation—the wonderful Charlotte Le Page was to be present. Until now Jeremy had never taken the slightest interest in girls. Mary and Helen, being his sisters, were necessities and inevitabilities, but that did not mean that he could not get along very easily without them, and indeed Mary with her jealousies, her strange sulky temper and sudden sentimental repentances was certainly a burden and restraint. As to the little girls in Polchester, he had frankly found them tiresome and stupid, thinking of themselves, terrified of the most natural phenomena and untruthful in their statements. He had been always independent and reserved with everyone, and had never, in all his life, had a close friend, but there

had been, especially of late, boys with whom it had
been amusing to spend an hour or two, and since his
fight with the Dean's Ernest he had thought that it
would be rather interesting to make a further trial
of strength with whomsoever . . .

Girls were stupid, uninteresting, conceited and
slow.  He never, in all his life, wanted to have anything to do with girls.  But Charlotte Le Page was
another matter.  She had, in the first place, become
quite a tradition in the Cole family.  She was the
daughter of a wealthy landowner, who always spent
his holidays in Rafiel.  She and her very beautiful,
very superior mother had been seen on many occasions by the Coles driving about the Glebeshire roads
in a fine and languid manner, a manner to which the
Coles knew, very well, they themselves could never
attain.  Then Mrs. Cole had called, and Mrs. Le
Page and Charlotte had come to tea at Cow Farm.
This had been a year ago, when Jeremy had been
only seven ; nevertheless, he had been present during
the first part of the ceremony, and Charlotte had
struck him as amazing.

He had simply gazed at her with his mouth open,
forgetting all his good manners.  She was at this
time nine or ten years of age but very small and, as
they say of the most modern kind of doll, " perfect
in every particular."  She had wonderful hair of a
bright rippling gold ; her cheeks were pink and her
eyes were blue, and she was so beautifully dressed
that you could not take in details but must simply
surrender yourself to a cloudy film of white or blue,
with everything so perfectly in its place that it
seemed to the rough and ready Jeremy quite un-
earthly.  Of course she had to be very careful how

she walked, when she sat down, in what way she
moved her hands and feet, and how she blew her
nose.  It was wonderful to see her do these things,
she did them so naturally and yet always with a
sense of an effort overcome for the good of humanity.
Her mother never ceased to empty praises at her
feet, appealing to visitors with : " Isn't Charlotte
too lovely to-day ? " or " Really, Mrs. Cole, did
you ever see anything like Charlotte's hair ? " or
" Just a moment, Mrs. Cole, I'm sure you've never
seen such hands and feet on any human being
before ! "—and it was impossible to tell whether or
no Charlotte was moved by these praises, because
she never said anything at all.  She was almost
completely silent, and once, at the tea-gathering in
Cow Farm, when she suddenly said : " I'm tired,
Mamma," Jeremy nearly jumped from his chair, so
astonished he was.

Jeremy had, during the year that intervened
between that visit and this, sometimes thought of
Charlotte, and he had looked back upon her, not as a
little girl but as something strange, fantastic, won-
derfully coloured, whom it would be interesting to
see again.  He wondered why Mary and Helen could
not be like that, instead of running about and
screaming and becoming red in the face.  He said
once to Mary that she should imitate Charlotte, and
the scene that followed was terrible.  Mary, from that
moment, hated Charlotte with an overpowering
hatred.

Here this year they were again, Mrs. Le Page with
her long neck, her beautiful pearl ear-rings, her pale
watery eyes and her tapering fingers ; Charlotte just
as before, silent, beautiful and precious.  There was

again a tea-party at Cow Farm, and on this occasion
Jeremy was asked to show Hamlet. But Hamlet
behaved badly, trying to jump upon Charlotte's
white frock and soil her blue ribbons. Charlotte
screamed exactly as a doll screams when you press
it in the stomach, and Hamlet was so deeply astonished at the unexpected noise that he stopped his
bad behaviour, sat on his hind legs, and gazed up at
her with an anxious wondering expression. In spite
of this unfortunate incident, the visit went off well,
and Mrs. Cole said that she had never seen anything
so lovely as Charlotte, and Mrs. Le Page said, " No,
had anyone ever ? " and Charlotte never turned a
hair. The final arrangement was that there should
be a picnic and soon, because " Mr. Le Page has to
return to Warwickshire to look after the Estate—
so tiresome, but I've no doubt it's all going to wrack
and ruin without him."

After the picnic had been arranged the Coles were,
frankly, a little uneasy. The family of Le Page was
not the easiest in the world to entertain, and the
thought of a whole day with Mr. Le Page, who was a
very black, very silent gentleman and looked as
though he were always counting sums over in his
head, was truly alarming. Moreover, in the ordinary
way, a picnic, which depended so entirely for its
success on the weather, was no great risk, because
the Coles were indifferent to rain, as all true Glebeshire people must be. But that the Le Pages should
be wet was quite another affair ; the thought of a
dripping Mrs. Le Page was intolerable, but of a
dripping Charlotte quite impossible ; moreover, the
plain but excellent food—pasties, saffron cake, apples
and ginger beer—enjoyed by the Coles seemed quite

too terrestrial for the Le Pages. Mrs. Le Page and
ginger beer! Charlotte and pasties! . . . nevertheless, the invitation had been given and accepted.
The Coles could but anxiously inspect the sky. . . .

2

There was another reason why Jeremy looked
forward to the picnic with impatience. A funny
old lady, named Miss Henhouse, who lived near
Cow Farm, in a little cottage all by herself, called
sometimes upon the Coles and told them stories
about the people and the place, which made them
" sit up in their chairs." She was an old lady with
sharp eyes, a black moustache and a double chin,
wore an old shabby bonnet, grey mittens and large
shoes which banged after her as she walked. She
leant on a cane with a silver knob to it, and she wore
a huge cameo brooch on her breast with a miniature
of herself inside it. She was what is called in novels
" a character." There was no one who knew so
much about Rafiel and its neighbourhood ; she had
lived here for ever, her father had been a friend of
Wellington's and had known members of the local
Press Gang intimately. It was from her that
Jeremy heard, in detail, the famous story of the
Scarlet Admiral. It was, of course, in any case, a
well-known story, and Jeremy had often heard it
before, but Miss Henhouse made it a new, a most
vivid and realistic thing. She sat forward in her
chair, leaning on her silver-headed cane, her eyes
staring in front of her, her two chins bobbing, gazing,
gazing as though it all had happened before her very
nose.

How one night outside Rafiel Cove there was a terrible storm, and on the morning afterwards a wonderful, smiling calm, and how the village idiot, out for his early morning stroll, saw a splendid ship riding beyond the Cove, a ship of gold with sails of silk and jewelled masts. As he watched, from the ship a boat pushed out, and then landed on the sand of the Cove a wonderful company in cocked hats of gold lace, plush breeches of red, and shoes with diamond buckles. The leader of them was a little man with a vast cocked hat and a splendid sword all studded with jewels. The fool, peering over the hedge, saw him give orders to his men, and then walk, alone, up the little winding path to the cliff-top. Straight up the path he came, then right past the fool himself, standing at last upon the turnip field of Farmer Ede, one of the greatest of the farmers of those parts. And here he waited, staring out to sea, his arms crossed, his eyes very fierce and very, very sad. Then a second time from the golden ship a boat pushed out, cutting its way through the glassy sea—and there landed on the beach a young man, very beautiful, in a suit of blue and gold, and he, without a glance at the waiting sailors, also slowly climbed the sea-path, and at last he too reached Farmer Ede's turnip field. Then he and the Scarlet Admiral bowed to one another, very beautifully, very sadly, and very, very fiercely. As the sun rose high in the sky, as the cows passed clumsily down the lane behind the field, so the fool, with eyes staring and heart thumping, saw these two fight a duel to the death. There could be no question, from the first, how it would end. The beautiful young man in his fine blue suit and his white cambric shirt had despair upon his face. He knew that his hour had come. And the eyes of the Scarlet Admiral were ever sadder and ever fiercer. Then, with a sudden move, a little turn of his agile body, the Scarlet Admiral had the young man through the breast. The young man threw up his arms and cried ; and, as the Scarlet Admiral withdrew his sword, dripping with blood from his body, the young man fell backwards over the cliff into the sea. Then the Scarlet Admiral wiped his sword on the grass and, slowly and sadly, walked down the cliff-path even as he had walked up. He joined his men, they found their boat, pushed out to their ship, and even as they landed upon her she had disappeared. A moment later the fool saw the parson of Rafiel Church coming round the corner for his morning bathe, and two minutes afterwards nothing human was to be seen save the naked limbs of the parson and his little bundle of black clothes lying neatly upon a stone. Then the fool ran all the way home to his mother, who was a widow, and sat and cried and cried for the beautiful young man who had been slain, nor would he eat, nor taste the excellent Rafiel beer, and he pined away, and at last he died, first telling this history to his mother who, like all widows, was a garrulous woman and loved a good story. . . .

Impossible to imagine with what life and fire old Miss Henhouse gave this history. You could see with your own eyes the golden ship, the diamond buckles of the Scarlet Admiral, the young man's sad eyes, the parson's black clothes. When she had finished it seemed to Jeremy that it must have been just so. She told him that now on a summer morning or evening the Scarlet Admiral might still be

seen, climbing the cliff-path, wiping his sword upon
the grass, gazing out with sad eyes to sea. Jeremy
swore to himself that on the next occasion of visiting
the Cove he would watch . . . he would watch—
but to no single human being would he speak anything of this.

This was the second reason why he had looked
forward so eagerly to the sea-picnic.

### 3

The day arrived, and it was marvellously fine—one
of those days in August when heat possesses the
world and holds it tranced and still, but has in the
very strength of its possession some scent of the
decay and chill of autumn that is to follow so close
upon its heels. There was no breeze, no wind from
the sea, only a sky utterly without cloud and a world
without sound.

Punctually at eleven of the morning the splendid
Le Page equipage arrived at Cow Farm. Splendid it
was! A large wagonette, with a stout supercilious
fellow on the box who sniffed at the healthy odours of
the farm and stared haughtily at Mrs. Monk as
though she should be ashamed to be alive. The
Coles had provided a small plump jingle with a small
plump pony, their regular conveyance; the pony
was Bob, and he would not go up hills unless persuaded with sugar, but Jeremy loved him and would
not have ridden behind any other steed in the whole
world. How contemptuously the big black horses of
the wagonette gazed down their nostrils at Bob and
how superbly Mrs. Le Page, sitting very upright
under her white sunshade, greeted Mrs. Cole!

"Dear Mrs. Cole. Such a hot morning, isn't it? Lovely, of course, but so hot."

"I'm afraid," Jeremy heard his mother say, "that your carriage will never get down the Rafiel Lane, Mrs. Le Page. We hoped you'd come in the dogcart. Plenty of room. . . ."

Superb to witness the fashion in which Mrs. Le Page gazed at the dogcart.

"For all of us? . . . Dear Mrs. Cole, I scarcely think—— And Charlotte's frock. . . ."

Then Jeremy turned his eyes to Charlotte. She sat under a miniature sunshade of white silk and lace, a vision of loveliness. She was a shimmer of white, a little white cloud that had settled for a moment upon the seat of the carriage to allow the sun to dance upon it, to caress it with fingers of fire, so to separate it from the rest of the world for ever as something too precious to be touched. Jeremy had never seen anything so lovely.

He blushed and scraped his boots the one against the other.

"And this is Jeremy?" said Mrs. Le Page as though she said: "And this is where you keep your little pigs, Mr. Monk?"

"Yes," said Jeremy, blushing.

"Charlotte, you know Jeremy. You must be friends."

"Yes," said Charlotte, without moving. Then Jeremy tumbled into the stern gaze of Mr. Le Page who, arrayed as he was in a very smart suit of the whitest flannels, looked with his black beard and fierce black eyebrows like a pirate king disguised.

"How are you?" said Mr. Le Page in a deep voice.

"Very well, thank you," said Jeremy.

To tell the truth, Mrs. Cole's heart sadly misgave her when she saw the Le Page family all sitting up so new and so bright in their new and bright carriage. She thought of the simple preparations that had been made—the pasties, the saffron buns and the ginger beer; she looked around her at the very plain but useful garments worn by her family, her husband in faded grey flannel trousers and a cricketing shirt, Helen and Mary in the simplest blue cotton, and Jeremy in his two-year-old sailor suit. She had intended to bring their bathing things in a bundle, but now she put them aside. It was obvious that the Le Pages had no intention of bathing. She sighed and foresaw a difficult day ahead of her.

It was evident that the Le Pages did not intend to come one step farther into Cow Farm than was necessary.

" Dear Mrs. Cole, on a hot day—how can you endure the smells of a farm . . . such a charming farm, too, with all its cows and pigs, but in this weather. . . . Charlotte darling, you don't feel the heat ? No ? Hold your sunshade a little more to the right, love. That's right. She was not quite the thing last night, Mrs. Cole. I had some doubts about bringing her, but I knew you'd all be so disappointed. She's looking rather lovely to-day, don't you think ? You must forgive a mother's partiality. . . . Oh, you're not bringing that little dog, are you ? Surely——"

Jeremy, who had from the first hated Mrs. Le Page, forgot his shyness and brought out fiercely:

" Of course he's coming. Hamlet always goes everywhere with us."

" Hamlet ! " said Mr. Le Page in his deep bass voice.

" What a strange name for a dog ! " said Mrs. Le Page in tones of vague distrust.

At last it was settled that one member of the Cole party should ride with the Le Pages, and Mary was selected. Poor Mary ! inevitably chosen when something unpleasant must be done. To-day, it was especially hard for her, because she entertained so implacable a hatred for the lovely Charlotte and looked, it must be confessed, so plain and shabby by the side of her. Indeed, to any observer with a heart it must have been touching to see Mary driven away in that magnificent black carriage, staring with agonized hostility in front of her through her large spectacles, compelled to balance herself exactly between the magnificent sunshade of Mrs. Le Page and the smaller but also magnificent sun-shade of the lovely Charlotte. Mrs. Cole, glancing in that direction, may have felt with a pang that she would never be able to make her children handsome and gay as she would like to do—but it was certainly a pang of only a moment's dura-tion.

She would not have exchanged her Mary for a wagon-load of Charlottes.

And Jeremy, bumping along in the jingle, also felt the contrast. Why could not Mary wear her straw hat straight, and why must she have elastic under her chin ? Why did she look so cross and so stupid ? Why did she bother him so with her worries ? Charlotte would never worry him. She would just sit there, looking beautiful, with her golden hair, and blue eyes and pink cheeks. Next

week was to be Miss Jones's birthday, and in pre-
paration for this he had bought for her in Polchester
a silver thimble. He wondered whether he would
not give Charlotte this thimble instead of Miss Jones.
He could give Miss Jones some old thing he would
find somewhere, or he would go out and pick for her
some flowers. She would be pleased with anything.
He wondered what Charlotte would say when he
gave her the thimble. She would like it, of course.
She would smile. She would open her eyes and look
at him. Fortunately he had the thimble even now
in his pocket. He had bought it when he was
wearing this same suit. Yes, he would give it to
her. As he decided this he looked at Miss Jones
guiltily, but she was making such odd faces as she
squinted to escape from the sun that he did not feel
ashamed.

They came to that steep hill just beyond Garth
woods, and Bob, of course, refused to move. The
superb Le Page affair dashed past them, shouted
something at them, and disappeared over the brow
of the hill. The last thing to be seen of them were
the fierce despairing eyes of the imprisoned Mary.
A strange sensation of relief instantly settled upon
the Coles. For a moment they were alone ; they
began slowly to walk up the hill, dragging with them
the reluctant Bob. About them was peace, absolute and unstained. The hard glitter of the day
shone upon the white road, but behind them the
wood was dark and cool, a green cloud against the
sky. Behind the steep hedges the harvesters were
moving. In the air a lark was singing, and along
the ditch at the roadside a tiny stream tumbled.
And beyond these sounds there was silence.

The Coles moved up the hill very slowly, only Hamlet racing ahead to find spots of shadows where he might lie down and pant. They would not confess to themselves that this promised to be the happiest moment of their day. They went bravely forward.

On the bend of the hill the Le Pages were waiting. What Mrs. Cole had foreseen had in truth occurred. The Le Page carriage would not go down the Rafiel Lane. No, it would not. . . . Nothing would induce it to.

" James," said Mrs. Le Page to her stout and disdainful attendant.

" Nothing, ma'am," said James.

" Dear me, dear me," said Mrs. Le Page. " Well, then, we must walk," said the deep despairing voice of the Pirate King.

And walk they did.

That walk was, as Mrs. Cole afterwards said, " a pity," because it destroyed the Le Page tempers when the day was scarcely begun. Mr. Le Page was, it was quickly descried, not intended for walking. Strong and fierce though he seemed, heat instantly crumpled him up. The perfect crease of his white trousers vanished, his collar was no longer spotless, little beads of perspiration appeared almost at once on his forehead, and his black beard dripped moisture. Mrs. Le Page, with her skirts raised, walked as though she were passing through the Valley of Destruction ; every step was a risk and a danger, and the difficulty of holding her skirts and her sunshade at the same time, and of seeing that her shoes were not soiled and her hat not caught by an offending bough gave her face an expression of desperate despair.

o

4

There was, unfortunately, one spot very deep down in the lane where the ground was never dry.

A little stream ran here across the path, and the ground on either side was soft and sodden.  Mrs. Le Page, struggling to avoid an overhanging branch, stepped into the mud ; one foot stuck there, and it needed Mr. Cole's strong arm to pull her out of it.

" Charlotte ! Charlotte ! " she cried.  " Don't let Charlotte step into that !  Mr. Cole ! Mr. Cole ! I charge you—my child ! "  Charlotte was conveyed across, but the damage was done.  One of Mrs. Le Page's beautiful shoes was thick with mud.

When, therefore, the party, climbing out of the Lane, came suddenly upon the path leading down to the Cove, with the sea, like a blue cloud in front of them, no one exclaimed at the view.  It was a very beautiful view—one of the finest of its kind in the United Kingdom, the high rocks closing in the Cove and the green hills closing in the rocks.  On the hill to the right was the Rafiel Old Church, with its graveyard that ran to the very edge of the cliff, and behind the Cove was a stream and a green orchard and a little wood.  The sand of the Cove was bright gold, and the low rocks to either side of it were a dark red—the handsomest place in the world, with the water so clear that you could see down, far down, into green caverns laced with silver sand. Unfortunately, at the moment when the Coles and their friends beheld it, it was blazing in the sun ; soon the sun would pass and, during the afternoon, half of it would lie in shadow, but the Le Pages could not be expected to think of that.

The basket was unloaded from the jingle and carried down to the beach by Mr. Cole and Jim. Jeremy, finding himself at the side of the lovely Charlotte, was convulsed with shyness, the more that he knew that the unhappy Mary was listening with jealous ears. Charlotte, walking like Agag, " delicately," had a piteous expression in her eyes as though she were being led to the torture.

Jeremy coughed and began : " We always come here every year. Don't you like it ? "

" Yes," she said miserably.

" And we paddle and bathe. Do you like bathing ? "

" Going into the sea ? "

" Yes."

" Oh, no ! Mother says I mustn't, because it'll hurt my hair. Do you like my hair ? "

" Yes," said Jeremy, blushing at so direct an invitation to compliment.

" Mother says I've got to be very careful of my hair because it's my chief beauty."

" Yes," said Jeremy.

" I have a maid, Alice, and she brushes a whole hour every morning and a whole hour every evening."

" Don't you get very tired ? " asked Jeremy. " I know I should."

" Mother says if you have such beautiful hair you must take trouble with it," Charlotte gravely replied.

Her voice was so like the voice of a parrot that Jeremy's grandmother had once possessed that it didn't seem as though a human being was speaking at all. They were near the beach now and could see the blue slipping in, turning into white bubbles, then slipping out again.

" Do you like my frock ? " said Charlotte.

" Yes," said Jeremy.

" It was bought in London. All my clothes are bought in London."

" Mary's and Helen's aren't," said Jeremy with some faint idea of protecting his sisters. " They're bought in Polchester."

" Mother says," said Charlotte, " that if you're not pretty it doesn't matter where you buy your clothes."

They arrived on the beach and stared about them. It became at once a great question as to where Mrs. Le Page would sit. She could not sit on the sand, which looked damp, nor equally, of course, on a rock, that was spiky and hard. What to do with her ? She stood in the middle of the beach, still holding up her skirts, gazing desperately about her, looking first at one spot and then at another.

" Oh, dear, the heat ! " she exclaimed. " Is there no shade anywhere ? Perhaps in that farm-house over there. . . ." It was probable enough that no member of the Cole family would have minded banishing Mrs. Le Page into the farm-house, but it would have meant that the whole party must accompany her. That was impossible. They had come for a picnic, and a picnic they would have.

Mrs. Cole watched, with growing agitation, the whole situation. She saw from her husband's face that he was rapidly losing his temper, and she had learnt, after many experiences, that when he lost his temper he was capable of anything. That does not mean, of course, that he was ever angry to the extent of swearing or striking out with his fists—no, he simply grew sadder, and sadder, and sadder, and this melancholy had a way of reducing to despair all the people with whom he happened to be at the time.

" What does everyone say to our having lunch now ? " cried Mrs. Cole cheerfully. " It's after one, and I'm sure everyone's hungry."

No one said anything, so preparations were begun. A minute piece of shade was found for Mrs. Le Page, and here she sat on a flat piece of rock with her skirts drawn close about her as though she were afraid of rats or crabs. A tablecloth was laid on the sand and the provisions spread out—pasties for everybody, egg-sandwiches, seed-cake, and jam-puffs—*and* ginger beer. It looked a fine feast when it was all there, and Mrs. Cole, as she gave the final touch to it by placing a drinking glass containing two red rose-buds in the middle, felt proud of her efforts and hoped that after all the affair might pass off bravely. But alas, how easily the proudest plans fall to the ground.

" I hope, Alice, you haven't forgotten the salt ! "

Instantly Mrs. Cole knew that she had forgotten it. She could see herself standing there in Mrs. Monk's kitchen forgetting it. How could she ? And Mrs. Monk, how could *she ?* It had never been forgotten before.

" Oh, no," she said wildly. " Oh, no ! I'm sure I can't have forgotten it."

She plunged about, her red face all creased with anxiety, her hat on one side, her hands searching everywhere, under the tablecloth, in the basket, amongst the knives and forks.

" Jim, you haven't dropped anything ? "

" No, mum. Beggin' your pardon, mum, the basket was closed, so to speak—closed it was."

No, she knew that she had forgotten it.

" I'm so sorry, Mrs. Le Page, I'm afraid——"

" My dear Mrs. Cole ! What does it matter ? Not in the least, I assure you. In this heat it's impossible to feel hungry, isn't it ? I assure you I don't feel as though I could touch a thing. A little fruit, perhaps—an apple or a peach——"

Fruit ? Why hadn't Mrs. Cole brought fruit ? She might so easily have done so, and she had never thought about it. They themselves were rather tired of fruit, and so——

" I'm afraid we've no fruit, but an egg-sandwich——"

" Eggs need salt, don't you think ? Not that it matters in the very least, but so that you shouldn't think me fussy. Really, dear Mrs. Cole, I never felt less hungry in my life. Just a drop of milk and I'm perfectly satisfied."

" Jeremy shall run up to the farm for the milk. You don't mind, Jeremy dear, do you ? It's only a step. Just take this sixpence, dear, and say we'll send the jug back this afternoon if they'll spare one."

Jeremy did mind. He was enjoying his luncheon, and he was gazing at Charlotte, and he was teasing Hamlet with scraps—he was very happy. Nevertheless, he started off.

As soon as he left the sands the noise of the sea was shut off from him, and he was climbing the little green path up which the Scarlet Admiral had once stalked.

Suddenly he remembered—in his excitement about Charlotte he had forgotten the admiral. He stood for a moment, listening. The green hedge shut off the noise of the sea—only above his head some birds were twittering. He fancied that he heard footsteps, then that beyond the hedge something was moving. It seemed to him that the birds were also listening for something. " Well, it's the middle of the afternoon, anyway." He thought to himself, " He never comes there—only in the morning or evening," but he hurried forward after that, wishing that he had called to Hamlet to accompany him. It was a pleasant climb to the farm through the green orchard, and he found at the farm door an agreeable woman, who smiled at him when she gave him the milk. He had to come down the hill carefully, lest the milk should be spilt. He walked along very happily, humming to himself and thinking in a confused summer afternoon kind of manner of Charlotte, Hamlet, Mrs. Le Page and himself. " Shall I give her the thimble or shan't I ? I could take her to the pools where the little crabs are. She'd like them. I wonder whether we're going to bathe. Mrs. Le Page will look funny bathing. . . ." Then he was in the green lane again, and at once his discomfort returned to him, and he looked around his shoulder and into the hedges, and stopped once and again to listen. There was no sound. The birds, it seemed, had all fallen to sleep. The hedges, he thought, were closer about him. It was very hot here, with no breeze and no comforting sound of the sea. " I wonder whether he really does come," he thought. " It must be horrid to see him—coming quite close." And the thought of the Fool also frightened him. The Fool with his tongue out and his shaking legs, like the idiot who lived near the Cathedral at home. At the thought of this Jeremy suddenly took to his legs and ran, covering the top of his jug with his hand ; then, when he came out on to the strip of grass that crossed the top of the beach, he stopped, suddenly ashamed of himself. Scarlet Admirals! Scarlet Admirals! How could there be Scarlet Admirals in a world that also contained so blazing a sun, so blue a sea, and the gorgeous realities of the Le Page family. He arrived at the luncheon party hot and proud and smiling, so cheerful and stolid and agreeable that even Mrs. Le Page was compelled to say, " Really, Mrs. Cole, that's a very nice little boy of yours. Come here, little Jeremy, and talk to me ! " How deeply he hated being called " little Jeremy " only Mary and Helen knew. Their eyes flew to his face to see how he would take it. He took it very well. He sat down beside Mrs. Le Page, who very gracefully and languidly sipped at her glass of milk.

" How old are you, Jeremy, dear ? " she asked him.

" Eight," he answered, wriggling.

" What a nice age ! And one day you'll go to school ? "

" In September."

" And what will you be when you're a man ? "

" Oh, I don't know. I'll be a soldier, perhaps."

" Oh, I'm sure you wouldn't like to be a soldier and kill people."

" Yes, I would. There's lots of people I'd like to kill."

Mrs. Le Page drew her skirts back a little.

" How horrible !  I'm sure your mother wouldn't like to hear that."

But Mr. Cole had caught the last words of the dialogue and interrupted with :

" But what could be finer, Mrs. Le Page, than the defence of one's country ?  Would you have our young lads grow up faint-hearted and fail their Motherland when she calls ?  What can be finer, I say, than to die for Queen and country ?  Would not every mother have her son shed his blood for liberty and freedom ? . . . No, Jeremy, not another.  You've had quite enough.  It would indeed be a disheartening sight if we elders were to watch our sons and grandchildren turning their swords into ploughshares——"

He was interrupted by a shrill cry from Mrs. Le Page :

" Charlotte, darling, do hold your sunshade up. All the left side of your face is exposed.  That's better, dear.  I beg your pardon, Mr. Cole ? "

But Mr. Cole was offended.

" I hope no son of mine will ever show himself a faint heart," he concluded, severely.

The luncheon, in fact, had been a most dismal failure.  The Coles could fling their minds back to luncheons on this same beach that had been simply riotous successes.  What fun they had had ! What games !  What bathes !  Now the very sight of Mr. Le Page's black beard was enough.  Even Jeremy felt that things were wrong.  Then he looked at Charlotte and was satisfied.  There she sat, straight and stiff, her hands on her lap, her hair falling in lovely golden ripples down her back, her gaze fixed on distance.  Oh !  she was beautiful !

He would do whatever she told him ; he would give
her Miss Noah and the apple tree ; he would——
A sound disturbed his devotions. He turned.
Both Mr. and Mrs. Le Page were fast asleep.


### 5

" Children," whispered Mrs. Cole, " very quietly
now, so that you don't disturb anyone, run off to
the farther beach and play. Helen, you'll see that
everything is all right, won't you ? "

It was only just in time that Jeremy succeeded in
strangling Hamlet's bark into a snort, and even
then they all looked round for a moment at the
sleepers in the greatest anxiety. But no, they had
not been disturbed. If only Mr. Le Page could have
known what he resembled lying there with his
mouth open ! But he did not know. He was
doubtless dreaming of his property.

The children crept away. Charlotte and Jeremy
together. Jeremy's heart beat thickly. At last he
had the lovely creature in his charge. It was true
that he did not quite know what he was going to do
with her, and that even now, in the height of his
admiration, he did wish that she would not walk
as though she were treading on red-hot ploughshares, and that she could talk a little instead of
giving little shivers of apprehension at every step.

" I must say," he thought to himself, " she's rather
silly in some ways. Perhaps it wouldn't be fun to
see her always."

They turned the corner round a projecting finger
of rock, and a new little beach lay in front of
them.

" Well," said Jeremy, " here we are. What shall we play ? "

There was dead silence.

" We might play pirates," he continued. " I'll be the pirate, and Mary can sit on that rock until the water comes round her, and Charlotte shall hide in that cave——"

There was still silence. Looking about him, he discovered from his sisters' countenances that they were resolved to lend no kind of assistance, and he then from that deduced the simple fact that his sisters hated Charlotte and were not going to make it pleasant for her in any way if they could help it. Oh ! it was a miserable picnic ! The worst that he'd ever had.

" It's too hot to play," said Helen loftily. " I'm going to sit down over there."

" So am I," said Mary.

They moved away, their heads in the air and their legs ridiculously stiff.

Jeremy gazed at Charlotte in distress. It was very wicked of his sisters to go off like that, but it was also very silly of Charlotte to stand there so helplessly. He was beginning to think that perhaps he would give the thimble to Miss Jones after all.

" Would you like to go and see the pool where the little crabs are ? " he asked.

" I don't know," she answered, her upper lip trembling as though she were going to cry. " I want to go home with Mother."

" You can't go home," he said firmly, " and you can't see your mother, because she's asleep."

" I've made my shoes dirty," she said, looking

down at her feet, " and I'm so tired of holding my sunshade."

" I should shut it up," Jeremy said, without any hesitation. " I think it's a silly thing. I'm glad I'm not a girl. Do you have to take it with you everywhere ? "

" Not if it's raining. Then I have an umbrella."

" I think you'd better come and see the crabs," he settled. " They're only just over there."

She moved along with him reluctantly, looking back continually to where her mother ought to be.

" Are you enjoying yourself ? " Jeremy asked politely.

" No," she said without any hesitation. " I want to go home."

" She's as selfish as anything," he thought to himself. " We're giving the party, and she ought to have said ' Yes ' even if she wasn't."

" Do you like my dog ? " he asked, with another effort at light conversation.

" No," she answered with a little shiver. " He's ugly."

" He isn't ugly," Jeremy returned indignantly. " He isn't perhaps the very best breed, but Uncle Samuel says that that doesn't matter if he's clever. He's better than any other dog. I love him more than anybody. He isn't ugly ! "

" He is," cried Charlotte with a kind of wail. " Oh ! I want to go home."

" Well, you can't go home," he answered her fiercely. " So you needn't think about it."

They came to the little pools, three of them, now clear as crystal, blue on their surface, with green depths and red shelving rock.

" Now you sit here," he said cheerfully. " No one will touch you. The crabs won't get at you."

He looked about him and noticed with surprise where he was. He was sitting on the farther corner of the very beach where the Scarlet Admiral had landed with his men. It was out there beyond that bend of rock that the wonderful ship had rode, with its gold and silk, its jewelled masts and its glittering board. Directly opposite to him was the little green path that led up the hill, and above it the very field —Farmer Ede's field !

For a long, long time they sat there in silence. He forgot Charlotte in his interest over his discovery, staring about him and watching how quickly the August afternoon was losing its heat and colour, so that already a little cold autumnal wind was playing about the sand, the colours were being drawn from the sky, and a grey web was slowly pulled across the sea.

" Now," he said cheerfully at last to Charlotte, " I'll look for the crabs."

" I hate crabs," she said. " I want to go home."

" You can't go home," he answered furiously. " What's the good of saying that over and over again ? You aren't going yet, so it's no use saying you are."

" You're a horrid little boy," she brought out with a kind of inanimate sob.

He did not reply to that ; he was still trying to behave like a gentleman. How could he ever have liked her ? Why, her hair was not so much after all. What was hair when you come to think of it ? Mary got on quite well with hers, ugly though it was. She was stupid, stupid, stupid ! She was like someone dead. As he searched for the crabs that weren't there he felt his temper growing. Soon he would lead her back to her mother, and leave her there and never see her again.

But this was not the climax of the afternoon.

When he looked up from gazing into the pool the whole world seemed to have changed. He was still dazzled perhaps by the reflection of the water in his eyes, and yet it was not altogether that. It was not altogether because the day was slipping from afternoon into evening.

The lazy ripple of the water as it slutched up the sand and then broke, the shadows that were creeping farther and farther from rock to rock, the green light that pushed up from the horizon into the faint blue, the grey web of the sea, the thick gathering of the hills as they crept more closely about the little darkening beach . . . it was none of these things.

He began hurriedly to tell Charlotte about the Scarlet Admiral. Even as he told her he was himself caught into the excitement of the narration. He forgot her ; he did not see her white cheeks, her mouth open with terror, an expression new to her, that her face had never known before, stealing into her eyes. He told her how the Fool had seen the ship, how the Admiral had landed, then left his men on the beach, how he had climbed the little green path, how the young man had followed him, how they had fought, how the young man had fallen. What was that ? Jeremy jumped from his rock. " I say, did you hear anything ? "

And that was enough for Charlotte. With one scream, a scream such as she had never uttered in her life before, she turned, and then, running as indeed she had never run before, she stumbled, half fell, stumbled, finally ran as though the whole world of her ghosts was behind her. Her screams were so piercing that they may well have startled the villagers of Rafiel.

Jeremy followed her, but his mind was not with her. Was he going to see something ? What was it ? Who was it ?

Then the awful catastrophe that finished the afternoon occurred. Turning the corner of the rock, Charlotte missed her footing and fell straight into a pool. Jeremy, Mary and Helen were upon her almost as she fell. They dragged her out, but alas ! what a sight was there ! Instead of the beautiful and magnificent Charlotte there was a bedraggled and dirty little girl.

But also, instead of an inanimate and lifeless doll, there was at last a human being, a terrified soul.

The scene that followed passes all power of description. Mrs. Le Page wailed like a lost spirit ; Mr. Le Page was so rude to Mr. Cole that it might confidently be said that those two gentlemen would never speak to one another again. Mrs. Cole, dismayed though she was, had some fatalistic consolation that she had known from the first that the picnic would be a most dreadful failure and that the worst had occurred ; there was no more to come.

Everyone was too deeply occupied to scold Jeremy. They all moved up to the farm, Charlotte behaving most strangely, even striking her mother and crying, " Let me go ! Let me go ! I don't want to be clean ! I'm frightened ! I'm frightened ! "

Jeremy hung behind the others. At the bottom

of the little lane he stood and waited. Was there
a figure coming up through the dusk ? Did someone pass him ? Why did he suddenly feel no longer
afraid, but only reassured and with the strangest
certainty that the lane, the beach, the field belonged
to him now ? He would come there and live when
he grew up. He would come often. Had the
Scarlet Admiral passed him ? If not the Scarlet
Admiral, then the other.

The sea picnic had, after all, been not quite a
misfortune.

Jeremy had been made free of the land.

And Charlotte ? Charlotte had been woken up,
and never would go to sleep again.

# CHAPTER X

## MARY

### I

MARY COLE had been, all her life, that thing beloved of the sentimental novelist, a misunderstood child. She was the only misunderstood member of the Cole family, and she was misunderstood, as is very often the case, in a large measure because she was so plain. Had she been good-looking as Helen, or independent as Jeremy, she would have either attracted the world in general, or have been indifferent as to whether she attracted it or no. As it was, she longed to attract everyone, and, in truth, attracted nobody. She might have found consolation in books or her own highly-coloured imaginations had it not been for the burning passions which she formed, at a very early age, for living people. For some years now her life had centred round her brother Jeremy. Had the Coles been an observant family, they might, perhaps, have found some pathos in the way in which Mary, with her pale sallow complexion, her pear-shaped face with its dull, grey eyes, her enormous glasses, her lanky colourless hair, and her thin, bony figure, gazed at her masculine and independent brother.

Uncle Samuel might have noticed, but he was occupied with his painting. For the rest they were not observant. Mary was only seven years of age, but she had the capacity for being hurt of a person of thirty. She was hurt by everything and everybody. When somebody said : " Now, Mary, hurry up. You're always so slow," she was hurt. If Helen told her that she was selfish, she was hurt, and would sit wondering whether she was selfish or no. If Mrs. Cole said that she must brush her hair more carefully she was hurt, and when Jeremy said anything sharp to her she was in agony. She discovered very quickly that no one cared for her agonies. The Coles were a plain, matter-of-fact race, and had the day's work to finish. They had no intention of thinking too much of their children's feelings. Thirty years ago that was not so popular as it is now. Meanwhile, her devotion to her brother grew with every month of her life. She thought him, in all honesty, the most miraculous of all human beings. There was more in her worship than mere dog-like fidelity. She adored him for reasons that were real and true ; for his independence, his obstinacy, his sense of fun, his sudden, unexpected kindnesses, his sudden helplessness, and above all, for his bravery. He seemed to her the bravest hero in all history, and she felt it the more because she was herself compact of every fear and terror known to man. It was not enough for her, the ordinary panic that belongs to all human life at every stage of its progress. She feared everything and everybody, and only hid her fear by a persistent cover of almost obstinate stupidity, which deceived, to some extent, her relations, but never in any degree herself. She knew that she was plain, awkward and hesitating, but she knew also that she was clever. She knew that she could do everything twice as fast

as Jeremy and Helen, that she was often so impatient
of their slow progress at lessons that she would beat
her foot on the ground in a kind of agonized impatience. She knew that she was clever, and she
wondered sometimes why her cleverness did not
give her more advantage. Why, for instance,
should Helen's good looks be noticed at once by
every visitor and her own cleverness be unnoticed ?
Certainly, on occasions, her mother would say :
" And Mary ? I don't think you've met Mary.
Come and say, how do you do, Mary. Mary is
the clever one of the family ! " but it was always
said in a deprecating, apologetic tone, which made
Mary hang her head and hate both herself and her
mother.

She told herself stories of the times when Jeremy
would have to depend entirely upon the splendour of
her brains for his delivery from some horror—death,
torture or disgrace. At present those times were,
she was bound to confess to herself, very distant.
He depended upon no one for anything ; he could
not be said to need Mary's assistance in any particular. And with this burning desire of hers
came, of course, jealousy. There are some happy,
easy natures to whom jealousy is, through life,
unknown. They are to be envied. Jealousy in a
grown-up human being is bad ; in a child it is
terrible. Had you told Mrs. Cole—good mother
though she was—that her daughter Mary, aged
seven, suffered tortures through jealousy, she would
have assured you that it was not, in reality, jealousy,
but rather indigestion, and that a little medicine
would put it right.

Mary was quite helpless. What is a child to do

if she is jealous ?   Other children do not understand
her, her elders laugh at her.   Mary, with a wisdom
greatly beyond her years, realized very quickly that
this was some sort of horrible disease, with which she
must wrestle alone.   Above all, she must never
allow Jeremy to know anything about it.   He was,
of course, sublimely unaware of the matter ; he
knew that Mary was silly sometimes, but he attributed that to her sex ; he went on his way, happily
indifferent whether anyone cared for him or no. . . .

Mary suffered agonies when, as sometimes happened, Jeremy sat with his arm round Helen's neck
and his cheek up against hers.   She suffered when,
in a mood of tempestuous affection to the whole
world, he kissed Miss Jones.   She even suffered
when he sat at his mother's feet whilst she read
" The Dove in the Eagle's Nest " or " Engel the
Fearless."

Most of all, however, she suffered over Hamlet.
She knew that at this present time Hamlet was the
one creature for whom Jeremy passionately cared.
He loved his mother, but with the love that custom
and habit has tamed and modified, although since
Mrs. Cole's illness in the early summer he had cared
for her in a manner more demonstrative and openly
affectionate.   Nevertheless, it was Hamlet who
commanded Jeremy's heart, and Mary knew it.
Matters were made worse by the undoubted truth
that Hamlet did not care very much for Mary—
that is, he never gave any signs of caring, and very
often walked out of the room when she came into
it.   Mary could have cared for the dog as enthusi-
astically as Jeremy—she was always sentimental
about animals—but now she was shut out from

their alliance, and she knew that when she came
up to them and began to pat or stroke Hamlet,
Jeremy was annoyed and Hamlet's skin wriggled
in a kind of retreating fashion under her fingers.
Wise people will say that it is impossible for this
to be a serious trouble to a child. It was increasingly
serious to Mary.

Jeremy was not, perhaps, so tactful as he might
have been. " Oh, bother, Mary ! " he would say.
" You've gone and waked Hamlet up ! " or " Don't
stroke Hamlet that way, Mary ; he hates it ! " or
" No, I'm going for a walk with Hamlet ; we don't
want anyone ! " Or Hamlet himself would suddenly
bark at her as though he hated her, or would bare
his teeth and grin at her in a mocking, sarcastic
way that he had. At first, as an answer to this,
she had the ridiculous idea of herself adopting an
animal, and she selected, for this purpose, the
kitchen cat, a dull, somnolent beast, whose sleek
black hair was furtive, and green, crooked eyes
malignant. The cat showed no signs of affection
for Mary, nor could she herself honestly care for it.
When she brought it with her into the schoolroom,
Hamlet treated it in a scornful, sarcastic fashion
that was worse than outrageous attack. The cat
was uncleanly, and was speedily banished back
into the kitchen. Mary's jealousy of Hamlet then
grew apace, and with that jealousy, unfortunately,
her secret appreciation of his splendours. She
could not help admitting to herself that he was the
most attractive dog in the world. She would look
at him from under her spectacles when she was
supposed to be reading and watch him as he rolled,
kicking his legs in the air, or lay stretched out, his

black wet nose against his paws, his eyes gleaming, his gaze fixed like the point of a dagger raised to strike, upon some trophy, or enemy, or spoil, or sat, solemn and pompous, like the Lord Mayor holding a meeting, as Jeremy said, up against his master's leg, square and solid as though he were cut out of wood, his peaked beard supercilious, his very ears at a patronizing angle ; or, as Mary loved best of all to see him, when he was simply childish, playing, as though he was still a new-found puppy, with pieces of paper or balls of string, rolling and choking, growling, purring, staggering and tumbling. At such times, again and again, her impulse would be to go forward and applaud him, and then the instinct that she would be checked by Jeremy stayed her.

She knew very well that Jeremy realized nothing of this. Jeremy was not given to the consideration of other people's motives—his own independence saved him from anxiety about others. He had the English characteristic of fancying that others must like and dislike as he himself liked and disliked. Of sentiment he had no knowledge whatever.

As this year grew towards summer Mary had the feeling that Jeremy was slipping away from her. She did not know what had happened to him. In the old days he had asked her opinion about many things ; he had seemed to enjoy the long stories that she had told him—at any rate, he had listened to them very politely—and he had asked her to suggest games or to play with his toys. Now, as the summer drew near, he did none of these things. He was frankly impatient with her stories, never asked her advice about anything, and never played with her. Was he growing very conceited ? Was it because he was going to school, and thought himself too old for his sisters ? No, he did not seem to be conceited—he had always been proud, but never conceited. It was rather as though he had lately had thoughts of his own, almost against his will, and that these had shut him off from the people round him.

Then, when their mother was so ill and Barbara made her startling appearance Jeremy kept more to himself. He never talked about his mother's illness, as did the others, and yet Mary knew that he had been more deeply concerned than any of them. She had been miserable, of course, but to Jeremy it had been as though he had been led into a new world altogether ; Helen and she were still in their old places, and Jeremy had left them.

At last just before they all moved to Cow Farm Mary made a silly scene. She had not intended to make a scene. Scenes seemed to come upon her, like evil birds, straight out of the air, to seize her before she knew where she was, to envelop and carry her up with them ; at last, when all the mischief was done, to set her on her feet again, battered, torn and bitterly ashamed. One evening she was sitting deep in " Charlotte Mary," and Hamlet, bunched up against his master's leg, stared at her. She had long ago told herself that it was ridiculous to mind what Hamlet did, that he was not looking at her, and, in any case, he was only a dog—and so on.

But to-night she was tired, and had read so long that her head ached—Hamlet was laughing at her, his eyes stared through his hair at her, cynically, superciliously, contemptuously. His lip curled and his beard bristled. Moved by a sudden wild impulse she picked up "The Chaplet of Pearls" and threw it at him. It hit him (not very severely), and he gave the sharp, melodramatic howl that he always used when it was his dignity rather than his body that was hurt. Jeremy looked up, saw what had happened, and a fine scene followed. Mary had hysterics, stamped and howled. Jeremy, his face white, stood and said nothing, but looked as though he hated her, which at that moment he undoubtedly did. It was that look which more than anything else in the world she dreaded.

She made herself sick with crying; then apologized with an abjection that only irritated him the more; finally remembered the smallest details of the affair long after he had forgotten all about it.

2

During the first few weeks at Cow Farm Mary was happy. She had then many especial private joys, such as climbing into one of the old apple trees behind the house and reading there, safe from the world, or inventing for herself wonderful adventures out of the dark glooms and sunlit spaces of the orchard, or creeping about the lofts and barns as though they were full of the most desperate dangers and hazards that she alone had the pluck and intelligence to overcome. Then Mrs. Monk was kind to her, and listened to her imaginative chatter with a most marvellous patience. Mary did not know that, after these narrations, she would shake her head and say to her husband: "Not long for this world, I'm thinking, poor worm . . not long for this world."

Then, at first Jeremy was kind and considerate.
He was so happy that he did not mind what anyone
did, and he would listen to Mary's stories quite
in the old way, whistling to himself, not thinking
about her at all perhaps, really, but very patient.
After the first fortnight he slipped away from her
again—and now more than ever before. He went
off for long walks with Hamlet, refusing to take
her with them; he answered her questions so
vaguely that she could see that he paid her no
attention at all; he turned upon her and rent her
if she complained. And it was all, she was sure,
that horrible dog. Jeremy was always with Hamlet
now. The free life that the farm gave them, no
lessons, no set hours, no care for appearances, left
them to choose their own ways, and so developed
their individualities. Helen was now more and
more with her elders, was becoming that invaluable
thing, " a great help to her mother," and even, to
her own inexhaustible pride, paid two calls with Mrs.
Cole on the wives of neighbouring farmers. Then, Barbara absorbed more than ever of Helen's attention,
and Mary was not allowed to share in these rites and
services because " she always made Barbara cry."

She was, therefore, very much alone, and felt all
her injuries twice as deeply as she had felt them
before. Hamlet began to be an obsession with her.
She had always had a habit of talking to herself,
and now she could be heard telling herself that if
it were not for the dog, Jeremy would always be
with her, would play with her, walk with her, laugh
with her as he used to do. She acquired now an
awkward habit of gazing at him with passionate
intensity. He would raise his eyes and find the

great moon-faced spectacles fixed upon him with a beseeching, reproachful glare in the light of them. This would irritate him intensely. He would say :

" You'll know me next time, Mary."

She would blush crimson and then, with trembling mouth, answer :

" I wasn't looking."

" Yes, you were."

" No, I wasn't."

" Of course you were—staring as though I were an Indian or Chinaman. If my face is dirty, say so."

" It isn't dirty."

" Well, then——"

" You're always so cross."

" I'm not cross—only you're so silly——"

" You usen't always to say I was silly. Now you always do—every minute."

" So you are." Then as he saw the tears coming he would get up and go away. He didn't mean to be unkind to her ; he was fond of her—but he hated scenes.

" Mary's always howling about something now," he confided to Helen.

" Is she ? " Helen answered with indifference. " Mary's such a baby."

So Mary began to attribute everything to the dog. It seemed to her that she met the animal everywhere. Cow Farm was a rambling building, with dark, uneven stairs, low-ceilinged rooms, queer, odd corners, and sudden unexpected doors. It seemed to Mary as though in this place there were two Hamlets. When, in the evening she went to her room, hurrying through the passages for fear of what she might see, stumbling over the uneven

boards, sniffing the mice and straw under the smell
of her tallow candle, suddenly out of nowhere at
all Hamlet would appear scurrying along, like the
White Rabbit, intent on serious business.

He came so softly and with so sudden a flurry
and scatter when she did hear him that her heart
would beat for minutes afterwards, and she would
not dare that night to search, as she usually did,
for burglars under her bed, but would lie, quaking,
hot and staring, unable to sleep. When at last
dreams came they would be haunted by a monstrous
dog, all hair and eyes, who, with padding feet, would
track her round and round a room from which there
was no escape. Hamlet, being one of the wisest
of dogs, very quickly discovered that Mary hated
him. He was not a sentimental dog, and he did
not devote his time to inventing ways in which he
might placate his enemy, he simply avoided her.
But he could not hinder a certain cynical and
ironic pleasure that he had of, so to speak, flaunting
his master in her face. He clung to Jeremy more
resolutely than ever, would jump up at him, lick
his hands and tumble about in front of him whenever
Mary was there, and then suddenly, very straight
and very grave, would stare at her as though he
were the most devout and obedient dog in the place.
Indeed, he bore her no malice ; he could afford to
disregard the Marys of this world, and of women
in general he had a poor opinion. But he loved
to tease, and Mary was an easy prey. He had his
fun with her.

After the affair of the sea picnic, Jeremy was for
some time under a cloud. It was felt that he was
getting too big for anyone to manage. It was not

that he was wicked, not that he kept bad company
with the boys on the farm, or was dishonest, or told
lies, or stole things—no, he gave no one that kind
of anxiety—but that he was developing quite
unmistakably a will of his own, and had a remarkable
way of doing what he wanted without being actually
disobedient, which was very puzzling to his elders.
Being a little in disgrace he went off more than
ever by himself, always appearing again at the
appointed time, but telling no one where he had
been or what he had been doing. His father had
no influence over him at all, whilst Uncle Samuel
could make him do whatever he wanted—and this,
as Aunt Amy said, " was really a pity."

" It's a good thing he's going to school in September," sighed his mother. " He's getting out of
women's hands."

Mary longed with feverish longing to share in
his adventures. If only he would tell her what
he did on these walks of his. But no, only Hamlet
knew. Perhaps, if he did not go with the dog he
would go with her. When this idea crept into her
brain she seized it and clutched it. That was all
he wanted—a companion. Were Hamlet not there
he would take her. Were Hamlet not there. . . .
She began to brood over this. She wondered. . . .
She considered. She shuddered at her own wickedness ; she tried to drive the thoughts from her
head, but they kept coming.

After all, no one need know. For a day or two
Jeremy would be sorry and then he would forget.
She knew the man who went round selling dogs
—selling dogs and buying them.

She shuddered at her wickedness.

## 3

The last days of August came, and with them the last week of the holiday. Already there was a scent of autumn in the air, leaves were turning gold and red, and the evenings came cool and sudden, upon the hot summer afternoons. Mary was not very well ; she had caught a cold somewhere, and existed in the irritating condition of going out one day and being held indoors the next. This upset her temper, and at night she had nightmares, in which she saw clouds of smoke crawling in at her window, snakes on the floor, and crimson flames darting at her from the ceiling. It was because she was in an abnormal condition of health that the idea of doing something with Hamlet had gained such hold upon her. She considered the matter from every point of view. She did not want to be cruel to the dog ; she supposed that after a week or two he would be quite happy with his new master, and, in any case, he had strolled in so casually upon the Cole family that he was accustomed to a wandering life.

She did not intend that anyone should know. It was to be a deep secret all of her own.

Jeremy was going to school in September, and before then she must make him friendly to her again. She saw stretching in front of her all the lonely autumn without him and her own memories of the miserable summer to make her wretched. She was an extremely sentimental little girl.

As always happens when one is meditating with a placated conscience a wicked deed, the opportunity was suddenly offered Mary of achieving her purpose.

One morning, Jeremy, after refusing to listen to one of Mary's long romances, lost his temper :

" I can't stop," he said. " You bother and bother and bother. Aunt Amy says you nearly make her mad."

" I don't care what Aunt Amy says," Mary on the edge of tears replied.

" Hamlet and I are going out. And I'm sick of your silly old stories." Then he suddenly stopped and gazed at Mary, who was beginning, as usual, to weep.

" Look here, Mary, what's been the matter with you lately ? You're always crying now or something. And you look at me as though I'd done something dreadful. I haven't done anything."

" I—never—said you—had," Mary gulped out. He rubbed his nose in a way that he had when he was puzzled——

" If it's anything I do, tell me. It's so silly always crying. The holidays will be over soon, and you've done nothing but cry."

" You're—never—with me—now," Mary sobbed.

" Well, I've been busy."

" You haven't. You can't be busy all—by yourself."

" Oh, yes, you can." He was getting impatient. " Anyway, you might let Hamlet and me alone. You're always bothering one of us."

" No, I'm not." She choked an enormous sob and burst out with : " It's always Hamlet now. I wish he'd never—come. It was much nicer before."

Then he lost his temper. " Oh, you're a baby ! I'm sick of you and your nonsense," he cried, and stamped off.

In Mary's red-rimmed eyes, as she watched him go, determination grew.

It happened that upon the afternoon of that same day Miss Jones announced that she would take Mary for a walk ; then, just as they passed through the farm gates, Hamlet, rushing out, joined them. He did not often honour them with his company, despising women most especially when they walked, but to-day his master was busy digging for worms in the vegetable garden, and, after a quarter of an hour's contemplation of this fascinating occupation, he had wandered off in search of a livelier game. He decided to join Miss Jones ; he could do what he pleased, he could amuse himself with her ineffectual attempts to keep him in order and he could irritate Mary ; so he danced along, with his tail in the air, barking at imaginary rats and poking his nose into hedges.

Mary, with a sudden tightened clutching of the heart, realized that her hour was upon her. She felt so wicked as she realized this that she wondered that the ground didn't open up and swallow her, as it had done with those unfortunate people in the Bible. But no, the world was calm. Little white milky clouds raced in lines and circles across the sky, and once and again a leaf floated from a tree, hung for a moment suspended and then turned slowly to the ground. The hedges were a dark black-green, high and thick above the dusty road ; there had been no rain for weeks. Truly a stable world. Mary, glaring at Fate, wondered how it could be done.

Miss Jones, who was happy and optimistic to-day, talked in a tenderly reminiscent tone of her **youth.** This vein of reminiscence Mary, on her normal day, loved. To-day she did not hear a word that Miss Jones said.

" I remember my mother saying so well to my dear brother : 'Do what you like, my boy. I trust you.' And indeed Alfred was to be trusted if ever a boy was. It is a remarkable thing, but I cannot remember a single occasion of dishonesty on Alfred's part. 'A white lie,' he would often say, 'is a lie, and a lie is a sin—white or black, always a sin'; and I remember that he would often put Mother to a serious inconvenience by his telling callers that she was in when she had wished it to be said that she was not at home. He felt it his serious duty, and so he told Mother. 'Don't ask me to tell a lie, Mother,' I remember his saying. 'I cannot do it.'"

" Like George Washington," said Mary, suddenly catching the last words of Miss Jones's sentence.

" He was like many famous characters in history, I used to think. Once I remember reading about Oliver Cromwell. . . . Where is that dog ? Hamlet ! Hamlet ! Perhaps he's gone after the sheep. Ah ! there he is ! Hamlet, you naughty dog !"

They were approaching one of their favourite pieces of country—Mellot Wood. Here, on the wood's edge, the ground broke away, running down in a field of corn to a little green valley with clustered trees that showed only their heads, so thickly embedded were they, and beyond the valley the sea. The sea looked quite close here, although it was in reality four miles distant. Never was such a place as this view for light and shadow. The clouds raced like the black wings of enormous birds across the light green valley, and the red gold of the cornfield was tossed into the haze and swept like a golden shadow across the earth, bending back again when the breeze had died. Behind Mellot Wood was Mellot Farm, an old eighteenth-century house about which there was a fine tragic story with a murder and a ghost in it, and this, of course, gave Mellot Wood an additional charm. When they arrived at the outskirts of Mellot Wood Mary looked about her. It was there on the edge of the Rafiel Road that skirted the wood, that she had once seen the dog-man eating his luncheon out of a red pocket handkerchief. There was no sign of him to-day. All was silent and still. Only the little wood uttered little sighs of content beneath the flying clouds. Hamlet, tired with his racing after imaginary rabbits, walked quietly along by Mary's side. What was she to do? She had once again the desperate feeling that something stronger than she had swept down upon her and was forcing her to do this thing. She seemed to have no will of her own, but to be watching some other commit an act whose dangerous wickedness froze her heart. How could she? But she must. Someone was doing it for her.

And in very truth it seemed so. Miss Jones said that now they were here she might as well call upon Miss Andrews, the sister of the Mellot farmer. Miss Andrews had promised her some ducks' eggs. They pushed open the farm gate, passed across the yard and knocked on the house door. Near Mary was a large barn with a heavy door, now ajar. Hamlet sat gazing pensively at a flock of geese, his tongue out, panting contentedly.

"Wait here one minute, Mary," said Miss Jones. "I won't stay."

Q

Miss Jones disappeared. Mary, still under the strange sense that it was not she, but another, who did these things, moved back to the barn, calling softly to Hamlet. He followed her, sniffing a rat somewhere. Very quickly she pulled back the door ; he, still investigating his rat, followed into the dark excitements of the barn. With a quick movement she bent down, slipped off his collar, which she hid in her dress, then shut him in. She knew that for a moment or two he would still be pursuing his rat, and she saw, with guilty relief, Miss Jones come out to her just as she had finished her evil deed.

" Miss Andrews is out," said Miss Jones. " They are all away at Liskane Fair."

They left the farm and walked down the road. Hamlet had not begun his cry.

<h3 style="text-align:center">4</h3>

Miss Jones was pleased. " Such a nice servant," she said. " One of the old kind. She had been with the family fifty years, she told me, and had nursed Mr. Andrews on her knee. Fancy ! Such a large fat man as he is now. Too much beer, I suppose. I suppose they get so thirsty with all the straw and hay about. Yes, a really nice woman. She told me that there was no place in Glebeshire to touch them for cream. I dare say they're right. After all, you never can tell. I remember at home . . ."

She broke off then and cried : " Where's Hamlet ? "

Mary, wickeder than ever, stared through her spectacles down the road. " I don't know, Miss Jones," she said. They had left the wood and the farm, and there was nothing to be seen but the long white ribbon of road hemmed in by the high hedges.

" Perhaps he stayed behind at the farm," said Miss Jones.

Then Mary told her worst lie.

" Oh, no, Miss Jones. He ran past us just now. Didn't you see him ? "

" No, I didn't. He's gone on ahead, I suppose. He runs home sometimes. Naughty dog ! We shall catch him up."

But of course they did not. They passed through the gates of Cow Farm and still nothing of Hamlet was to be seen.

" Oh dear ! Oh dear ! " said Miss Jones. " I do hope that he's arrived. Whatever will Jeremy say if anything has gone wrong ? "

Mary was breathing hard now, as though she had been running a desperate race. She would at this moment have given all that she possessed, or all that she was ever likely to possess, to recall her deed. If she could have seen Hamlet rushing down the road towards her she would have cried with relief ; there seemed now to be suddenly removed from her that outside agency that had forced her to do this thing ; now, having compelled her, it had withdrawn and left her to carry the consequences. Strangely confused in her sentimental soul was her terror of Jeremy's wrath and her own picture of the wretched Hamlet barking his heart out, frightened, thirsty, and lonely. Her teeth began to chatter ; she clenched her hands together.

Miss Jones went across the courtyard, calling :

" Hamlet ! Hamlet ! " The family was collected,

having just sat down to tea, so that the announce-
ment received its full measure of excitement.

" Has Hamlet come back ?   We thought he was
ahead of us."

A chair had tumbled over.   Jeremy had run round
the table to Miss Jones.

" What's that ?   Hamlet ?   Where is he ? "

" We thought he must be ahead of us.   He ran
past us down the road, and we thought——"

They thought !   Silly women !   Jeremy, as though
he were a challenging god, stood up against Miss
Jones, hurling questions at her.   Where had they
been ?   What road had they taken ?   Had they gone
into the wood ?   Whereabouts had he run past them ?

" I don't know," said Miss Jones to this last.   " I
didn't see him, Mary did."

Jeremy turned upon Mary.   " Where was it you
saw him ? "

She couldn't speak.   Her tongue wouldn't move,
her lips wouldn't open ;   she could but waggle her
head like an idiot.   She saw nothing but his face.   It
was a desperate face.   She knew so much better
than all the others what the thought of losing Hamlet
was to him.   It was part of the harshness of her fate
that she should understand him so much better
than the others did.

But she herself had not realized how hardly he
would take it.

" I didn't——   I couldn't——"

" There's the dog-man," he stammered.   " He'll
have stolen him."   Then he was off out of the room
in an instant.

And that was more than Mary could bear.   She
realized, even as she followed him, that she was giving

her whole case away, that she was now, as always, weak when she should be strong, soft when she should be hard, good when she should be wicked, wicked when she should be good. She could not help herself. With trembling limbs and a heart that seemed to be hammering her body into pieces she followed him out. She found him in the hall, tugging at his coat.

" Where are you going ? " she said weakly.

" Going ? " he answered fiercely. " Where do you think ? " He glared at her. " Just like you." He broke off, suddenly appealing to her. " Mary, *can't* you remember ? It will be getting dark soon, and if we have to wait until to-morrow the dog-man will have got him. At any rate, he had his collar——"

Then Mary broke out. She burst into sobs, pushed her hand into her dress, and held out the collar to him.

" There it is ! There it is ! " she said hysterically.

" You've got it ? " He stared at her, suspicion slowly coming to him. " But how——? What have you done ? "

She looked up at him wild-eyed, the tears making dirty lines on her face, her hand out towards him.

" I took it off. I shut Hamlet into the barn at Mellot Farm. I wanted him to be lost. I didn't want you to have him. I hated him—always being with you, and me never."

Jeremy moved back, and at the sudden look in his eyes her sobbing ceased, she caught her breath and stared at him with a silly fixed stare as a rabbit quivers before a snake.

Jeremy said in his ordinary voice :

" You shut Hamlet up ? You didn't want him to be found ? "

She nodded her head several times as though now she must convince him quickly of this—

" Yes, yes, yes. I did. . . . I know I shouldn't, but I couldn't help it——"

He clutched her arm, and then shook her with a sudden wave of fierce physical anger that was utterly unlike him, and, therefore, the more terrifying.

" You wicked, wicked—— You beast, Mary ! "

She could only sob, her head hanging down. He let her go.

" What barn was it ? "

She described the place.

He gave her another look of contempt and then rushed off, running across the courtyard.

There was still no one in the hall ; she could go up to her room without the fear of being disturbed. She found the room, all white and black now with the gathering dusk. Beyond the window the evening breeze was rustling in the dark trees of the garden and the boom of the sea could be heard faintly. Mary sat, where she always sat when she was unhappy, inside the wardrobe with her head amongst the clothes. They in some way comforted her ; she was not so lonely with them, nor did she feel so strongly the empty distances of the long room, the white light of the window-frames, nor the mysterious secrecy of the high elms knocking their heads together in the garden.

She had a fit of hysterical crying, biting the hanging clothes between her teeth, feeling suddenly sick and tired and exhausted, with flaming eyes and a dry, parched throat. Why had she ever done such a thing, she loving Jeremy as she did ! Would he ever forgive her ? No, never ; she saw that in his face.

Perhaps he would—if he found Hamlet quickly and came back. Perhaps Hamlet never would be found. Then Jeremy's heart would be broken.

She slept from utter exhaustion, and was so found, when the room was quite dark and only shadows moved in it, by her mother.

" Why, Mary ! " said Mrs. Cole. " What are you doing here ? We couldn't think where you were. And where's Jeremy ? "

" Jeremy ! " She started up, remembering everything.

" Hasn't he come back ? Oh, he's lost and he'll be killed, and it will be all my fault ! " She burst into another fit of wild hysterical crying.

Her mother took her arm. " Mary, explain—what have you done ? "

Mary explained, her teeth chattering, her head aching so that she could not see.

" And you shut him up like that ? Whatever—— Oh, Mary, you wicked girl ! And Jeremy—— He's been away two hours now——"

She turned off, leaving Mary alone in the black room.

## 5

Mary was left to every terror that can beset a lonely, hysterical child—terror of Jeremy's fate, terror of Hamlet's loss, terror of her own crimes, above all, terror of the lonely room, the waving elms and the gathering dark. She could not move ; she could not even close the door of the wardrobe, into whose shelter she had again crept. She stared at the white sheet of the window, with its black bars like railings and its ghostly hinting of a moon that

would soon be up above the trees. Every noise
frightened her, the working of the " separator " in
a distant part of the farm, the whistling of some farm-
hand out in the yard, the voice of some boy, " coo-
ee "-ing faintly, the lingering echo of the vanished
day—all these seemed to accuse her, to point fingers
at her, to warn her of some awful impending punishment. " Ah! you're the little girl," they seemed
to say, " who lost Jeremy's dog and broke Jeremy's
heart." She was sure that someone was beneath
her bed. That old terror haunted her with an almost
humorous persistency every night before she went to
sleep, but to-night there was a ghastly certainty
and imminence about it that froze her blood. She
crouched up against the hanging skirts, gazing at
the black line between the floor and the white sheets,
expecting at every second to see a protruding black
mask, bloodshot eyes, a coarse hand. The memory
of the burglary that they had had in the spring
came upon her with redoubled force. Ah! surely,
surely someone was there! She heard a movement,
a scraping of a boot upon the floor, the thick hurried
breathing of some desperate villain. . . .

Then these fears gave way to something worse
than them all, the certainty that Jeremy was dead.
Ridiculous pictures passed before her, of Jeremy
hanging from a tree, Jeremy lying frozen in the wood,
the faithful Hamlet dead at his side, Jeremy stung by
an adder and succumbing to his horrible tortures,
Jeremy surrounded by violent men, who snatched
Hamlet from him, beat him on the head and left
him for dead on the ground.

She passed what seemed to her hours of torture
under these horrible imaginings, tired out, almost out

of her mind with the hysteria of her loneliness, her imagination and her conscience ; she passed into a kind of apathy of unhappiness, thinking now only of Jeremy, longing for him, beseeching him to come back, telling the empty moonlit room that she never meant it ; that she would do everything he wanted if only he came back to her ; that she was a wicked girl ; that she would never be wicked again. . . . And she took her punishment alone.

After endless ages of darkness and terror and misery she heard voices—then *his* voice ! She jumped out of the wardrobe and listened. Yes ; it *was* his voice. She pushed back the door, crept down the passage, and came suddenly upon a little group, with Jeremy in its midst, crowded together at the top of the stairs. Jeremy was wrapped up in his father's heavy coat, and looked very small and impish as he peered from out of it. He was greatly excited, his eyes shining, his mouth smiling, his cheeks flushed.

His audience consisted of Helen, Mrs. Cole, Miss Jones, and Aunt Amy. He described to them how he had run along the road " for miles and miles and miles," how at last he had found the farm, had rung the bell, and inquired, and discovered Hamlet licking up sugary tea in the farm kitchen ; there had then been a rapturous meeting, and he had boldly declared that he could find his way home again without aid. " They wanted me to be driven home in their trap, but I wasn't going to have that. They'd been at the fair all day, and didn't want to go out again. I could see that." So he and Hamlet started gaily on their walk home, and then, in some way or another, he took the wrong turn, and suddenly

they were in Mellot Wood. " It was dark as anything, you know, although there was going to be a
moon. We couldn't see a thing, and then I got
loster and loster. At last we just sat under a tree.
There was nothing more to do ! " Then, apparently,
Jeremy had slept, and had, finally, been found in
the proper romantic manner by Jim and his father.

" Well, all's well that ends well," said Aunt Amy
with a sniff. In spite of that momentary softness
over the defeat of the Dean's Ernest she liked her
young nephew no better than of old. She had
desired that he should be punished for this, but as
she looked at the melting eyes of Mrs. Cole and Miss
Jones she had very little hope.

Mary was forgotten ; no one noticed her.

" Bed," said Mrs. Cole.

" Really, what a terrible affair," said Miss Jones.
" And I can't help feeling that it was my fault."

" What Mary——" began Mrs. Cole. And then
she stopped. She had perhaps some sense that Mary
had already received sufficient punishment.

Mary waited, standing against the passage wall.
Jeremy, who had not seen her, vanished into his
room. She waited, then plucked up all her courage
with the desperate suffocating sense of a prisoner
laying himself beneath the guillotine, she knocked
timidly on his door.

He said : " Come in," and, entering, she saw
him, in his braces, standing on a chair trying to put
the picture entitled " Daddy's Christmas " straight
upon its nail. The sight of this familiar task—the
picture would never hang straight, although every
day Jeremy, who, strangely enough, had an eye to
such matters, tried to correct it—cheered her a little.

" Won't it go straight ? " she said feebly.

" No, it won't," he began, and then, suddenly realizing the whole position, stopped.

" I'm sorry, Jeremy," she muttered, hanging her head down.

" Oh, that's all right," he answered, turning away from her and pulling at the string. " It was a beastly thing to do all the same," he added.

" Will you forgive me ? " she asked.

" Oh, there isn't any forgiveness about it. Girls are queer, I suppose. I don't understand them myself. There, that's better. . . . I say, it was simply beastly under that tree——"

" Was it ? "

" Beastly ! There was something howling some-where—a cat or something."

" You do forgive me, don't you ? "

" Yes, yes. . . . I say, is that right now ? Oh, it won't *stay* there. It's the wall or something."

He came down from the chair yawning.

" Jim's nice," he confided to her. " He's going to take me ratting one day ! "

" I'm going," Mary said again, and waited.

Jeremy coloured, looked as though he would say something, then, in silence, presented a very grimy cheek. " Good night," he said, with an air of relief.

" Good night," she said, kissing him.

She closed the door behind her. She knew that the worst had happened. He had passed away, utterly beyond her company, her world, her interests. She crept along to her room, and there, with a determination and a strength rare in a child so young and so undisciplined, faced her loneliness.

# CHAPTER XI

I

THE holidays were over. The Coles were once more back in Polchester, and the most exciting period of Jeremy's life had begun. So at any rate he felt it. It might be that in later years there would be new exciting events, lion-hunting for instance, or a war, or the tracking of niggers in the heart of Africa—he would be ready for them when they came—but these last weeks before his first departure for school offered him the prospect of the first real independence of his life. There could never be anything quite like that again. Nevertheless, school seemed still a long way distant. It was only his manliness that he was realizing and a certain impatience and restlessness that underlay everything that he did.

September and October are often very lovely months in Polchester ; autumn seems to come there with greater warmth and richness than it does elsewhere. Along all the reaches of the Pol, right down to the sea, the leaves of the woods hung with a riotous magnificence that is glorious in its recklessness. The waters of that silent river are so still, so glassy, that the banks of gold and flaming red are reflected in all their richest colour down into the very heart of the

256

stream, and it is only when a fish jumps or a twig falls from the overhanging trees that the mirror is broken and the colours flash into ripples and shadows of white and grey. The utter silence of all this world makes the Cathedral town sleepy, sluggish, forgotten of all men. As the autumn comes it seems to drowse away into winter to the tune of its Cathedral bells, to the scent of its burning leaves and the soft steps of its Canons and clergy. There is every autumn here a clerical conference, and long before the appointed week begins, and long after it is lawfully concluded, clergymen, strange clergymen with soft black hats, take the town for their own, gaze into Martin the pastry-cook's, sit in the dusk of the Cathedral listening to the organ; walk, their heads in air, their arms folded behind their backs, straight up Orange Street as though they were scaling Heaven itself; stop little children, pat their heads, and give them pennies; stand outside Poole's bookshop and delve in the 2d. box of thumb-marked sermons; stand gazing in learned fashion at the great West Door, investigating the saints and apostles portrayed thereon; hurry in their best hats and coats along the Close to some ladies' tea-party, or pass with solemn and anxious mien into the palace of the Bishop himself.

All these things belong to autumn in Polchester, as Jeremy very well knew, but the event that marks the true beginning of the season, the only way by which you may surely know that summer is over and autumn is come is Pauper's Fair.

This famous fair has been, from time immemorial, a noted event in Glebeshire life. Even now, when fairs have yielded to cinematographs as attractions

were told that " they would be stolen by the gipsies
if they weren't careful," and, although some of them
in extreme moments of rebellion and depression
felt that the life of adventure thus offered to them
might, after all, be more agreeable than the dreary
realism of their natural days, the warning may be
said to have been effective.

No family in Polchester was guarded more carefully in this matter of the Pauper's Fair than the
Cole family. Mr. Cole had an absolute horror of
the fair. Sailors and gipsies were to him the sign
and seal of utter damnation, and although he tried,
as a Christian clergyman, to believe that they
deserved pity because of the disadvantages under
which they had from the first laboured, he confessed to his intimate friends that he saw very little
hope for them either in this world or the next.
Jeremy, Helen and Mary were, during Fair Week,
kept severely within doors ; their exercise had to
be taken in the Cole garden, and the farthest that
they poked their noses into the town was their
visit to St. John's on Sunday morning. Except
on one famous occasion. The Fair Week of Jeremy's
fifth year saw him writhing under a terrible attack
of toothache, which became, after two agonized
nights, such a torment and distress to the whole
household that he had to be conveyed to the house
of Mr. Pilter, who had his torture-chamber at
No. 3, Market Square. It is true that Jeremy
was conveyed thither in a cab, and that his pain
and his darkened windows prevented him from
seeing very much of the gay world ; nevertheless,
in spite of the Jampot, who guarded him like a
dragon, he caught a glimpse of flags, a gleaming

brass band and a Punch and Judy show, and he heard the trumpets and the drum, and the shouts of excited little boys, and the blowing of the Punch and Judy pipes, and he smelt roasting chestnuts, bad tobacco, and beer and gin. He returned, young as he was, and reduced to a corpse-like condition by the rough but kindly intentioned services of Mr. Pilter, with the picture of a hysterical, abandoned world clearly imprinted upon his brain.

" I want to go," he said to the Jampot.

" You can't," said she.

" I will when I'm six," said he.

" You won't," said she.

" I will when I'm seven," said he.

" You won't," said she.

" I will when I'm eight," he answered.

"Oh, give over, do, Master Jeremy," said she. And now he was eight, very nearly nine, and going to school in a fortnight. There seemed to be a touch of destiny about his prophecy.

2

He had no intention of disobedience. Had he been once definitely told by someone in authority that he was not to go to the fair he would not have dreamt of going. He had no intention of disobedience—but he had returned from the Cow Farm holiday in a strange condition of mind.

He had found there this summer more freedom than he had been ever allowed in his life before, and it had been freedom that had come, not so much from any change of rules, but rather from his own attitude to the family—simply he had wanted to

R

do certain things, and he had done them and the family had stood aside. He began to be aware that he had only to push and things gave way—a dangerous knowledge, and its coming marks a period in one's life.

He seemed, too, during this summer, to have left his sisters definitely behind him and to stand much more alone than he had done before. The only person in his world whom he felt that he would like to know better was Uncle Samuel, and that argued, on his part, a certain tendency towards rebellion and individuality. He was no longer rude to Aunt Amy, although he hated her just as he had always done. She did not seem any longer a question that mattered. His attitude to his whole family now was independent.

Indeed, he was, in reality, now beginning to live his independent life. He was perhaps very young to be sent off to school by himself, although in those days for a boy of eight to be plunged without any help but a friendly word of warning into the stormy seas of private school life was common enough— nevertheless, his father, conscious that the child's life had been hitherto spent almost entirely among women, sent him every morning during these last weeks at home down to the Curate of St. Martin's-in-the-Market to learn a few words of Latin, an easy sum or two, and the rudiments of spelling. This young curate, the Rev. Wilfred Somerset, recently of Emmanuel College, Cambridge, had but two ideas in his head—the noble game of cricket and the jolly qualities of Mr. Surtees's novels. He was stout and strong, red-faced, and thick in the leg, always smoking a large black-looking pipe, and wearing trousers very short and tight. He did not strike Jeremy with fear, but he was, nevertheless, an influence. Jeremy, apparently, amused him intensely. He would roar with laughter at nothing at all, smack his thigh and shout, " Good for you, young 'un," whatever that might mean, and Jeremy, gazing at him, at his pipe and his trousers, liking him rather, but not sufficiently in awe to be really impressed, would ask him questions that seemed to him perfectly simple and natural, but that, nevertheless, amused the Rev. Wilfred so fundamentally that he was unable to give them an intelligible answer.

Undoubtedly this encouraged Jeremy's independence. He walked to and from the curate's lodging by himself, and was able to observe many interesting things on the way. Sometimes, late in the afternoon, he would have some lesson that he must take to his master who, as he lodged at the bottom of Orange Street he was a safe and steady distance from the Coles.

Of course Aunt Amy objected :

" You allow Jeremy, all by himself, into the street at night, and he only eight. Really, you're too strange ! "

" Well, in the first place," said Mrs. Cole, mildly, " it isn't night—it's afternoon ; in the second place, it is only just down the street, and Jeremy's most obedient always, as you know, Amy."

" I'm sure that Mr. Somerset is wild," said Aunt Amy.

" My dear Amy, why ? "

" You've only got to look at his face. It's ' flashy.' That's what I call it."

" Oh, that isn't the sort of man who'll do Jeremy harm," said Mrs. Cole, with a mother's wisdom.

Certainly he did Jeremy no harm at all ; he taught him nothing, not even " mensa," and how to spell " receive " and " apple." The only thing he did was to encourage Jeremy's independence, and this was done, in the first place, by the walks to and fro.

He had only been going to Mr. Somerset's a day or two when the announcements of the Fair appeared on the walls of the town. He could not help but see them ; there was a large one on the boarding half-way down Orange Street, just opposite the Doctor's ; a poster with a coloured picture of " Wombwell's Circus," a fine affair, with spangled ladies jumping through hoops, elephants sitting on stools, tigers prowling, a clown cracking a whip, and, best of all, a gentleman, with an anxious face and a scanty but elegant costume, balanced above a gazing multitude on a tight-rope. There was also a bill of the Fair setting forth that there would be a " Cattle Market, Races, Roundabout, Swings, Wrestling, Boxing, Fat Women, Dwarfs, and the Two-Headed Giant from the Caucasus." During a whole week, once a day, Jeremy read this bill from the top to the bottom ; at the end of the week he could repeat it all by heart.

He asked Mr. Somerset whether he was going.

" Oh, I shall slip along one evening, I've no doubt," replied that gentleman. " But it's a bore —a whole week of it—upsets one's work."

" It needn't," said Jeremy, " if you stay indoors."

This amused Mr. Somerset immensely. He laughed a great deal.

" We always have to," said Jeremy, rather hurt.
" We're not allowed farther than the garden."

" Ah, but I'm older than you are," said Mr.
Somerset. " It was the same with me once."

" And what did you do ? Did you go all the
same ? "

" You bet, I did," said the red-faced hero, more
intent on his reminiscences than on the effect that
this might have on the morals of his pupil.

Jeremy waited then for the parental command
that was always issued. It was : " Now, children,
you must promise me never to go outside the house
this week unless you have asked permission first."
And then : " And on no account to speak to any
stranger about anything whatever." And then :
" Don't look out of the back windows, mind."
(From the extreme corners of the bedroom windows
you could see a patch of the meadow whereon the
gipsy-vans settled.) These commands had been
as regular as the Fair, and always, of course, the
children had promised obedience. Jeremy told
his conscience that if, this year, he gave his promise
he would certainly keep it. He wondered, at the
same time, whether he might not possibly manage
to be out of the house when the commands were
issued. He formed a habit of suddenly slipping
out of the room when he saw his father's mouth
assuming the shape of a " command." He took
the utmost care not to be alone with his father.

But he need not have been alarmed. This year
no command appeared. Perhaps Mr. Cole thought
that it was no longer necessary ; it was obvious
that the children were not to go, and they were,
after all, old enough now to think for themselves  Or,

perhaps, it was that Mr. Cole had other things on his mind ; he was changing curates just then ; and a succession of white-faced, soft-voiced, and loud-booted young men were appearing at the Coles' hospitable table.

" Here's this tiresome Fair come round again," said Mrs. Cole.

" Wicked ! " said Aunt Amy, with an envious shudder. " Satan finds work, indeed, in this town."

" I don't suppose it's worse than anywhere else," said Mrs. Cole.

On the late afternoon of the day before the open-ing, Jeremy, on his way to Mr. Somerset's, caught the tail-end of Wombwell's Circus Procession moving, in misty splendour, across the market.

He could see but little, although he stood on the pedestal of a lamp-post ; but Britannia, rocking high in the air, flashing her silver sceptre in the evening air, and followed by two enormous and melancholy elephants, caught his gaze. Strains of a band lingered about him. He entered Mr. Somerset's in a frenzy of excitement, but he said nothing. He felt that Mr. Somerset would laugh at him.

He returned to his home that night haunted by Britannia. He ate Britannia for his supper ; he had Britannia for his dreams ; and he greeted Rose as Britannia the next morning when she called him. Early upon that day there were borne into the heart of the house strains of the Fair. It was no use whatever to close the windows, lock the doors, and read Divinity. The strains persisted, a heavenly murmur rising at moments into a muffled shriek or a jumbling shout, hanging about the walls as a

romantic echo, dying upon the air a chastened wail.
No use for Mr. Cole to say :

" We must behave as though the Fair was
not."

For a whole week it would be there, and everyone knew it.

Jeremy did not mean to be disobedient, but after
that glimpse of Britannia he knew that he would go.


### 3

It had, at first, been thought advisable that
Jeremy should not go to Mr. Somerset's during
Fair Week. Perhaps Mr. Somerset could come to
the Coles' ? No, he was very sorry. He must be
in his rooms at that particular hour in case parishioners should need his advice or assistance.

" Pity for him to miss all this week, especially as
there will be only four days left after that. I am
really anxious for him to have a little grounding in
Latin."

Mrs. Cole smiled confidently. " I think Jeremy
is to be trusted. He would never do anything that
you wouldn't like."

Mr. Cole was not so sure. " He's not quite so
obedient as I should wish. He shows an independence——"

However, after some hesitation it was decided
that Jeremy might be trusted.

But even after that he was never put upon his
honour. " If I don't promise, I needn't mind,"
he said to himself, and waited breathlessly ; but
nothing came. Only Aunt Amy said :

" I hope you won't speak to little boys in the

street, Jeremy." To which he replied scornfully :
" Of course not."

He investigated his money-box, removing the top
with a tin-opener. He found that he had there
3s. 3½d. ; a large sum, and enough to give him a
royal time.

Mary caught him.

" Oh, Jeremy, what are you doing ? "

" Just counting my money," he said, with would-
be carelessness.

" You're going to the Fair ? " she whispered
breathlessly.

He frowned. How could she know ? She always
knew everything.

" Perhaps," he whispered back ; " but if you tell
anyone I'll——"

" Oh course I wouldn't tell," she replied, deeply
offended.

This little conversation strengthened his purpose.
He had not admitted to himself that he was really
going. Now he knew.

Wednesday would be the night. On Wednesday
evenings his father had a service which prevented
him from returning home until half-past eight. He
would go to Somerset's at half-past four, and would
be expected home at half-past six ; there would be
no real alarm about him until his father's return from
church, and he could, therefore, be sure of two hours'
bliss. For the consequences he did not care at all.
He was going to do no harm to anyone or anything.
They would be angry, perhaps, but that would not
hurt him, and, in any case, he was going to school
next week. No one at school would mind whether
he had been to the Fair or no.

He felt aloof and apart, as though no one could touch him. He would not have minded simply going in to them all and saying : " I'm off to the Fair." The obvious drawback to that would have been that he would have been shut up in his room, and then they might make him give his word. . . . He would not break any promises.

When Wednesday came it was a lovely day. Out in the field just behind the Coles' house, they were burning a huge bonfire of dead leaves. At first only a heavy column of grey smoke rose, then flames broke through ; little, thin golden flames like paper ; then a sudden fierce red tongue shot out and went licking up into the air until it faded like tumbling water against the sunlight. On the outer edge of the bonfire there was thin grey smoke through which you could see as through glass. The smell was heavenly, and even through closed windows the crackling of the burnt leaves could be heard. The sight of the bonfire excited Jeremy. It seemed to him a signal of encouragement, a spur to perseverance. All the morning the flames crackled, and men came with wheelbarrows full of leaves and emptied them in thick heaps upon the fire. At each emptying the fire would be for a moment beaten, and only the white, thick, malicious smoke would come through ; then a little spit of flame, another, another ; then a thrust like a golden hand stretching out ; then a fine, towering, quivering splendour.

Under the full noon-day sun the fire was pale and so unreal, weak, and sickly, that one was almost ashamed to look at it. But as the afternoon passed it again gathered strength, and with the faint, dusky evening it was a giant once more.

" You come along," it said to Jeremy. " Come
along !   Come along ! "

" I'm going to Mr. Somerset's, Mother," he said,
putting two exercise books and a very new and shining blue Latin book together.

" Are you, dear ?   I suppose you're  safe ? "
Mrs. Cole asked, looking through the drawing-room
window.

" Oh, it's all right," said Jeremy.

" Well, I think it is," said Mrs. Cole. " The
street seems quite empty.   Don't speak to any odd-
looking men, will you ? "

" Oh, that's all right," he said again.

He walked down Orange Street, his books under
his arm, the 3s. 3½d. in his pocket.  The street was
quite deserted, swimming in a cold, pale light ;  the
trees, the houses, the church, the garden-walls, sharp
and black ; the street, dim and precipitous, tumbling
forward into the blue, when lights, one, two,
three, now a little bunch together, came pricking
out.

The old woman opened the door when he  rang
Mr. Somerset's bell.

" Master's been called away," she said in her
croaking voice.  " A burial.  'E 'adn't time to let
you know.  ' Tell the little gen'l'man,' 'e said, ' I'm
sorry.' "

" All right," said Jeremy ;  " thank you."

He descended the steps, then stood where he was,
in the street, looking up and down.  Who could
deny that it was all being arranged for him ?  He
felt more than ever like God as he looked proudly
about him.  Everything served his purpose.

The jingling of the money in his pocket reminded

him that he must waste no more time.   He started
off.

Even his progress through the town seemed
wonderful, quite unattended at last, as he had
always all his life longed to be.   So soon as he left
Orange Street and entered the market he was caught
into a great crowd.   It was all stirring and humming
with a noise such as the bonfire had all day been
making.   It was his first introduction to the world—
he had never been in a large crowd before—and it
is not to be denied but that his heart beat thick and
his knees trembled a little.   But he pulled himself
together.   Who was he to be afraid of ?   But the
books under his arm were a nuisance.   He suddenly
dropped them in amongst the legs and boots of the
people.

There were many interesting sights to be seen in
the Market Place, but he could not stay, and he
found himself soon, to his own surprise, slipping
through the people as quietly and easily as though
he had done it all his days, only always he kept his
hand on his money lest that should be stolen and his
adventure suddenly come to nothing.

He knew his way very well, and soon he was at
the end of Finch Street which, in those days, opened
straight into fields and hedges.

Even now, so little has Polchester grown in thirty
years, the fields and hedges are not very far away.
Here there was a stile, with a large wooden fence on
either side of it, and a red-faced man saying :
" Pay your sixpences now !   Come along . . . pay
your sixpences now."   Crowds of people were
passing through the stile, jostling one another,
pressing and pushing, but all apparently in good

temper, for there was a great deal of laughter and
merriment.   From the other side of the fence came
a torrent of sound, so discordant and so tumultuous
that it was impossible to separate the elements of it
one from another—screams, shrieks, the bellowing
of animals, and the monotonous rise and fall of
scraps of tune, several bars of one and then bars of
another, and then everything lost together in the
general babel ; and to the right of him Jeremy
could see not very far away quiet fields with cows
grazing, and the dark grave wood on the horizon.

Would he venture ?   For a moment his heart
failed him—a wave of something threatening and
terribly powerful seemed to come to him through the
stile, and the people who were passing in looked
large and fierce.   Then he saw two small boys,
their whole bearing one of audacious boldness, push
through.   He was not going to be beaten.   He
followed a man with a back like a wall.   " One,
please," he said.

" Come along, now . . . pay your sixpences . . .
pay your sixpences," cried the man.   He was
through.   He stepped at once into something that
had for him all the elements of the most terrifying
and enchanting of fairy tales.   He was planted, it
seemed, in a giant world.   At first he could see
nothing but the high and thick bodies of the people
who moved on every side of him ; he peered under
shoulders, he was lost amongst legs and arms, he
walked suddenly into waistcoat buttons and was
flung thence on to walking-sticks.

But it was, if he had known it, the most magical
hour of all for him to have chosen.   It was the
moment when the sun, sinking behind the woods

and hills, leaves a faint white crystal sky and a world transformed in an instant from sharp outlines and material form into coloured mist and rising vapour. The Fair also was transformed, putting forward all its lights and becoming, after the glaring tawdriness of the day, a place of shadow and sudden circles of flame and dim obscurity.

Lights, even as Jeremy watched, sprang into the air, wavered, faltered, hesitated, then rocked into a steady glow, only shifting a little with the haze. On either side of him were rough, wooden stalls, and these were illuminated with gas, which sizzled and hissed like angry snakes. The stalls were covered with everything invented by man ; here a sweet stall, with thick, sticky lumps of white and green and red, glass bottles of bulls' eyes and peppermints, thick slabs of almond toffee and pink coconut icing, boxes of round chocolate creams and sticks of liquorice, lumps of gingerbread, with coloured pictures stuck upon them, saffron buns, plum cakes in glass jars, and chains of little sugary biscuits, hanging on long red strings. There was the old-clothes stall with trousers and coats and waistcoats, all shabby and lanky, swinging beneath the gas, and piles of clothes on the boards, all nondescript and unhappy and faded ; there was the stall with the farm implements, and the medicine stall, and the flower stall, and the vegetable stall, and many, many another. Each place had his or her guardian, vociferous, red-faced, screaming out the wares, lowering the voice to cajole, raising it again to draw back a retreating customer, carrying on suddenly an intimate conversation with the next-door shop-keeper, laughing, quarrelling, arguing.

falling again with an implication of restrained force
as though he would say : " I have only to let myself
go and there, my word, you *would* see where I'd get
to." His bold black eyes turned beseechingly to
Jeremy—surely it was not only a trick of the waving
gas ; the boy drew closer and closer, never moving
his gaze from the horses who had hitherto been
whirling at a bacchanalian pace, but now, as at
some sudden secret command, suddenly slackened,
hesitated, fell into a gentle jog-trot, then scarcely
rose, scarcely fell, were suddenly still. Jeremy saw
what it was that you did if you wanted to ride. A
stout dirty man came out amongst the horses and,
resting his hands on their backs as though they were
less than nothing to him, shouted : " Now's your
chance, lidies and gents ! Now, lidies and gents !
Come along hup ! Come along hup ! The ride of
your life now ! A 'alfpenny a time ! A 'alfpenny
a time, and the finest ride of your life ! "

People began to mount the steps that led on to
the platform where the horses stood. A woman,
then a man and a boy, then two men, then two
girls giggling together, then a man and a girl.

And the stout fellow shouted : " Come along
hup ! Come along hup ! Now, lidies and gents !
A 'alf-penny a ride ! Come along hup ! "

Jeremy noticed then that the fine horse with the
black mane had stopped close beside him. Impossible to say whether the horse had intended it or no.
He was staring now in front of him with the innocent
stupid gaze that animals can assume when they do
not wish to give themselves away. But Jeremy
could see that he was taking it for granted that
Jeremy understood the affair. " If you're such a

fool as not to understand," he seemed to say, " well
then, I don't want you." Jeremy gazed, and the
reproach in those eyes was more than he could
endure. And at any moment someone else might
settle himself on that beautiful back ! There, that
stupid fat giggling girl ! No—she had moved elsewhere. . . . He could endure it no longer and, with
a thumping heart, clutching a scalding penny in a
red-hot hand, he mounted the steps. " One ride—
little gen'elman. 'Ere you are ! 'Old on now !
Oh, you wants that one, do yer ? Right yer are
—yer pays yer money and yer takes yer choice."
He lifted Jeremy up. " Put yer arms round 'is
neck now—'e won't bite yer ! "

Bite him indeed ! Jeremy felt, as he clutched the
cool head and let his hand slide over the stiff black
mane, that he knew more about that horse than his
owner did. He seemed to feel beneath him the
horse's response to his clutching knees, the head
seemed to rise for a moment and nod to him
and the eyes to say : " It's all right. I'll look
after you. I'll give you the best ride of your
life ! "

He felt, indeed, that the gaze of the whole world
was upon him, but he responded to it proudly,
staring boldly around him as though he had been
seated on merry-go-rounds all his days. Perhaps
some in the gaping crowd knew him and were saying
" Why, there's the Rev. Cole's kid——" never
mind ; he was above scandal. From where he was
he could see the Fair lighted up and translated into
a fantastic splendour. Nothing was certain,
nothing defined—above him a canopy of evening
sky, with circles and chains of stars mixed with the

s

rosy haze of the flame of the Fair ; opposite him
was the Palace of " The Two-Headed Giant from
the Caucasus," a huge man as portrayed in the
picture hanging on his outer walls, a giant naked,
save for a bearskin, with one black head and one
yellow, and white protruding teeth in both mouths.
Next to him was the Fortune Teller's, and outside
this a little man with a hump beat a drum. Then
there was " The Theatre of Tragedy and Mirth,"
with a poster on one side of the door portraying a
lady drowning in the swiftest of rivers, but with
the prospect of being saved by a stout gentleman
who leaned over from the bank and grasped her
hair. Then there was the " Chamber of the Fat
Lady and the Six Little Dwarfs," and the entry
to this was guarded by a dirty sour-looking female
who gnashed her teeth at a hesitating public, before
whom, with a splendid indifference to appearance,
she consumed, out of a piece of newspaper, her
evening meal.

All these things were in Jeremy's immediate
vision, and beyond them was a haze that his eyes
could not penetrate. It held, he knew, wild beasts,
because he could hear quite clearly from time to
time the lion and the elephant and the tiger ; it
held music, because from somewhere through all the
noise and confusion the tune of a band penetrated ;
it held buyers and sellers and treasures and riches,
and all the inhabitants of the world—surely all the
world *must* be here to-night. And then, beyond
the haze, there were the silent and mysterious gipsy
caravans. Dark with their little square windows,
and their coloured walls, and their round wheels,
and the smell of wood fires, and the noise of hissing

kettles and horses cropping the grass, and around them the still night world with the thick woods and the dark river.

He did not see it all as he sat on his horse—he was, as yet, too young ; but he did feel the contrast between the din and glare around him and the silence and dark beyond, and, afterwards, looking back, he knew that he had found in that same contrast the very heart of romance. As it was, he simply clutched his horse's beautiful head and waited for the ride to begin. . . .

They were off ! He felt his horse quiver under him, he saw the Mansions of the Two-Headed Giant and the Fat Lady slip to the right, the light seemed to swing like the skirt of someone's dress, upwards across the floor, and from the heart of the golden woman and the king and the minstrel a scream burst forth as though they were announcing the end of the world. After that he had no clear idea as to what occurred. He was swung into space, and all the life that had been so stationary, the booths, the lights, the men and women, the very stars went swinging with him as though to cheer him on ; the horse under him galloped before, and the faster he galloped the wilder was the music and the dizzier the world. He was exultant, omnipotent, supreme. He had long known that this glory was somewhere if it could only be found, all his days he seemed to have been searching for it ; he beat his horse's neck, he drove his legs against his sides. " Go on ! Go on ! Go on ! " he cried. " Faster ! Faster ! Faster ! "

The strangest things seemed to rise to his notice and then fall again—a peaked policeman's hat,

flowers, a sudden flame of gas, the staring eyes and
dead white arms of the golden woman, the flying
forms of the horses in front of him. All the world
was on horseback, all the world was racing higher
and higher, faster and faster. He saw someone
near him rise on to his horse's back and stand on
it, waving his arms. He would like to have done
that, but he found that he was part of the horse,
as though he had been glued to it. He shouted, he
cried aloud, he was so happy that he thought of
no one and nothing. . . . The flame danced about
him in a circle, he seemed to rise so high that there
was a sudden stillness, he was in the very heart
of the stars ; then came the supreme moment when,
as he had always known, that one day he would be,
he was master of the world. . . . Then, like Lucifer,
he fell. Slowly the stars receded, the music
slackened, people rocked on to their feet again. . . .
The Two-Headed Giant slipped back once more
into his place, he saw the sinister lady still devour-
ing her supper, women looking up at him gaped,
his horse gave a last little leap and died.

This marvellous experience he repeated four times,
and every time with an ecstasy more complete than
the last.

He rushed to a height, he fell, he rushed again, he
fell, and at every return to a sober life his one
intention was instantly to be off on his steed once
more. He was about to start on his fifth journey,
he had paid his half-penny, he was sitting forward
with his hands on the black mane, his eyes, staring,
were filled already with the glory that he knew was
coming to him, his cheeks were crimson, his hat on
the back of his head, his hair flying. He heard a

voice, quiet and cool, a little below him, but very near :

" Jeremy. . . . Jeremy.   Come off that.   You've got to go home."

He looked down and saw his Uncle Samuel.


4

It was all over ; he knew at once that it was all over.   As he slipped down from his dear horse he gave the glossy dark mane one last pat ; then, with a little sigh, he found his feet, stumbled over the wooden steps and was at his uncle's side.

Uncle Samuel looked queer enough with a squashy black hat, a black cloak flung over his shoulders, and a large cherry-wood pipe in his mouth.   Jeremy looked up at him defiantly.

" Well," said Uncle Samuel sarcastically.   " It's nothing to you, I suppose, that the town-crier is at this moment ringing his bell for you up and down the Market Place ? "

" Does Father know ? " Jeremy asked quickly.

" He does," answered Uncle Samuel.

Jeremy cast one last look around the place ; the merry-go-round was engaged once more upon its wild course, the horses rising and falling, the golden woman clashing the cymbals, the minstrel striking, with his dead eyes fixed upon space, his harp.   All about men were shouting ; the noise of the coconut stores, of the circus, of the band, of the hucksters and the charlatans, the crying of children, the laughter of women—all the noise of the Fair bathed Jeremy up to his forehead.

He swam in it for the last time.   He tried to catch

one last glimpse of his coal-black charger, then, with a sigh, he said, turning to his uncle : " I suppose we'd better be going."

" Yes, I suppose we had," said Uncle Samuel.

They threaded their way through the Fair, passed the wooden stile, and were once again in the streets, dark and ancient under the moon, with all the noise and glare behind them. Jeremy was thinking to himself : " It doesn't matter what Father does, or how angry he is, *that* was worth it." It was strange how little afraid he was. Only a year ago to be punished by his father had been a terrible thing. Now, since his mother's illness in the summer, his father had seemed to have no influence over him.

" Did they send you, or did you just come your-self, Uncle ? " asked Jeremy.

" I happened to be taking the air in that direction," said Uncle Samuel.

" I hope you didn't come away before you wanted to," said Jeremy politely.

" I did not," said his uncle.

" Is Father very angry ? " asked Jeremy.

" It's more than likely he may be. The Town Crier's expensive."

" I didn't think they'd know," explained Jeremy. " I meant to get back in time."

" Your father didn't go to church," said Uncle Samuel. " So your sins were quickly discovered."

Jeremy said nothing.

Just as they were climbing Orange Street he said :

" Uncle Samuel, I think I'll be a horse-trainer."

" Oh, will you. Well, before you train horses you've got to train yourself. Think of others beside yourself. A fine state you've put your mother into to-night."

Jeremy looked distressed. " She'd know if I was dead, someone would come and tell her," he said. " But I'll tell Mother I'm sorry. . . . But I won't tell Father," he added.

" Why not ? " asked Uncle Samuel.

" Because he'll make such a fuss. And I'm not sorry. He never told me not to."

" No, but you knew you hadn't to."

" I'm very good at obeying," explained Jeremy, " if someone says something ; but if someone doesn't, there isn't anyone to obey."

Uncle Sam shook his head. " You'll be a bit of a prig, my son, if you aren't careful," he said.

" I think it will be splendid to be a horse-trainer," said Jeremy. " It was a lovely horse to-night. . . . And I only spent a shilling. I had three and three-pence halfpenny."

At the door of their house Uncle Samuel stopped and said :

" Look here, young man, they say it's time you went to school, and I don't think they're far wrong. There are things wiser heads than yours can understand, and you'd better take their word for it. In the future, if you want to go running off somewhere, you'd better content yourself with my studio and make a mess there."

" Oh, may I ? " said Jeremy delighted.

That studio had been always a forbidden place to them, and had, therefore, its air of enchanting mystery.

" Won't you really mind my coming ? " he asked.

" I shall probably hate it," answered his uncle;
" but there's nothing I wouldn't do for the family."

The boy walked to his father's study and knocked
on the door. He did have then, at the sound of that
knock, a moment of panic. The house was so silent,
and he knew so well what would follow the opening
of the door. And the worst of it was that he was
not sorry in the least. He seemed to be indifferent
and superior, as though no punishment could touch
him.

" Come in ! " said his father.

He pushed open the door and entered. The scene
that followed was grave and sad, and yet, in the end,
strangely unimpressive. His father talked too
much. As he talked Jeremy's thoughts would fly
back to the coal-black horse, and to that moment
when he had seemed to fly into the very heart of
the stars.

" Ah, Jeremy, how could you ? " said his father.
" Is obedience nothing to you ? Do you know how
God punishes disobedience ? Think what a terrible
thing is a disobedient man ! " Then on a lower
scale : " I really don't know what to do with you.
You knew that you were not to go near that wicked
place."

" You never said——" interrupted Jeremy.

" Nonsense ! You knew well enough. You will
break your mother's heart."

" I'll tell her I'm sorry," he interrupted quickly.

" If you *are* really sorry——" said his father.

" I'm not sorry I went," said Jeremy, " but I'm
sorry I hurt Mother."

The end of it was that Jeremy received six strokes
on the hand with a ruler. Mr. Cole was not good at

this kind of thing, and twice he missed Jeremy's hand altogether, and looked very foolish. It was not an edifying scene. Jeremy left the room, his head high, his spirit obstinate; and his father remained, puzzled, distressed, at a loss, anxious to do what was right, but unable to touch his son at all.

Jeremy went up to his room. He opened his window and looked out. He could smell the burnt leaves of the bonfire. There was no flame now, but he fancied that he could see a white shadow where it had been. Then, on the wind, came the music of the Fair.

" Tum—te—Tum . . . Tum—te—Tum . . . Whirr —Whirr—Whirr—Bang—Bang."

Somewhere an owl cried, and then another owl answered.

He rubbed his sore hand against his trousers; then, thinking of his black horse, he smiled.

He was a free man. In a week he would go to school; then he would go to college; then he would be a horse-trainer.

He was in bed; faintly into the dark room stole the scent of the bonfire and the noise of the Fair.

" Tum—te—Tum . . . Tum—te—Tum. . . ."

He was asleep, riding on a giant charger across boundless plains.

# CHAPTER XII

## HAMLET WAITS

### I

THE last day! Jeremy, suddenly waking, realized this with a confusion of feeling as though he were sentenced to the dentist's, but oddly enough, looked forward to his visit. Going to school, one had, of course, long ago perceived, was a mixed business; but the balance was now greatly to the good. It was a step in the right direction towards liberty and freedom. Thank Heaven! No one in the family was likely to make a fuss about his departure, unless it were possibly Mary, and she had, of late, kept very much to herself and worried him scarcely at all. Indeed, he felt guilty about Mary. He was fond of her, really. . . . Funny kid. . . . If only she didn't make fusses!

Yes, it was unlike his family to make fusses. He realized that very plainly to-day. Everyone went about his or her daily business with no implication whatever that something extraordinary was going to happen to-morrow. Perhaps they were all secretly relieved that he was off. He had been, he knew, something of a failure during these last months; one trouble after another; the scandal of his visit to the Fair as the grand finale. He felt that there was, in some way, some injustice in all this. He had no desire to be bad or rebellious—on the contrary he wished to do all that his elders ordered him—but he could not prevent the rising of his own individuality, which showed him quite clearly whether he should do a thing or no. It was as though something inside him *pushed* him . . . whereas they, all of them, only checked him.

He loved his mother best, and he was secretly disappointed to find how ordinary an affair his departure was to her. He realized, with a perception that was beyond his years, that the infant Barbara was now rapidly occupying the position, as centre of the family, that he had held. Barbara, everyone declared, was a charming baby—the house revolved, to some extent, round Barbara. But, then again, this isolation was his own fault. During the summer holidays he had gone his own way, and had wanted no one but Hamlet as his companion. He had no right to complain.

After breakfast he did not know quite what to do, and it was obvious, also, that no one knew quite what to do with him.

Mrs. Cole said : " Jeremy, dear, Ponting hasnever sent that paper and envelopes that he promised, and Father must have them to-day. Would you go down and bring them back ? Father will write a note."

No one seemed to realize what an abysmal change from earlier conditions this casual sentence marked. That he should go to Ponting's, which was on the farther side of the town, alone and unattended, seemed to no one peculiar ; and yet, only six months ago, a walk without Miss Jones was undreamt of ; and, before her, no more than nine months back, there was the Jampot ! He was delighted to go ; but, of course, he did not show his delight.

All he said was : " Yes, Mother."

He was in his new clothes : stiff black jacket, black knickerbockers, black stockings, black boots. No more navy suits with white braid and whistles ! Perhaps he would see the Dean's Ernest. It was his most urgent desire !

He started off, accompanied by a barking, bounding Hamlet, who showed no perception of the calamity that threatened to tumble upon him. For Jeremy, leaving Hamlet was a dreadful affair. In three months a dog can change more swiftly than a human being, and Hamlet, although not a supremely greedy dog, had shown of late increasing signs of a love of good food, and a regrettable tendency to fawn upon the giver of the same, even when it was Aunt Amy. Jeremy had checked this tendency, and had issued punishments when necessary, and Hamlet had accepted the same without a murmur. So long as Jeremy was there Hamlet's character was secure ; but now, during this long absence, anything might happen. There was no one to whom Jeremy might leave him ; no one who had the slightest idea what a dog should do and what he should not.

These melancholy thoughts filled Jeremy's mind when he started upon his walk, but soon he was absorbed by his surroundings. He realized even more drastically than the facts warranted that he was making his farewell to the town.

He was not making his final farewell ; he would not make that until his death and, perhaps, not then ; but he was making farewell to some of his sense of his wonder in it, only not, thank God, to the sense of wonder itself !

As he went he met the daily figures of all his walks, and he could not help but speculate on their realization of the great change that was coming to him. It was absurd to suppose that they were saying to themselves : " Ah, there's young Jeremy Cole ! He's off to school to-morrow. I wonder what he feels about it ! . . ." No, that was incredible, and yet they must realize something of the adventure.

He, on his part, stared at them with a new interest. They had before shared in the inevitable background without individuality. But now that he was leaving them, and they would grow, as it were, without his permission, he was forced to grant them independence. At the bottom of Orange Street he met Mr. Dawson, the Cathedral Organist ; he was a little, plump man, in a very neat grey suit, a shiny top hat, and very small spats. He was always dressed in the same fashion, and carried a black music-case under his arm. He had an eternal interest for Jeremy, because, whenever he was mentioned, the phrase was : " Poor little Mr. Dawson ! " Why he was to be pitied Jeremy did not know. He looked spruce and bright enough, and generally whistled to himself as he walked, but " poor " was an exciting adjective, and Jeremy, when he passed him, felt a little shudder of drama run down his spine.

Outside Poole's bookshop there was, of course, Mr. Mockridge. Mr. Mockridge was the poorest of the Canons ; so poor, that it had become a proverb in the place : " As poor as Mr. Mockridge " ; and also another proverb, I am afraid, from the same source : " As dirty as Mr.

Mockridge." He was a very long, thin man, with a big, pointing nose, coloured red, not from indigestion, and most certainly not from drink, but simply, I think, because the wind caught it. His passion was for books, and he might be seen every afternoon, between three and four o'clock, bending over Poole's 2d. box, a dirty handkerchief flying out of the tail of his long, black coat, and a green, bulging umbrella, pointing outwards, under his arm, to the infinite danger of all the passers-by. He was so commonplace a figure to Jeremy that, on ordinary days, he was shrouded by an invisibility of tradition. But, to-day, he was fresh and strange. "He'll be here to-morrow poking his nose into that box just the same, and I shall be——"

Then, on the outskirts of the Market Place, Jeremy paused and looked about him. There was all the usual business of the place—the wooden trestles with the flower-pots, the apple-woman under her umbrella, the empty cattle-pens, where the cows and sheep stood on market days, and behind them the dark, vaulted arches of the actual market, now empty and deserted. Bathed in sunlight it lay very quiet and still ; some pigeons pecking at grain, a dog or two, and children playing round the empty cattle-stalls. From the hill above the square the Cathedral boomed the hour, and all the pigeons rose in a flight, hovered, then slowly settled again.

Jeremy sighed, and, with a strange pain at his heart that he could not analyse, moved up the hill. The High Street is, of course, the West End of Polchester, and in the morning, between ten and one, every lady in the town may be seen at her shopping. It had always been the ambition of the Cole children to be taken for their walk up High Street in the morning ; but it was an ambition very rarely gratified, because they stopped so often and were always in everyone's way. And here was Jeremy, at this gay hour, strolling up the High Street all by himself. He lifted his head, pushed out his chest, and looked the world in the face. He might meet the Dean's Ernest at any moment. The first people whom he saw were the Misses Cragg—always known, of course, as " The Cragg girls." They were, perhaps, Polchester's most constant and obvious feature. There were four of them, all as yet unmarried, all with brown-red faces and hard straw hats, short skirts, and tremendous voices ; forerunners, in fact, of a type now almost universal. They played croquet and lawn-tennis, were prominent members of the Archery Club, and hunted when their father would let them. They were terrible Dianas to Jeremy. He had met one of them once at a Children's Dance, and she had whirled him around until, with a terrified scream, he broke, howling, from her arms, and hid himself in the large bosom of the Jampot. He was always ashamed of this memory, and he could never see them without blushing ; but, to-day, he seemed less afraid of them, and actually, when he passed them, touched his hat and looked them in the face. They all smiled and nodded to him, and when they had gone he was so deeply astonished at this adventure that he had to stop and consider himself. If the Craggs were nothing to him, what might he not face ?

" Come here, Hamlet. How dare you ? " he

ordered in so sharp and military a voice that Hamlet, who had merely cast a most innocent glance at a disdainful and conceited white poodle, looked up at his master with surprise.

Nevertheless, his new-found hardihood received, in the very midst of his self-congratulation, its severest test. He stumbled into the very path of the Dean's wife.

Mrs. Dean could never have seemed to anyone a large woman, but to Jeremy she had always been a terror. She was thick and hard, like a wall, and wore the kind of silken clothes that rustled—like the whispering of a whole meeting of frightened clergy-men's wives—as she moved. She had a hard, con-demnatory voice, and she spoke as though she were addressing an assembly ; but, worst of all, she had black, beetling eyebrows, and these frightened Jeremy into fits. He did not, of course, know that the poor old lady suffered continually from nervous headaches.

He suddenly heard that voice in his ear : " Good morning, Jeremy, and where are you off to so early ? " Mrs. Dean was never so awful as when she was jolly, and Jeremy, caught up by the eye-brows as though they had been hooks and hung thus in mid-air for all the street to laugh at, nearly lost his command of his natural tongue. He found his voice just in time :

" To Ponting's," he said.

" All alone ? Ah, no, I see you have your little dog. Nice little dog. And how's your mother ? "

" She's quite well, thank you."

" That's right—that's right. We haven't seen you lately. You must come up to tea with your sisters. I'm afraid you won't find Ernest, he's gone back to school—but I dare say you're not too big to play with little girls."

Jeremy felt some triumph at his heart.

" I'm going to school to-morrow," he said. But if he expected Mrs. Dean to be pitiful at this statement he was greatly mistaken.

" Are you, indeed ? Such a pity you couldn't have gone with Ernest—but he'd be senior to you, of course. . . . Good-bye. Good-bye. Give my love to your mother," and she pounded her way along.

" She's a beastly woman anyway," thought Jeremy. " I wish I'd found something to say to her. I wonder whether she knows I knocked Ernest down in the summer and trod on him ? "

But the sight of the High Street soon restored his equanimity. On other occasions he had been pushed through it, either by the Jampot or Miss Jones, so rapidly that he could gather only the most fleeting impressions. To-day he could linger and linger ; he did. The two nicest shops were Mannings' the hairdressers and Ponting's the book-shop, but Rose the grocer's, and Coulter's the confectioner's were very good. Mr. Manning was an artist. He did not simply put a simpering bust with an elaborate head of hair in his window and leave it at that— he did, indeed, place there a smiling lady with a wonderful jewelled comb and a radiant row of teeth, but around this he built up a magnificent world of silver brushes, tortoise-shell combs, essences and perfumes and powders, jars and bottles and boxes. Manning was the finest artist in the town. Ponting, at the top of the street just at the corner of the Close,

T

was an artist too, but in quite another fashion. Ponting was the best established, most sacred and serious bookseller in the country. In the days when the new " Waverley " was the sensation of the moment Mr. Ponting, grandfather of the present Mr. Ponting, had been in quite constant correspondence with Mr. Southey, and Mr. Coleridge, and had once, when on a visit to London, spoken to the great Lord Byron himself. This tradition of aristocracy remained, and the present Mr. Ponting always advised the Bishop what to read and was consulted by Mrs. Lamb, our only authoress, on questions of publishers and editions and such technical points. For all this Jeremy, at his present stage of interest, would have cared nothing even had he known it, but what he did care for were the rows of calf-bound books with little ridges of gold, that made a fine wall across the window with an old print of the Cathedral and the Close in the middle of them. Inside Ponting's there was a hush as of the study and the church combined. It was a rather dark shop with rows and rows of books disappearing into the ceiling, and one grave and unnaturally old young man behind the counter. Jeremy did not know what he should do about Hamlet, so he brought him inside, only to discover to his horror that the fiercest of all the Canons, Canon Waterbury, held the floor of the shop. Canon Waterbury had a black beard and a biting tongue. He had once warned Jeremy off the Cathedral grass in a voice of thunder, and Jeremy had never forgotten it. He glared now and pulled his beard, but Hamlet fortunately behaved well, and the old young man discovered Jeremy's notepaper within a very short period.

Then suddenly the Canon spoke.

" Dogs should not be inside shops," he said, as though he were condemning someone to death.

" I know," said Jeremy frankly. " I wanted to tie him up to something and there was nothing to tie him up to."

" What did you bring him out for at all ? " said the Canon.

" Because he's got to have exercise," said Jeremy, discovering, to his own delighted surprise, that he was not frightened in the least.

" Oh, has he ? I don't know what people keep dogs for."

And then he stamped out of the shop.

Jeremy regarded this in the light of a victory and marched away, his head more in the air than ever. He should now have hurried home. The midday chimes had rung out and Jeremy's duties were performed. But he lingered, listening to the last notes of the chimes, hearing the cries of the Cathedral choir-boys as they moved across the green to the choir-school, watching all the people hurry up and down the street. Ah, there was the Castle carriage ! Perhaps the old Countess was inside it. He had only seen her once, at some service in the Cathedral to which his mother had taken him, but she had made a great impression on him with her snow-white hair. He had heard people speak of her as " a wicked old woman." Perhaps she was inside the carriage . . . but he only saw the Castle coachman and footman and the coronet on the door. It rolled slowly up the hill with its fine air of commanding the whole world—then it disappeared around the corner of the Close.

Jeremy decided then that he would go home across the Green and down Orchard Lane. He had a wish to enter the Cathedral for a moment ; such a visit would, after all, complete the round of his experiences. He had never entered the Cathedral alone, and now, as he saw it facing him, so vast and majestic and quiet, across the sun-drenched green, he felt a sudden fear and awe. He found a ring in a stone near the west end through which he might fasten Hamlet's lead, then, slowly pushing back the heavy door, he passed inside. The Cathedral was utterly quiet. The vast nave, stained with reflections of purple and green and ruby, was vague and unsubstantial, all the little wooden chairs huddled together to the right and left, leaving a great path that swept up to the High Altar under shafts of light that fell like searchlights from the windows. The tombs and the statues peered dimly from the shadow, and the great east end window, with its deep purple light, seemed to draw the whole nave up into its heart and hold it there. All was space and silence, light and dusk ; a little doll of a verger moved in the far distance, an old woman, so quiet that she seemed only a shadow, passed him, wiping the little chairs with a duster.

It seemed to Jeremy that he had never been in the Cathedral before ; he stood there, breathless, as though in a moment something must inevitably happen. Although he did not think of it, the moment was one of a sequence that had come to him during the year—his entry into the theatre with his uncle, his first conversation with the sea-captain, the hour when his mother had been so ill, the evening on the beach when Charlotte had been frightened, the time when Hamlet had been lost and he had slept with him under a tree. All these moments had been something more than merely themselves, had had something behind them or inside them for which simply they stood as words stand for pictures. He analysed, of course, nothing, being a perfectly healthy small boy, but if afterwards he looked back these were the moments that he saw as one sees stations on a journey. One day he would know for what they stood.

He simply now waited there as though he expected something to happen. Thoughts slipped through his mind quite casually, whether Hamlet were behaving well outside, what the old lady did when she was tired of dusting, who the stone figure lying near him might be, a figure very fine with his ruff and his peaked beard, his arms folded, his toes pointing upwards, whether the body were inside the stone like a mummy or underneath the ground somewhere ; how strangely different the nave looked now from its Sunday show, and what fun it would be to run races all the way down and see who could reach the golden angels over the reredos first ; he felt no reverence, and yet a deep reverence, no fear, but, nevertheless, awe ; he was warm and happy and comfortable, and yet suddenly, giving a little shudder, he slipped out into the sunlight, released Hamlet and started for home.

2

Back again in the bosom of his family he felt that they were beginning to be aware of his departure.

" What shall we do this evening, Jeremy—your last evening ? " said his mother.

Everyone looked at him.

"Oh, I don't know," he said uncomfortably. "Just as usual, I suppose."

"You're making him feel uncomfortable," said Aunt Amy, who loved to explain quite obvious things.

"You want it to be just an ordinary evening, dear, don't you?"

"Oh, I don't know," he said again, hating his aunt.

"I don't think that quite the way to speak to your aunt, my son," said his father. "We only inquire out of kindness, thinking to please you. No, Mary, no more. Friday—one helping——"

"Jeremy might have another as it's his last day, I suggest," said Aunt Amy who was determined to be pleasant.

"I don't want any, thank you," said Jeremy, although it was treacle pudding, which he loved.

"Well, I think," said Mrs. Cole, "that we'll have high tea at half-past seven, and the children shall stay up afterwards and we'll have 'Midshipman Easy.'"

Jeremy loved his mother intensely at that moment. How did she know so exactly what was right? She made so little disturbance, was so quiet and was never angry, and yet she was always right when the others were always wrong. She knew that above all things he loved high tea—fish pie and boiled eggs and tea and jam and cake—a horrible meal that his later judgment would utterly condemn, but nevertheless something so cosy and so comfortable that no later meal would ever be able to rival it in those qualities.

" Oh, that will be lovely ! " he said, his face shining all over.

Nevertheless, as the afternoon advanced a strange new sense of insecurity, unhappiness and forlornness crept increasingly upon him. He realized that he had that morning said good-bye to the town, and now he felt as though he had, in some way, hurt or insulted it.

And, all the afternoon, he was saying farewell to the house. He did not wander from room to room, but rather sat up in the schoolroom pretending to mend a fishing rod which Mr. Monk had given him that summer. He did not really care about the rod —he was not even thinking of it. He heard all the sounds of the house as he sat there. He could tell all the clocks, that one booming softly the half hours was in his mother's bedroom, there was a rattle and a whirr and there came the cuckoo-clock on the stairs, there was the fast, cheap, careless chatter of the little clock on the school mantelpiece, there was the whisper of Miss Jones's watch which she had put out on the table to mark the time of Mary's sewing by. There were all the regular sounds of the house. The distant closing of doors, deep down in the heart of the house someone was using a sewing machine somewhere, voices came up out of the void and faded again, someone whistled, someone sang. His gloom increased. He was exchanging a world he knew for a world that he did not know, and he could not escape the feeling that he was, in some way, insulting this world that he was leaving. He bothered himself all the afternoon with unnecessary stupid affairs to cover his deep discomfort. He whistled carelessly and out of tune, he poked the fire and walked about. He was increasingly aware of Hamlet and Mary. Mary was determined so hard that she would show no emotion at all that she was a painful sight to witness. She scarcely spoke to him, and only answered in monosyllables if he asked her something.

And Hamlet had suddenly discovered that the atmosphere of the house was unusual. He had expected, in the first place, to be taken for a walk that afternoon ; then his master was very busy doing nothing, which was most unusual. Then at tea time his worst suspicions were confirmed. Jeremy suddenly made a fuss of him, pouring his tea into his saucer, giving him a piece of bread and jam and an extra lump of sugar. Hamlet drank his tea and ate his bread and jam thoughtfully. They were very nice, but what was the matter ?

He looked up through his hair and discovered that his master's eyes were restless and unhappy, and that he was thinking of things that disturbed him. He went away to the fire and, sitting on his haunches, gazing in his metaphysical way at the flames, considered the matter. Jeremy came over to him and, drawing him back to him, laid his head upon his knee and so held him. Hamlet did not move, save occasionally to sigh, and, once or twice, to snap in a sudden way that he had at an imaginary fly. He thought that in all probability his master had been punished for something, and in this he was deeply sympathetic, never seeing why his master need be punished for anything and resenting the stupidity of human beings with their eternal desire to be, in some way or other, asserting their authority.

Gradually, in front of the hot fire, both boy and

dog fell asleep. Jeremy's dreams were confused,
bewildering, distressing ; he was struggling to find
something, was always climbing higher and higher
to discover it, only to be told that, in the end, he was
in the place where he had begun.

Hamlet's dream was of an enormous succulent
bone that was pulled away from him so soon as he
snapped at it.

They both awoke with a start to find that it was
time for high tea.


3

Throughout the evening Jeremy was more and
more lonely. He had never before felt so deep an
affection for the family and never been so utterly
unable to express it. It was as though, during the
whole year he had, by his own will, been slipping
away from them, and now they had gone too far
for him to call them back.

He sat on the floor at his mother's feet whilst she
read " Midshipman Easy." It was all so cosy, the
room was so comfortable with all the familiar pictures and photographs and books, and Helen and
Mary diligently sewing, and Hamlet stretched out
in front of the fire, his nose on his paws—six months
ago Jeremy would have felt utterly and absolutely
part of it. Now he was outside it and, at the same
time, was inside nothing else. It might be that in
a week's time he would be so familiar with his new
world that he would be as happy as a cricket—he
did not know. He only knew that at this moment
he would have given all that he had to fling his
arms round his mother's neck, to be hugged and

kissed and nursed by her, and that, at the same time, he would have died rather than do such a thing.

The evening came to an end. The girls got up and said good night. His mother kissed him, holding him perhaps for a moment longer than usual, but at that same instant she said :

" Oh, I must remind Ella about the half-past seven breakfast again, she always has to be told everything twice."

The girls went on ahead, Jeremy and Hamlet following close behind. Jeremy found himself alone in the schoolroom, where the fire was very low, giving only little spurts and flashes that ran like golden snakes suddenly through the darkness.

Moved by an impulse, he went to the toy-cupboard and, opening it, put his hand quite by chance on the toy village. The toy village ! He laid it out and spread it on the floor. He could not see, but he knew every piece by heart, and he laid it all out, the church and the flower garden, and the Noah's house and the village street, the animals and the Noahs. What centuries ago that birthday was, what worlds away ! How excited he had been, and now—— !

With a sudden impatient gesture he tumbled the pieces over on to their sides, then quickly, as though he were afraid of the dark, went into his bedroom and began to undress.

4

In the morning events moved too quickly for thought. He had still the same lonely pain at his heart, but now he simply was not given time to consider it.

His father called him into the study. He gave him ten shillings and a new prayer-book. Jeremy knew that he was trying to come close to him and be a friend of a new kind to him.

He heard in a distance such words as : " . . . . a new world, full of trial and temptation. God sees us. . . . Work at your Latin . . . cricket and football . . . prayers every night. . . ." But he could feel no emotion, nothing but terror lest some sudden stupid emotional scene should occur. Nothing occurred. He kissed his father and went.

Then, quite suddenly, just as he came down in his hat and coat and heard that the cab was there, his restraint melted ; he was free and impulsive and natural. He kissed Mary, telling her :

" You have my toy village. I'd like you to—— Yes, rather. I mean it."

He kissed Helen and Barbara, and then held to his mother, not caring whether all the world was there to see. The old life was going with him ! He was not leaving it after all. The town and the house, and all the things to which he had thought that he had said good-bye, were going with him.

Hamlet ! He found the dog struggling to get into the cab. That was more than he could stand. He was not going to make a fool of himself, but the only way to be secure was to get into the cab and hide there. He caught Hamlet's head, gave it a kiss, then jumped in, catching a last glimpse of the family grouped at the door, the servants at the window, the old garden with the dead leaves gathered upon it, Hamlet held, struggling, in Mary's arms.

He choked down his sobs, felt the ten shillings in his pocket, then with a mighty resolve, to which it seemed that the labours of Hercules were as nothing, leaned out and waved his hand.

The cab rolled off.

Hamlet lay down upon the mat just inside the hall-door. Someone tried to pull him away. He growled, showing his teeth. His master had gone out. He would wait for his return—and no one should move him.

Made and Printed in Great Britain by
The Greycaine Book Manufacturing Company Limited, Watford
30.528